Bishop
&
Nun

A <u>Mormon</u> Bishop & the <u>Catholic</u> Nun adventure.

Book 1 (Bishop and Nun Series)

Brent Carr

BETHANY PUBLISHING GROUP

1603 Capitol Ave.,

Cheyenne, WY 82001

This is Book 1 of a series.

A. Brent Carr,

Bishop & Nun

ISBN-13: 978-1-939395-03-0

BETHANY PUBLISHING GROUP

DEDICATION

This novel is dedicated to three friends — indeed three great men — David Sanchez, Jacob Wenz and Elder Justin Hall. They have inspired me, and influenced greatly this novel. It is impossible to be around people who embrace the spirit of the Lord and not be uplifted.

David Sanchez is a spiritual leader, who answers my difficult, and complex religious questions. In speaking with love for people whose beliefs are different than ours, I have caused my friend grief and frustration. As a benchmark, you feel Christ's love in his presence.

I am also immensely grateful to David Sanchez for his dedication in editing *The Bishop & Nun*, and with assistance on religious doctrine. Nonetheless, the words herein are mine alone, and any inaccuracy falls squarely on my shoulders. Nonetheless, clearly without him this novel would have missed the mark.

Jacob Wenz – mission completed. Two years of exemplary service teaching about Heavenly Father and Jesus Christ. Now, he must be mindful that the tree grows as the twig is bent.

My beloved, Elder Hall, I love you for the eternities, for which, we must both endeavor. Your bold spirit fought back from a time adrift; for which I greatly admire. You are living an inspired mission. From Camarillo to shinny sea.

ACKNOWLEDGMENTS

There are many who have influenced this work of fiction, with the underpinnings to the truth of Christ, including my grandson, **Jacob**, who is 7-years-old and Catholic. His understanding and love of **Jesus** is amazing.

I recently said to Jacob, "Your entire family is Catholic – right?" Then, my precious 3-year-old grandson said, "I'm not Catholic – I am Lucas." The young are so priceless.

⌸⌸⌸⌸⌸⌸⌸

The resolute spirit of my wife **Terri** has provided me the drive to complete the novel. At times, I have waivered, because of adversity. My wife points out that challenges and how we meet them is part of God's plan of salvation.

Terri has fought stage IV metastatic breast cancer with valor for four years. During the final edit of this novel, she was hospitalized. It was doubtful she would come home; however, with faith and prayers of many faithful my bride of 40 years fights onward.

The beastly cancer has spread to her liver, spine, among other organs. Terri urges me forward – knowing that grace makes a soft landing to those who believe, and express their faith through keeping the **Commandments**, working to help others to return toe Heavenly Father, and showing love all around.

Chapter 1

ଔଔଔଔଔ

WHAT YOU SEE IS NOT WHAT YOU GET

"You're a Bishop? I don't think so?"

So said the pretty woman with high cheek-bones, large brown eyes – big, bright eyes.

"Astonishing eyes."

Dressed in the traditional black, Nun's habit, she stood erect. Her voice had an edge to it, a little combative.

Her stance declaring slight vengeance, as well. Devoid of peace – at the moment. Not a woman who fit with her Nun's motif. No love of Christ shown on her face.

Agitation. Ready for vigilance. But beautiful – drop-dead gorgeous.

"They told me you were a Marine," I said warily. She looked tough enough. A tad under 30-years-old, I guessed. Those brown eyes peered directly through me. Daggers.

The wary Nun checked me out, wondering about my title as the so-called 'Bishop'.

"An impostor," she thought.

She noticed his 6' 3" chiseled frame, square shoulders, with blonde hair and eyes of Caribbean-blue, staring back at her.

"Too good looking for a Bishop," she knew for sure. "Without a question, the wrong clothes for a Catholic man of God."

The power of his body belied the apparent peace in his demeanor. He had a confident, deep voice. Whoever he was, she observed, the guy didn't fidget. A calm, too-good looking smile on his face.

"I am a Marine," she said belligerently. "Well, I was. Now, what you see is what you get."

"Miss, that means?" I asked almost too rudely.

"I'm asking the questions," she shot back. "I asked you a question. What's your answer? You're no Bishop."

A playful smile now lit my face. Nearly impossible not to break into laughter. This gorgeous woman dressed as a Nun – barking out orders.

Her rigid expression and stony glare are too much to ignore. I imagine some of my FBI buddies having a good chuckle at our expense.

"You laugh at me. I'll knock the smirk right off your silly face. Who in the hell are you?" she continued with defiance. Unlike any Nun who I ever encountered.

She couldn't be ignored. The dangerous one wasn't goofing with me. This lady was deadly serious.

"What I see is a Nun. Where did you steal the outfit?"

Sister Claire Coogan had enough of this stranger, who was mocking her. She moved forward in a fighting stance; however, she was nearly fallen when her front foot stuck in her Nun's garb.

"Easy, Sister. You're going to hurt yourself."

"It's not me, who is in danger."

"Who are you looking for, Sister?"

"I was told by the Vatican to meet the Bishop here. That's what I know. You are not him."

"Well, Rome clued you correctly. I am the Bishop."

Sister Claire Coogan now had a confused, perplexed expression on her face. She understood full-well that Bishops didn't dress in $2,000 suits, with white shirts and matching blue ties. Bishops we're about God – not fashion statements. Furthermore, she knew the presiding Cardinal in Los Angeles – this wasn't him.

"I've been dispatched by the Pope on a matter of severe importance," she said. "Other than standing here at St. Anthony Catholic Parish, this is a hoax. You're a fraud."

"Who me?"

Then a faint outline of a pistol shown from under her clothing. My smile gone in an instant. I wondered who was kidding who?

"Sister, we've both been taken off guard."

Her eyes blazed. Big, bright, beautiful eyes. I saw her passion, which bore intelligence, able to summon quick and insightful actions. The eyes are the portal to the soul. To reason.

Nevertheless, I also realized potential menace – not love – emanating with hyper-awareness from her deep confident stance. She saw everything. Missed nothing. There certainly was no smile – more of a smirk.

Beyond her intense emotional state, stood an extremely attractive lady. Her face was exquisite. Her clothing masked the contours of her body. Yet, from her taught arms, I could imagine something to behold under her religious frock.

I'd better stop looking, and start thinking; I thought, returning to the moment.

"I am a Bishop – a Mormon Bishop. Someone forgot to tell you that little fact. Perhaps, they are playing with you. Just like some joker is playing with me when they say you are a Marine. Neglected to inform me, you're now a Nun."

"Great, I have to work with a cult member." She said begrudgingly. A quick, instantaneous transition.

I had heard that slight a thousand times in my lifetime. I said nothing. It was time to put the agitation to rest.

"This meeting isn't by chance. As bizarre as we might be, we have been drawn together for a mission of national importance. I am assigned to a general, who is stationed at the White House. Attached to the President. Appears we were assigned to our mission somewhat in the dark," I said.

"So," she pried, "What's going on Mr. Bishop?"

"What did they tell you in Rome?"

"You don't know why I'm in Los Angeles?" she questioned. She did not make it easy.

"Didn't say that, Sister. Some way or another, we have to get on the same wave length. Perhaps, I should call Washington, and you should telephone Italy."

"You really don't know? Right?" Sister Claire queried like a laser.

Even with the friction, I kept being drawn back to her innate beauty. Sister Claire had a sensually, pretty face, and large kissable lips.

I said to myself, "Not lusting Father, I'm merely observing that even though she is a Nun, she is a "WOW."

Nonetheless, the mission is too important to be played for a fool. You could rent her garb at a Hollywood actor store for $50.

"With $500, I could make ten women into pretend-Nuns. Hire then right off the movie set." I said to myself.

She looked ready to star in an extravaganza. The Sister would not take a back seat to any of the current-day stars.

"Who are you – other than pretending to be a Bishop?" she questioned. "We are gasoline together. Ready to explode. Dynamite. Sitting ducks here on the steps of a Catholic church," Sister Claire Coogan accurately reported.

"First thing you've said that makes perfect sense," I told her.

I extended my hand, taking hers too firmly. The Sister did not flinch; her grip was powerful. Could be too strong for a Nun.

"My name is Joseph Smith. Code name - Green Beret."

She knew the good-looking agent had provided the identifier correctly. Now, he should ask for her credentials.

"Where were you born?" she asked, still trying to be certain he wasn't a handsome actor – a Pierce Brosman lookalike – playing a role. Sister Claire knew danger. She wanted proof.

The Pontiff's agent didn't get sent on simple, non-invasive assignments. She was the Vatican's troubleshooter. Jeopardy always surrounded her.

"Lyons, Kansas. Code name – irascible," I said, still playing with her.

Now, I took her hand in earnest. Whatever she was; she wasn't a spy. She would shoot you in the eye in a second, if you were against Rome or endangered the Pope.

My assessment, "Loyal to the end."

Furthermore, my partner had tracked her movements from Italy, including the fictitious name under which she flew. We had an FBI agent planted on the plane. The agent never identified herself to the Sister.   This was Claire Coogan, a real-life Nun.

"Here's my ticket. I'm sure you CIA types trust no one."

"CIA. That's not me. Wrong ship, Sister."

I briefly glanced at her passport and travel documents, which all matched her itinerary. What's more, they described perfectly the data provided from my handler.

"Welcome," I said, smiling. "I'm FBI - not a spook. What do I call you?"

"Sister Claire or Claire. Your choice."

"Thanks Sister."

"You look too young to have founded the Mormon Church brother Joseph Smith," she said with a straight face.

Friendly banter. And quick wit.

"Or, perhaps, God gave you a special lease on life. Always remain young. And fit."

"Thanks for saying I'm youthful. Some days I believe my bones creak. So many battle scars."

She was mocking me, yanking playfully at the threads of the core beliefs. Two pranksters on one team might be one too many.

I could have gone off on her, but turn around is fair play. I knew it. I dish it out, so I should be ready to take ribbing.

Even though a former Green Beret, with deadly hands and feet, his demeanor showed humble, Claire noticed. He was quiet and unassuming.

"Really handsome," she thought again, her face flushing slightly.

"Call me Joe or Joseph. Your choice. However, my name is truly Joseph Smith. I didn't found the Church of Jesus Christ of Latter-day Saints. Nevertheless, I am a faithful member. Named after the founder. Probably, ten thousand followers who have been named after the Prophet."

"Where do we go from here?" She asked, not giving an inch.

"Let's find a quiet place. Check out, whether we're being set up or followed. Some of the irony of this meeting is too much for me – if not for you."

She grasped his concern. Claire, as well, felt an increasing agitation. Not against him. The locale and situation screamed vulnerability. Why had Rome sent her all the way from Italy? His Eminence gave her the order – not some underling.

"The Pope doesn't send Sisters on a fool's errand."

I noticed her intently looking around. The open, unprotected, surroundings obviously a concern.

"We finally agree on something." She said. "Let's move to cover?"

Chapter 2

ఇంఇంఇంఇంఇం

A PRECIOUS LIFE, TAKEN TOO SOON

Now, we have immediacy of purpose and safety. No doubt, it was only a crazy, somewhat sketchy plan. Move to the cover of the FBI vehicle. Then what?

The weird-teamed twosome moved from the steps of the Catholic Church with verb. Poetry in action.

Their fated meeting with one sent in "robes from Rome," and the other a messenger dispatched with "sabers from Washington." From the outset, both burned with intrigue.

They hurried away. Sister Claire hiking up her garb, so she could keep up with the long legs of her Green Beret so-called friend.

Reaching a beat up, black Chevy, I felt like a high school kid. Where I needed to explain about the dilapidated ride to my date.

There had been plenty of bad rides in the early years of dating...this was different. This was certainly no love outing. Instead, an unexplained secret mission.

"I have a friend - another agent – staked out around here," I told her. "In our church, a married man is prohibited from being alone with a female other than his wife. Even, a sharp-shooting Nun." I smiled.

"Afraid I'm going to jump you, Bishop?"

"Say – What?" I responded out of shock. This Sister is too much.

After getting quickly over her glib answer, I shook my head. She got me again.

"Even the famous Rev. Billy Graham of the Baptist faith and other ministers celebrate the wisdom of being alone only with your wife. I am smart enough to follow the concept."

The Sister nearly cut me off, saying, "Oh, I am sure she handles you just fine."

She must have read my expression.

"Lighten up, Bishop. I'm pulling your chain," Sister Claire responded, with a widening smile. This was the first time she flashed her pearly-white teeth. An actual grin.

"I already realized...I was a little slow in picking up that you are a nit-wit."

"No, only a righteous Sister with wit."

I need to watch her. She is quicker than a mountain lion. Maybe, as dangerous.

"Well, anyway," I almost stuttered, "My agent-buddy is around here somewhere. He drove the newer FBI sedan for our use. Better transportation."

"Expecting trouble?"

"With you, there is ever-present mischief. However, you're right. I think we might meet up with dangerous rodents. The kind with guns."

"Where is your agent-friend?"

"Probably at the other ride. We'll pick him up." I answered. "Never know what to expect; therefore, we left the unmarked FBI vehicle two blocks away. Always, plan for the unexpected."

"Might be. This guy isn't really such a putz," thought Sister Claire. Being with him presents one major problem. He is so athletic; it is radical keeping up with him in her Nun's clothes.

"I'll keep an eye out for danger," she said, climbing onto the passenger bench seating of the old car. A loose spring from the seat hit her hard in the butt, clanging. The ride was 20 years old. By appearance, the car was ready for the junk yard.

"That hurt," she said picking at the metal chard.

"Only the best of rides for the FBI."

Not a minute to pause for sympathy. I understood we would be scuffed – if not killed – on this assignment. A far greater problem than a misplaced spring.

The car's engine sprang to life, running far better than the exterior might indicate.

"Have no idea what to expect. This smells from the start." I told her.

"What now?" she asked, still with alarm registering on her face, and rubbing at her rear.

"Need someone to rub, Sister," I said trying to loosen the gloom.

Another faint smile. Some more teeth.

She started to bring a finger up at me – a flicker of reason as she thought the better of it.

"In your dreams, you get to rub."

"Not I - for I am a trusted husband. Loyal to the end."

"You are merely a man. Like all, you won't wander if I keep a gun on you."

"Really?"

"And I'm a Nun – you dummy." Her nose wrinkled up similar to a Pug dog. I can't explain her antics better than that.

"A full-fledged Nun? Or, seriously, did you buy the uniform at a costume store?"

She kicked my right driver's leg. She didn't pull the strike, either. I hurt like hell.

I said nothing. I'm not going to rub, complain or .... anything. Macho-like.

"We will drive and find my partner. The other car is newer. And abandon this monstrosity."

"Why did we come to this clunker, instead of the newer one?"

"Thought he was meeting me here – going to check you out."

"Afraid of the big, bad Sister, huh? Two burly FBI guys can't take a little ole Nun."

"Sure. Dream on." I now found myself wrinkling up my face. She was catching – like a disease.

"Why two cars in the first place?"

"More options. If we had to abandon a vehicle, this was the one that could go. If we are followed, adds chances for diversion. One car would dart one way, and the other vehicle another direction."

"You don't trust anyone, do you?"

"Trust my family, God and Jesus. On the job, I'm conflicted."

"I'll say."

As Sister Claire and I turned the corner, an explosion and fireball erupted. It rocked the neighborhood, as strong as an earthquake.

We moved cautiously, turning the corner, so we could view the humongous eruption.

"You have some dangerous friends," the Sister said caustically.

"No friends of mine."

I pulled the car slowly up to the cross-street. Looking for my partner and the Chevrolet Suburban. Nosing the old heap out inch-by-inch, I peered around the corner.

"Over there," said the Sister, pointing.

Her finger directed me to a car – three fierce-Army or special forces desperados inside. Dressed in fatigues. They had too much interest to be innocents. They were studying what appeared to be their handiwork.

The Suburban sat on its side. In flames.

Claire screamed, "Let's get the hell out of here."

As I accelerated too fast, I screeched the tires on the asphalt with the guerrillas looking up. Out of my peripheral vision – to my horror – I viewed the obliterated Chevy Suburban.

"I've seen car bombs before. With the amount of explosives they planted, they were trying to do more than kill us. They were sending a message."

"You think?" she said.

I studied my companion, seeing a wry combative look on her face. Sister Claire's eyes twinkled. Her fear of me was gone, and another side of her exposed.

"Was the person in the Chevy, a close friend?"

"Yes. So is his family – his wife is very sweet. Two children. Now, he's burned to a crisp - for what? We don't know a thing. We haven't even started an investigation."

I am intensely angry. Confused. Having to work with a Nun sent from Rome makes no sense. Unless my superiors are not looking for answers. They might feel Sister Claire will slow me down.

I grimaced. A generous, kind man is now in fragments. Too few pieces to fit in a box. This holocaust cremated him, because my agent friend did me a favor. For obedience to church protocol – not to be alone with a woman other than my wife – his family lost a husband and father.

The irony. Hereafter, I would serve with the Nun – alone. No choice.

The devil interferes hourly with worldly events. Puts obstacles in our path. Attempts to tempt. To drive us from faith.

"His wife is totally kind. She does homework with all the kids on the block. Parties are at their house. You get the idea."

"I'm sorry."

"A nasty business."

"You sort of indicated things on this assignment didn't add up. What is different?"

I was still shaken. Driving fast through the streets of West Los Angeles, heading toward the 405 freeway.

"The way I received the assignment. Never like this before. In fact, you! Why were you sent? "

"Now, we are most-definitely partnered. If not careful, we will die together." She said.

Claire put a hand gently on my arm. She said nothing - and yet, said everything with her touch.

I explained further, "Normally I have a sit-down when I receive orders. This time I was contacted from a secret e-mail account used for extraordinary circumstances."

"Out of the ordinary?"

"Rules calls for a portion of the confirming instructions to be delivered by a combination of e-mails, and telephone to an untraceable cell phone. I get a newly issued one each month."

"Hinky," she said.

I glanced over, seeing I had dumbfounded my companion.

"Sometimes, circumstances dictate that sensitive material is passed this way. This method makes it impossible to trace."

"If its convention, what's the concern?"

"I've been undercover for a decade; never before has the bureau implemented the technology. Moreover, no name assigned to the engagement. Insane."

"Washington?"

"Yes, clearly their hand print. Better said, their dirty work." I added, "The voice giving me orders unknown to me. Never heard him before."

"You think it's a set up – a sting?"

"Thinking so. Possibly, until you showed up. You came thousands of miles with instructions from Rome. From the top honcho."

"True. I received the travel itinerary from the highest authority. In person: face-to-face. The Pope does not screw around."

The Nun's chosen words were not susceptible to a double meaning. Strong, clear words.

"What did His Eminence tell you?"

"Among other things, I was instructed to read James 2 from the Bible."

I replied, "Faith without works is dead. To some, Jesus' brother James is controversial. Some Christians believe the Book of James should be dropped from the Bible."

"Not hard to understand; we are saved by faith in Christ. Even so, we must do more than saying idle words," Claire replied.

She looked at me, because of the expression painted on my face. No doubt.

"Surprised, I would understand that we show our love for Christ's gift of the atonement by serving others," she said. The Nun had a soft, loving expression. One, I had not seen.

"Sister, obviously, there is more that binds than separates Christian religions. The Bible is truth for Mormons, Catholics and others who have faith in Christ. Too often an individual church declares itself the only holders of the keys to heaven," I said.

"Now you do astonish me Bishop. You believe a mere Catholic Sister can sit at the foot of God?"

"Why not? Jesus loves you no less than me."

I could see her quick, jokester-mind working overtime. "Well, Bishop, I will have to talk to the Pope about getting you a pass to heaven – after all."

Never a dull moment with this Nun.

"There are times for scripture reading, and a time to repel bullets," I urged, pulling us back to reality.

We turned onto the southbound 405 freeway, which ultimately joins up with highway 5 to San Diego. We were south of Los Angeles International Airport.

Then, I looked in the rear-view mirror. I observed the same vehicle with the sinister men from the explosion. They were traveling fast.

Obliged, I stepped hard on the accelerator.

"Sister, we're being followed."

"I figured, since you're going 90 miles per hour."

Freeway traffic was light. Cars traveling 20 miles per hour slower at around 70. I weaved in an out, traversing from one lane to the other.

"Tell me more on your instructions from Rome."

"The Pope told me million of lives are at stake," she said. "Many are involved in sacking America. Something about making the Middle East not habitable."

"What?"

"I didn't understand. I tried to seek clarification, but was told Rome only had pieces of the intrigue."

"Strong words."

"This Pope is loving and sincere," Sister Claire said. "He is a patient, loving man, who seeks peace for all. Consider, your new Mormon Temple in Rome, built with the approval of the Papacy."

I drove feverishly; not able to outrun our pursuers. We were fleeing dangerously.

"This chase is beyond perilous. Why us? We don't know anything."

Claire, looking over her shoulder, paused. "The great-man told me, a friend and the world is in peril. On the trip over, I read and prayed for discernment and knowledge."

"The Pope ever challenge you? Words which initially appear out of context?"

"He's not afraid to make you think."

"How long have you been a Nun? And why are you stationed at the Vatican?"

"Left the Marines after too many bloody assignments. With a religious background, I will discuss some other time. Suffice it to say, the Catholic Church took notice of my training as a Marine."

"What do you do for Rome?"

"Special assignments. Matters that others aren't called to do. I trained with the Swiss Guards – to protect the Pope. My life is expendable; missions are not."

"I believe; I understand." I said – not understanding at all.

The race continued. Our two cars in tandem scooted down the 405 freeway at speeds approaching 100 miles per hour. Mile after mile clicked off.

"Where are we headed? Joe Hardy."

"A Hardy boys fan, huh – Sister. Reading boy's mystery novels might be a too light of reading for a Nun."

"Reading from my days growing up. However, your adventurous spirit reminded me of the good-old days."

I said nothing.

"About where we are headed."

"I've been formulating a plan as we've been fleeing. Don't know if I can trust the FBI or police, because of the cryptic manner I was given the assignment and.... the explosion."

"So?"

"We're headed toward Los Alamitos – the racetrack. Hopefully, that will confuse them. In addition, there is security."

"You mean a horse racetrack has the type of security to stop three mad bombers who appear to be special forces?" she said in disbelief.

"No. Probably not. We might slow them down a little. They won't expect the move. Give us time to avoid a confrontation. Time to reconnoiter – to talk and figure out a plan. Decide what is going on. For honestly, I don't have a clue."

The freeway chase became erratic. Perilous. My car might be old, but finely tuned with a supercharger. We needed all the power.

Our chaperones kept pace. Follow the leader always gives an advantage to the rabbit. Quick moves can temporarily shed the follower.

I left the San Diego bound freeway – heading north on the San Gabriel, nearly tipping us over. The move was dicey, and made at the last minute.

"Great move – Sherlock," said Claire. "That fooled no one. Shocks not too new, Bishop?"

"This gal is sort of a Nun, maybe," I thought. "Special assignments and Swiss Guard for the Vatican, I believe."

She sat as cool, totally motionless. Resting comfortably. Relaxed. Like at a church social or college dance.

"Need me to drive?" she asked. This beauty has spunk.

"No. I will keep it on the road."

"Barely."

Scurrying off the 605 at Katella toward Los Alamitos, I raced at 80. Twice the speed limit.

"Where are the cops when you need them?" she asked. "Thought the city crawled with police."

There was no longer a subterfuge. The sedan behind us catching up at a dangerous rate of speed.

Sister Claire asked, "In the messages from Washington, what instructions did you receive? Why don't you call your boss?"

"Consider, I'm a little busy! Traveling at nearly 90 miles per hour. Dialing will be a tad tricky."

She grinned, "Want me to hold the phone?"

"The boss-thing is a little complicated, too."

She blinked.

"You left something out?" She said making a fist.

"As to my assignment, here goes...."

I was talking and driving at excessive speeds that would unhinge any normal passenger. Sister Claire sat 'chilled out', occasionally looking behind to see the attacker closing in from behind.

"Was told the U.S. has an invader – an enemy of the highest quarter. Nothing specific. Traitors?"

"It sounds like Judas betraying Christ."

I said, "We'll have time for a Scripture chase later – right now, I'm trying to save our lives."

"How are you doing? You are careening all over the road, nearly missing vehicles," she said.

I said nothing.

Soon afterward, several bullets were fired; slugs imbedding into our speeding vehicle. The chase car was abreast.

One of the bullets hit the old car radio, missing my right arm by inches.

Without a word, Sister Claire drew her pistol, Billy the Kid quick. Seemed even faster.

The combatant was hanging out of the right front window of the enemy vehicle. Taking aim.

Sister Clare Coogan added ventilation between his eyes. Game over for one combatant.

"Good shooting, Annie Oakley. You fired twice. Where did the other bullet land?"

"I am the fastest draw on the planet. However, sometimes, I have trouble grouping my shots. One goes astray."

"Often, more deliberation while firing yields better results without innocence getting killed."

"Back to saving our lives," she said. "Mission over, otherwise. Bishop, put them into some light pole."

"No tread on our tires, Sister." I kidded.

"So, that is why you can't avoid them, huh?" she said unconvinced. "Not that you suck at driving?"

Chapter 3

ଔଔଔଔଔ

HE WHO LEARNS, BUT DOES NOT THINK IS LOST!
HE WHO THINKS, BUT DOES NOT LEARN IS IN GREAT DANGER.

Confuscius

As I drove toward the Los Alamitos trainer's gate, I directed the Sister in a calm, yet decisive voice to move quickly when I parked.

I took a sneak peak behind. The chase vehicle had stopped, trying to deduce why I had turned into the racetrack. The ruse worked for the second.

I pulled up as close to the guard shack as possible.

"Come on."

"I'm coming." She said, running.

I quickly retrieved my racing credentials from my wallet, and additionally showed the FBI identification.

"They've stopped five or six rows back," she said. "Impressive, your plan has slowed them thus far. They are not shooting."

"For how long?"

The guard seeing Joseph's racing license, and a Catholic sister waved us through the gate.

"What now?"

"My trainer, Duke Snyder, is also a private investigator. I'm calling him for assistance." Speed dialing Duke Snyder's barn.

"Hello," answered Duke, not recognizing the caller ID from the incoming call.

"Duke, this is Joe."

"My good Bishop, how are you?"

"Troubles. I just entered the training gate. Where are you?"

"What do you need?"

"Some thugs following me, who blew up my partner's car. I need you to walk me over to the front side."

Duke Snyder was a leading trainer. Moreover, he was quiet, insightful and quick to respond in emergency.

He acknowledged. "I'll grab a horse and meet you by the entrance to the path. I've got a horse to school, anyway."

Horses that had difficult times on race days were often taken to the paddock. Additional trips to the saddling area, helped to calm the rouges.

"Sister Claire, we should get you some non-conspicuous clothing. Excuse my thoughts, but you stand out like a sore thumb."

"Bishop, five Hail Marys."

I was known for having a good sense humor; however, I wasn't as quick with the witticisms, I thought.

"She's something else."

The twosome had hardly made tracks to the trail when Duke Snyder came trotting up with a large, chestnut racehorse.

The Sister said, "Bishops in your church can gamble, own racehorses?"

"Normal Bishops can't. Nevertheless, I can leap small buildings in a single bound." I said, keeping a straight face.

She said nothing – looking very confused.

When the trainer appeared, I realized immediately why Duke was working with this character. He was out of control. Dancing on all four feet. I also understood with embarrassment this maniac was a beast that carried my silks. Always sweated out before the race, and tired badly with no energy to finish the course.

For a second, there was almost a collision. Duke was in awe that I came with a Nun. And Sister Claire was put off-balance by the prancing steed at Duke's side.

"Who's your pretty acquaintance?" Duke asked. "Bishop, you converted? Always a man of mystery – now, a Catholic?"

"I'm okay with flying bullets, not so sure about prancing hoofs," the Sister replied.

Duke and I broke into spontaneous laughter.

"I'm not afraid to shoot both of you." Claire recovering her wit.

"Believe it or not Duke, this is a Sister. Sent to us from the Vatican. Oh, by the way, she is a former Marine, and actually could pulverize us."

Duke said, "Nice to meet you Sister. You might want to choose your company more wisely."

"I've been wondering about that," she responded, circumspectly. "Known him for less than an hour. And life is already flashing before my eyes."

"Wait until you've known him a week."

"Is this guy really a Bishop?"

"You're with a man who leads four lives – and one of them is that of a Bishop."

"Bishops own horses?" Claire asked.

"Subterfuge," Duke answered.

"What?"

I knew it was time for a straight answer.

"Many Middle Eastern billionaires race horses in America. Some sit at the seat of power in Saudi Arabia, and other countries. The FBI advances the funds as a means of getting me close to them."

"A means of spying?" The Sister said.

I nodded my head. "And making influential friends."

We were walking at a casual, normal pace. Attempting to throw off any onlookers conceivably observing, Joseph and Claire tracked on the inside of the path. The stallion blocked the view of anyone peering in from outside of the racetrack.

"However, when you have a woman meandering in a penguin suit it is hardly camouflage," I reasoned.

No matter what the event, I'm always enthralled by being at the track near the majesty of one of God's wondrous creations – the horse. For those who do not believe in God, how do they explain all the incredible animals – beyond man's imagination?

I glanced over my left shoulder, gazing over the track. For twenty years, I kept horses at the legendary Hollywood Park. After 75 years, it closed to the dismay of horse lovers.

Los Alamitos started in 1947 with a match race at Vessels Ranch. In 1951, it opened for para-mutual racing with the first week of racing being pelted by torrent rain. The track held mainly quarter horses on a 5/8th mile track for years, but when Hollywood closed its doors the race course was expanded to the traditional mile.

Thinking of my old stomping grounds at Hollywood Park, I said, "Man-made things do not last forever. The only thing that is certain is change, itself. If you want eternal relations, one must contemplate heaven. Only through Christ one may embrace eternity."

"Ouch," yelped Claire. Slapping at the now prancing gelding, the Sister said, "He bit me."

Duke, with a dead-pan expression, replied, "He likes the outfit. Additionally, this bugger thinks he is in love with you."

With changed attitude, Claire softly told the dancing steed, "My friend – be easy."

She braved the biting teeth; with a confidant smile, she patted the thousand-pound beast on his nose. Danger was averted as the chestnut became her new best friend.

"My feet hurt," said Claire smiling at Duke, who already knew the Sister was a combination of humor, beauty and smarts.

"Complain, complain, complain," I answered jovially. The words reminded me of a story I heard recently. I told my two friends:

"As a mother and son went to the husband's funeral, the country preacher talked at length of the marvelous traits of the deceased. What an honest man he was, and what a loving husband and kind father he was.

Finally, the widow leaned over and whispered to her son,

"Go up there and take a look in the coffin and see if that's your dad in there."

"Funny," replied Claire, not looking too amused. "The horse bit me, where the spring in the heap of a car snared me."

"What kind of word is 'snared.' Just wondering," I kidded her.

She put her hands on her hips, making a scrunched up face, "Snared is a word, and – you're a 'bugger' – not a Bishop."

Duke had not learned her playful spirit. He believed she was upset. Almost immediately, the Sister smiled easily.

"Joe," Duke asked, "What are you working on?"

"It's classified. What's more, you tell me, and we will both know? Candidly, I haven't a clue."

Claire chipped in, "Other than almost getting us killed."

As we approached the front of the newly redecorate race event, I shook hands with my trainer.

"See you Duke. Thanks. I owe you."

Pointing at the grandstands, I told the good Sister, "Claire, there is nowhere to hide. We must a make a run for it."

The trainer held my arm. "Joe, I thought you might need a vehicle. Scrap is bringing my truck around. It's in trainer's parking. Try not to get it blown up."

"What is a Scrap?" Claire asked.

"A 400-pound groom, who never stops eating."

A quick glance was exchanged between comrades. Duke and I worked together on cases numerous times. We went to combat as owner and trainer. However, above all, a relationship based on honesty and respect existed for more than a decade.

"Claire, this way."

She hurried to keep up. This two-legged creature, Joseph Smith, could run – really move, she thought.

Trying to get her to catch up, I yelled, "Claire."

"Too informal, Bishop?"

"Sister, you told me I could call you plain-Claire."

I looked at her. Dang gone it. She pulled off another zinger without even trying.

"Trying to make the windows to make a bet, Bishop?"

"Don't bet unless it is in the line of duty. Don't think you are a Sheik."

She said in an inquisitive, but playful tone, "Oh, by the way, Bishop, I thought you Mormons weren't supposed to be alone with a woman, other than your wife?"

"Right you are, Sister. I pray Jesus is along with us on this trek. Otherwise, I know I will meet him in Paradise. You – well, I not quite so sure. It depends on whether God and Jesus appreciate people with wit."

I knew I wasn't being humble. However, time for a chop of my own.

She said nothing. Her face said it all.

The parking lot attendant immediately recognized Joseph Smith. The Bishop had administered to his sick son on a minute's notice. Doctors had said the son's condition was touch and go. He might not make it through the night.

Joseph Smith counseled the young boy who attended the Presbyterian Church. Told the boy to pray with a sincere heart.

In the Blessing, the Bishop revealed what the Spirit told him. "The youth would regain health, so long as he had faith."

The boy recovered.

"Bishop, how are you? Randy, says hello."

"I am borrowing Duke Snyder's vehicle."

"Yes, Scrap brought it over for you."

The truck was parked at the front of the lot, waiting on the Bishop. Then, for the first time, the valet recognized that Bishop Smith was escorting a Nun.

"I owe you an explanation, when I'm here next. I promise," Joseph explained to the confused man.

The parking lot attendant answered, "The Father works in mysterious ways."

"Doesn't he?" Sister Claire said.

The attendant tugged on my arm, stopping me. "Bishop, did you hear of the nuclear blast in Iran today?"

"What?"

"It was a news-break that came over the radio. Someone attacked, without warning."

"You are sure it was nuclear?"

"Bishop, that's what they reported."

"Who?"

"Don't know. They didn't say who detonated the device."

Chapter 4

ଔଔଔଔଔ

THE SNOW CRAB IS DEAD

"Sister, tune the radio to a news channel. Let's find out about the bombing in Iran. It most probably ties to our mission."

"You think?"

Claire searched the radio for a news broadcast. Finally, I pushed Duke's preset selections. The first was a country; the second selection more country, and the third news.

After several inconsequential news events, the announcer turned to international stories. The anchor asked a reporter located abroad to file the report.

"Little is known. However, Iran reports the port city of Jask has been attacked by nuclear bomb. Officials are tight-lipped about the source of the nuclear weapon."

"Any reports of casualties?"

"The city of Jask reports 11,000 citizens, with a major Iranian naval base. Initially, they say the navy base has been destroyed with a total loss of civilian life."

"Steve, anything else to report at this hour?"

"Experts are saying the launch of the weapon was from the Gulf of Oman in the Arabian Sea."

"Who?" The anchor asked.

"No one is saying for certain. Only speculation."

"Israel, the United States, or...?" asked the anchor, trying to pull more information from the reporter.

"The rankest of speculation. No one has claimed responsibility," the reporter concluded.

Once reports moved to other stories, I asked the Sister how the nuclear event would impact our mission. On the other hand, was this our assignment. How could it be?

The Sister queried, "Do you think the nuke was fired from an American submarine?"

I shook my head. "Why would we attack Jask? Never heard about the place until today. If we're going to nuke someone, why not Tehran? A city of 9 million?"

"Conceivably, the point was to attack a smaller city. Get notoriety without killing millions. In any case, the United States will be blamed."

I agreed, nodding my head. I said nothing.

"This cranks up possible military activity against the US," she speculated. "The attack is connected; the blast is our doing. Must be."

"Who else would fire a nuclear weapon from the Gulf of Oman?"

I took note of Sister Claire Coogan, decked out in her Nun habit. Realizing that we are now a team – like it or not. I understood the need to find clothing uniformity.

"We've got to find you some new duds. Your costume is a liability."

"Costume, huh? At least, our faithful can recognize our allegiance to God."

"Sister?" I said. Speechless.

"You can face bullets, but not an enlightened Sister?"

"We have Sister Missionaries in our church. They are not quite like you."

"Not so good, huh."

She might act tough. However, I already knew she was a woman who had love within her heart, witticism in her mind, and hands and arms that felt combat.

Traffic flowed slowly at the racetrack, coming out of the trainer's lot.

"Claire, hunker down, so you can't be seen. I'm trying to get us away from the track alive. Evade the mad bombers."

His instructions clear and concise – received as an order. She ducked.

"Even hiding, you can view the glow of a Catholic."

"Wow. You ever get scared."

"More mouth, when I am under fire." She admitted.

Driving with one hand and reaching with the other, I grabbed Duke Snyder's jacket out of the back seat and slipped it on. Then, I put on a baseball cap.

I drove out of the track as if I'd made a million dollars training horses – no cares in the world. Any onlooker would see a truck with "Duke Snyder Racing Stables" painted on the side. One passenger. Not give it another glance.

"Stay focused – an eye out. We need to determine whether we're clear."

"How can I duck, and keep an eye out?"

"I thought you Catholics could see through walls – a little thing like doors shouldn't hinder you."

She slugged my shoulder. She possessed fists of steel. My arm hurt. Claire didn't hit like a woman, and certainly not a Nun. Not that I knew many.

Five minutes passed as we hurried to seclusion. I was keeping a wary eye out for interlopers. Sister Claire took fleeting glances to scan cars, faces, and side streets.

My personal cell phone rang. The phone I use every day. Not my FBI throwaway. I peaked quickly at the caller ID; noted it was Duke Snyder calling.

"Joseph, this is Duke. Two men – heavily armed with guns – broke through the security gate here at the park. They slugged several grooms looking for you."

"Please, no."

"That's not the worst of it. They shot a security guard."

"Did they get away?"

"One of them did. One is dead. No ID."

"Did you have any contact with them?"

"Are you asking if they know you're in my truck?

"That's good for starters."

"You know me better. I didn't talk with them. And I'm going to the races now – avoiding questions that will come on the backside."

"As always, Duke, thanks. I owe you."

"Doesn't even start to make up for what you've done for me. Consider it a payment on account."

I laughed.

"See you soon. Win a race for me. More correctly, for Uncle Sam."

I explained the events to the Sister. "Who pockets the winnings?" she asked.

"Winnings?"

Claire said, "We are into something bigger than the two of us – enormous. Give me the details on our mission. Before they riddle me with holes."

"You keep asking. I keep telling you, I don't have any notion."

I pulled up in front of a discount clothing store. She looked at the motherish-looking clothing in the window.

"You need a change of pace, Sister." I pointed.

"You're kidding, right?"

"Nope."

"If you want me to break my vows, you must do better than this. I'll look 80-years-old."

"I promise if they riddle your body with bullets, I'll buy some stylish clothing for the funeral – okay?"

"In all seriousness, where is the store in the 20th century? Oh, I remember – you Mormons crossed the plains to Salt Lake City in covered wagons."

To Joseph's surprise, Sister Claire escaped the car; hiked her Nun's dress up, and began hoofing step-by-step across the Boulevard. To a small department store.

"Coming?" She asked sarcastically.

"Right on your heels. Do you wear heels?"

Stares and snickers were lofted inside. The sight was comical. A Nun sprinting ahead of a man scantly keeping up.

Sister Claire didn't back down an inch. I'm cut from a conservative cloth and embarrassed by ruckus. Not the Sister. She picked out three stylish outfits and changed in and out of them. Not noticing the pointed fingers.

"I'll take these," she said to the rude clerk. "God is testing you today to consider if you are kind to a poor innocent one," said Claire, with a straight face.

The clerk looked down, saying nothing.

Sister Claire – now somewhat stylish Claire – picked out modest, but appealing clothing. She wore a blue blouse, with matching skirt. A little long for the current style. Nonetheless, the outfit looked good on her. She bought sneakers, so she wouldn't have as much trouble keeping up.

She put her habit folded neatly into a bag. "Thanks for the help."

"Are you really a Nun?" asked the clerk, thinking this was a department store trick – checking on how she treated customers.

Sister Claire nodded respectfully. Said nothing. The woman was hopelessly confused. Moving from the counter, she almost skipped away.

"The skirt's long enough to be appropriate," said the Sister.

She was stunningly beautiful in street clothing. I wondered whether her willingness to abandon her Nun's clothing was recognition of the danger ahead. Knowing circumstances demanded a necessity to blend.

"She may talk rough, but is endowed with a good sense," I thought. "Some people pretend to have values and have none. She takes you into her heart, and warms you with a kind spirit."

"You're staring, Bishop. Never seen a pretty lady before?"

"Not one who was a Nun one minute, and a sophisticate the next."

We walked confidently out of the department store, and strode to the Ford. Back in the horse-hauler, we paused, surveyed the streets. Studying for menace.

"Maybe, I should wait down the street, until you've started the truck. I don't want to wrinkle my new clothes when the truck explodes," Claire said with a straight face.

"We're in this together. If you'd gone into the store, I picked, I would've waited in the truck. We would know there was no bomb."

"Now I would appear to be a 90-year-old bag lady. I think I'll chance an explosion."

I turned the key, the truck groaning to life.

Claire said, "See, Catholicism is correct. I asked God to dismantle the bomb."

I shook my head in astonishment. No way of keeping up with her.

"Let me fill you in. There's very little I know. I'm certain there's much more I don't understand."

"One wonders, whether this isn't Clint Eastwood in the Gauntlet," she said seriously. "A total set up."

"Could be right."

"Who can you check with that you trust?" Claire asked. "Seriously!"

"Here's the story first. I've been told a Muslim Middle East group is stealing secrets, undermining America."

"How?"

"Don't know."

I shrugged, not comprehending the full story. "Obtaining the most sensitive national secrets of our armament; handing them to Muslim extremists and countries sworn to attack us," I guessed.

"You believe them?"

"After what's happened today, I would say yes. I believe. It's not coincidental that a nuclear event befalls Iran. "

"What's the plan? Do you have one?"

Her question hit the mark. What was a plausible plan? I hadn't thought that far ahead. We barely started. We had been on the run since I met her. Got my orders an hour before.

"Outside Palmdale, two major airframe manufacturers build aircraft and avionics for the Air Force and Navy. Rumor says they have the next-generation fighter. Perhaps, more hardware the Muslim warriors would envy."

"I have some contacts. I can check," she said.

"I forgot; you were a big deal in the military."

"I rose quickly in rank. I have many ties, including those in military intelligence."

"Not much brainpower there."

"Old. The joke is older than I am."

Claire paused. "Perhaps, your contacts are why you've been chosen. The question is who did the choosing, and who's doing the killing?"

Claire smiled briefly.

I realized how pretty she was. Under her witticism and brash savvy is a stunning woman. Why is she a Nun? More to her story, I knew for sure. Being a Swiss Guard-trained agent for the Pope stands her in an elite group.

The Sister questioned, "Let's get back to whom you should call. One who could address the truthfulness of the mission? We need some light. We need to get out of the closet."

"The Los Angeles FBI station-chief cursorily touches my duties on some assignments. We can check with him."

"What do you mean the head of the local FBI offices only sort of understands who you are?"

"You heard Duke say I lead four lives?"

"I thought he was giving some reference to you being a cat – some sort of sarcasm. Like cats have four lives or nine lives or whatever," she said.

"Hardly."

"Well then?"

"I am not a normal, every-day FBI agent. I am undercover. I report to a special branch at the White House. They search for terrorists, spies and others who mean madness. I report to a Four-Star General in Washington."

"Damn."

"Been occasions when I've interfaced with the head of the Los Angeles bureau. Local deeds only. Therefore, he knows me by my distinct code name."

"Why don't we call the Four Star?"

"Not protocol."

"Protocol be damned. Our lives are on the line. Not to mention the world."

I glanced at her. "That's why we set protocol. The riskier the situation, the more important. Last resort. As a Marine, you understand."

She nodded her head. She didn't like it, but she understood. No jokes – no witticism.

"How long would it take to get a response from the general?"

"Forever."

"What?"

"When he wants a report, he will contact me. He will whistle for me – otherwise, we're out in the cold."

"Whistle. Why should he hiss at his own agent?"

She was scrunching her nose again. A pit bull this time.

"Call your local contact!"

Claire and I were traveling on the 405 freeway headed to Palmdale. No one in pursuit. Unlike the earlier driving escapades, I was following the speed limits and driving etiquette.

This time, I followed her instructions. I dialed the cell phone for the Los Angeles FBI bureau chief. I put the call on the speaker, so Claire could hear. The phone rang four times and was answered.

"Donnelly."

"Chief, this is the Snow Crab."

Silence on the phone.

"Chief Donnelly, this is Snow Crab – can you hear me?"

"The Snow Crab is dead, who is this? Identify yourself, immediately."

I hung up.

"I thought you were Green Beret," she said, considering.

"Different names for different folks. Need to know."

"Why did you hang up, so rapidly?"

"Chief Donnelly said the identifier – the Snow Crab – is dead. My death would have been reported in FBI briefings given to station chiefs. A report out of Washington. He thinks I am already dead" – I repeated. "Perhaps, this is the way our assignment is to end."

Claire said, "Someone with wishful thinking. The Snow Crab is an endangered species, huh?"

Chapter 5

ଔଔଔଔଔଔ

B-2 AIRCRAFT - THE PAINT SHOP

"Who are you masked man?" Claire asked, after hearing the senior boss in Los Angeles say I am dead.

"I'm beginning to wonder." This time the Nun gave a playful smile. A pat on the arm.

"What's next?"

I took a burner phone and dialed a series of numbers. Claire looked at me questioning; my attention drawn totally to the call.

"Four Star, this is Green Beret – calling you for instruction. FBI – LA says the Snow Crab is dead. Being followed by killers. Innocents shot at the racetrack. The Iran nuclear attack – relevant to us?"

Shorthand. The call was unwise. Not following orders. And with the FBI, orders were paramount. Nevertheless, I continued giving data to the general.

"Proceeding as instructed; however, need further clarification. Have met Rome's partner – a handful, but constructive. Out."

"Were you talking to anyone?"

"No. A drop, a call box number. Whether we will get a response or not, is a tossup. Won't be quick. We need to proceed on our own initiative."

We drove in silence for miles. Both creating game plans.

When Sister Claire first entered the tattered vehicle, she sat tucked far to the right as humanly possible. Now, she has moved over a bit toward the middle, showing she is indeed a partner. A friend. A sign of trust.

The drive from Los Alamitos to Palmdale was not quick in the diesel truck. The 405 is always busy. Out on Highway 5 – closer to our destination – travel was even slower.

"Not a bad ride," I said, killing time.

"Been thinking, we need to center our thoughts on the most outrageous theft an extremist could garner from the Palmdale defense plants," she said succinctly.

Right on the button.

"They paint the B-2 to be invisible, but as far as I know they only assemble fighters. In many cases, the plant trucks portions of a jet thousands of miles to another location for completion."

"We should visit the B-2 shop. Furthermore, track this new-generation fighter."

"Ditto."

Back to her mischievous self, she said, "See, a girl with pretty clothing can think."

I ignored the comment.

"We should cross examine our contacts; determine what other defense targets would benefit to our enemies."

Palmdale, Late Afternoon

I drove the truck up to the security gate and showed the FBI credentials – stamped Washington headquarters, Gene Michaels, supervisor. I, also, took out a driver's license from the District of Columbia. Same name.

"Wait here. I need to get clearance."

"Make it snappy. This is a national-security inspection. I'll give you two minutes."

I was brusque.

"You are being persnickety?" Claire said.

"Need their undivided attention. The big boss. Not some underling.

The sentry moved away noticeably upset.

"Who in the hell is Gene Michaels?"

"You want another dozen official identifiers. I thought it much preferred to go in undercover, rather than as Joseph Smith. We might be walking into a trap in any case. However, we will attain a minute of subterfuge."

The guard returned, pointing to a parking spot over to the right.

"Park by the fence. Sir. The head man will arrive in less than two minutes."

"What strategy will you employ when the escort comes?"

"First off, I'm considering who shows. I've worked these plants before. I've met the legitimate guards."

Closer to five minutes elapsed before a six-person electric golf cart arrived at the front gate. Immediately, the head of security recognized Joseph.

"How are you?" Asked the chief, looking somewhat confused.

Once seated inside the motorized vehicle, and heading toward the gigantic, city-sized aircraft plant, the chief said, "They told me my guest was Gene Michaels."

"My name today. I am undercover. This is a matter of national security. A potential breach."

"Who's this?" he asked — pointing at Claire, who rode a row behind us.

"This is Sister Claire, a Swiss-guard trained Nun. She's cleared top secret." I said, introducing my partner.

"Sister? Oh, right, you are a Bishop. She's a Mormon Sister?" Still not quite understanding. He didn't have the advantage of her normal Nun's garb.

I let the error go. Anything more would confuse the situation further.

"Any bizarre guests or occurrences?" Claire asked.

After thinking for only a split-second, the chief said, "Yes. We had a United States Senator here yesterday. He bounced our uniform-team. He had appropriate documentation. He made a real ass out of himself."

"What did he want?" I asked.

Claire broke in, "Where did he go in the plant?"

"Two places: to the B-2 hangar, and to our ultra-high security area. Our new fighter project."

"What's the haps about the fighter?"

"Not certain you have clearance for the information. You can go to the building — ask them. The building is most secure. I'm not going to divulge anything in that regard."

Something was amiss with this picture. First things first, I thought.

"Chief, take us to the paint shop, first," said Claire.

The chief looked at me — asking who was running the show. Essentially, who wore the pants.

"Go." I said, telling him informally, she did. This made him more perplexed; however, he followed orders.

The Sister might be a comic. However, when business was at the forefront, she was quick and incisive. On top of her game.

Arriving at the hangar, two B-2s were parked outside, under cover. And an additional craft inside a massive hangar.

The chief said, "I'm going to my headquarters and report."

"No, you're not." I ordered.

Thinking he'd misunderstood, he relayed, "I need to log the two of you. I'll be back for you in 10 minutes."

"Chief, you heard me accurately; you are staying."

"Not how it works."

Claire said, "That's how it works today."

The chief was armed, and started to reach for his sidearm concerned she was infiltrating a secure area... However, before he could touch the weapon on his side, Claire pointed an automatic at him.

"I don't understand."

"I already told you this was national security. We have reason to believe the Senator was bogus. We also think there are spies close by. Nobody − I mean nobody − leaves my side while I'm here." My tenor − stern and authoritative. No question in our resolve.

Claire said, "I think you already realize I'm much faster than you are. Go for your gun again, there will be no pleasantries."

"This the way you want it?" A little pout. He didn't like being shown up by Claire.

"Yes, sorry. I need it. Total control may help us escape this facility alive. Moreover, the only way we prevent secrets of calamity from being disseminated to foreign powers."

"Really." An unconvinced expression on his face.

Whatever he was; the security chief was a patriot. No one was going to steal information on his watch. If he could help.

"I trust you. Sorry, I lost my cool."

I smiled. "No problem"

He relaxed, his lips, which had been tight the second before had a small curl. The start of a smile. Certainly, an understanding.

Chapter 6

ঞেঞেঞেঞেঞে

MORE THAN PAINT WAS DRYING

The three of us marched into the paint shop, which had a bustle of activity. However, an ominous presence fell over the Herculean facility when workers saw their chief flanked by Claire and me.

"Chief," said the master in command of the painters, "Who are your friends?"

"This is Gene Michaels," said the chief, remembering the name I had given when entering the defense contractor's yard.

"Who is he?"

"He is FBI – national security."

The chief had dropped a bomb. As loud as the nuke someone fired on Jask, Iran today. All work abated. Everyone focused on us – the unknown.

I put out my hand in a sign of friendship. The man took it tentatively, but I noted sweat was rolling down his face.

"What's wrong?" I queried.

"Whata you mean?"

"You're perspiring profusely. Are you ill?"

No answer.

Sister Claire, always a Marine – even if she was sent from the Vatican – asked, "We understand you're selling national secrets here. How much are you getting?"

"Whata ya mean?" Asked the paint supervisor. "I'm selling nothing, here."

"Were you visited recently by a pretend United States Senator?" I asked, with all signs of friendship gone from my demeanor.

Absolute silence in the hundred-thousand square foot paint edifice. No answers. Not a word.

"I'm asking you man. Did a United States Senator come here or not?"

"Well.... A.... Yes."

"Was he handing out cigars, canvassing for votes?" Claire continued her assault.

No answer.

I extended both hands in front of me, palms down.

"I'm not accusing you of anything. I'm trying to understand exactly what the Senator wanted – that's all."

He seemed to relax a bit. Nonetheless, the little Hispanic painter was still tentative. He looked around at the other workers, seemingly anxious.

The security chief spoke softly, "They're not on your case. It's imperative we get the truth – the bottom line. The B-2 is at risk?"

The man nodded perceptively.

"I think so." He said.

"Tell us," I asked, again patiently.

Voices throughout the shop trickled to my ears. Several of the workers started to creep closer.

"Stay where you are," said Sister Claire, brandishing her weapon.

The men stopped. Silence returned through the structure.

I took another step toward the paint-crew supervisor, putting my arm around his shoulder.

"Relax. Who was the Senator?"

He leaned in cupping his hand to my ear – preventing anyone except me from hearing.

A shockwave, from a gun fired, rang out. Deafening the participants. Sister Claire was sidewinder fast, returning fire in the direction from which the offender had shot.

Another hail of bullets catapulted from another location in the gigantic hangar. The paint supervisor crumbled to the floor.

"I'm hit," I yelled, also feeling the sting of a bullet. I stood my ground, if you can say that falling to one knee is holding position. I returned fire with rapid volleys.

Still another offender opened the assault. Sister Claire took refuge behind a large tire of the attack aircraft. I was still kneeling on one knee. Holding my automatic in both hands.

"You got one of the bastards," yelled Claire.

I fired again – point blank – putting one in the forehead of one of the would-be assassins. I wasn't as quick as the Sister, but more accurate and deadly.

"Two down," I screeched.

"Any others?" Claire questioned.

"One. He's bugging out."

Remarkably, the chief of security did not fire a single shot. Didn't draw his gun.

He, likewise, did not run for cover. Instead, he knelt in the direct line of fire. He was covering his fallen friend. Bent over the head man, who was in command of keeping the B-2 secret in the skies.

"Do you see any more creeps?" I asked, with my right hand over the left arm, which was bleeding profusely. "Clearly, this suit will never make church again."

Claire was whirling as if she was undertaking some weird dance. Circling 360 degrees. You might say many things about the Sister, but she's not unobservant. Brave as the staunchest Marine.

"Everyone on the ground. Stand and you will be shot," she yelled.

No one doubted her sincerity. They hit the deck as if diving into foxholes.

"Should we chase the one who retreated?" she questioned.

"I want to check on the paint guy. Furthermore, I need some assistance."

"Okay."

I half walked, and crawled over to the still breathing supervisor – laying prone.

"I know you're in terrible pain. Can you answer a couple of questions?"

He nodded feebly.

"What did the Senator ask you to do?"

"He wants me to leave buckets of paint and primer out, unsecured, next Tuesday night. The formula too."

The supervisor must know there will be no tomorrow. However, he is answering bravely despite excruciating pain. Three slugs found their way home. Spelling his end.

I started to stand, when the man grappled for my sleeve. I winced, because I too felt the red-hot poker with blood running down the left arm.

"Sir?" I asked.

"Protect our new fighter. You'll need an army to get past their surveillance." He cringed with blood protruding from his nose.

"What do you mean?"

He was dead. No answer.

"Chief, tell me?" I asked my friend the head of security. He had implied there were problems with the fighter, but had refused to clarify earlier. "What is this new jet we must protect?"

"I've never been in the experimental hangar, where it was developed. They fly at night with absolute military coverage. No one can get close. The paint supervisor is correct."

"About what?" I asked.

"The two of you, including my patrol officers, aren't getting into that hangar. It's that simple."

"Why?"

"They've taken over. They have control."

"Who are 'they'? How many?

"Seven or eight. Heavily armed."

"Who are they?" I asked loudly. "And why haven't you called the Air National Guard, the police – everyone."

The chief spoke quietly. Obviously beleaguered. "They came in with the US Senator. And yes? He is a real Senator."

Claire and I looked at each other. The dark plan unfolding.

"Bishop, we need an Army to stop them from leaving with the new fighter." Claire said.

I was already calling. Locking down the airport. Notifying the Air National Guards stationed at Oxnard-Ventura under the control of a Colonel friend.

The police had no clearance into restricted areas; however, I called them too because of the shooting deaths in the paint hangar. Plus their guns would help at the secure jet hangar.

"The more help we get locking down this place, the better," said the former Marine Claire Coogan.

"If we can secure enough weapons, the traitors will be quickly out-gunned."

"They have machine guns," the chief repeated. "I saw the weapons."

A call came to the head security's man... The operator calling because of reports of "shots fired."

"We are at the paint shop," said the security chief. "Yes, guns were fired."

"Do you need ambulances?" Asked the lady on the phone.

"Yes, and the meat wagon," said the security chief.

Sister Claire said, "They are people...be respectful."

"Yes. I mean, certainly Sister. You're right."

Chapter 7

ଔଔଔଔଔ

A MESSAGE FROM A MAN
WHO THINKS HE'S GOD

I deliberated for an instant – arm on fire, oozing blood. I picked up my secure FBI issued telephone. Thinking, I started to text.

"Four Star, calamity at Palmdale secured, military contractor. Traitors killed. US Senator planning to steal paint for B-2 aircraft. Flying away with our new-generation fighter. Senator giving secrets to Muslim invaders? They are attempting to take flight – automatic weapons fired. Advice?"

I signed it Green Beret. I had no realistic expectations of a quick response.

"Really?" chided the Sister. "Wishful thinking that he will respond?"

"Absolutely. Nonetheless, he can't say I didn't tell him."

Bum arm and all, I joined Sister Claire, the security chief and one other armed guard in the six-man cart. The chief floored it.

We crept away. Heading to a massive hangar, housing the experimental fighter.

No one said a word. Although, we all knew we were light on fire power. Seven or eight machine gun toting military-types and, perhaps, an armed jet fighter awaited us.

My phone started playing the song the Star-Spangled Banner. I could hear the lyrics from the 1814 masterpiece in my head:

> *Oh, say can you see by the dawn's early light.*
> *What so proudly we hailed at the twilight's last gleaming?*
> *Whose broad stripes and bright stars thru the perilous fight,*
> *O'er the ramparts we watched were so gallantly streaming?*
> *And the rocket's red glare, the bombs bursting in air,*
> *Gave proof through the night that our flag was still there.*

The chief said, "A message from heaven, Bishop?"

"No, only from one who thinks of himself as God, sometimes. A Four-Star General."

I looked at the text I had received from Washington. Surprise, Surprise...the Four Star paid attention – when he wanted.

"New Air Force drone fighter may not be permitted to leave field, Palmdale. Protect at all cost. If it takes your life, and that of the Sisters, the flight is to be retarded – immediately!!! No excuses." The message read.

My reply, "General we have four small weapons, against probably eight with machine guns. Not to mention the fire power of the jet."

"Stop talking. Start fighting. Sniper rife being dispatched. Five minutes. Four Star out."

Claire scrunched up her pretty face. "Tell me?"
"Ready to die?"

"Do you Mormons ask yourselves that often?"

"For God – or country, I will."

"Well, then. Charge." She encouraged.

"The message said the new plane may not be permitted to leave the field. We die, if necessary, preventing take off." I told her.

The guard who was riding with us said, "I have a wife and family. I can't die." He was colorless. Looked deadly pale.

"Drop him off here. He has the cover of buildings; still has a reasonable firing angle," said the chief. The man got out. Staggering. Wetting his pants.

Claire said, "You have quite an army. A bunch of chickens."

"Most are good men."

"Want out, chief?" I asked.

"I'm with the two of you."

We pulled around the corner of a building, bringing the stadium-sized, super-secure hangar into view. The doors were being opened.

"Readying for flight," announced the chief.

Immediately, we started taking fire. One round clanged off the golf cart. Luckily, the combatant was a poor aim. Although, honestly, the distance was too far to accurately aim the machine guns of our enemy. Our weapons accuracy wasn't much better at the distance.

"We could throw fire crackers at them. For all the good, it will do." I said.

"Hitting someone from here is even a tad long for a Catholic," said Sister Claire, trying to get my goat.

The chief looked at her confused. Not understanding the reference. "I'm a Baptist," he confessed. "It's too far for me, as well."

The cart was abandoned. The three of us taking defensive positions. Candidly, however, we offered no real resistance to the enemy assailants. If they know how to handle the jet, they should be able to find the skies.

I was on both knees. My left arm dangling in pain. Presently, I had no target. Hangar doors were open. No plane. No enemy.

I was tapped on my injured arm. I whirled around.

"My name is Cory Bliggens, vice president of production."

"Stay under cover, sir," I instructed. "Nice to meet you."

"They probably are trying to fly the new bird. We killed their controls yesterday. Once we discovered a rouge US Senator, without proper authorization, put an elite crew of military mercenaries into our secure center, we pulled the plug."

"It can't fly?"

"A pile of bolts, without programming."

"Have you told them?"

A wry smile. "No."

"Obviously, the guys believe they can escape with the bird. They opened the hangar doors."

"Oh, and the idiots don't have access to the plans either." Said Bliggens.

I saw a figure moving toward my position. He held a sniper's rifle above his head. Yelling, "Green Beret, Green Beret."

There was no danger from the on-comer. Both hands held the rifle high in the air. He was attempting to stay clear of rounds that could be fired from the open hangar door...

"Here," I beckoned. "I'm the Green Beret."

"Identification, sir."

I first pulled the Gene Michaels creds. I replaced them. I was struggling because my movements were hampered by the winged shoulder.

"Here." I said, producing the correct identifying documents.

He handed me the rifle - glad to be rid of it. Then, he sat down a box of ammunition. Rid of both, the suit retreated to safety.

"Game on."

The distance with a scoped-sniper's weapon was trifling. Absolutely, no challenge. Now, the combatants were sitting ducks.

"Cory. Do me a favor? Call the plant and inform the invaders their bird will not fly. Secondly, tell them to surrender or be killed. They are surrounded."

"My pleasure."

He moved to a phone close by, and directed operations to connect him to the speakers in the experimental plane's hangar.

As he was making the call, I saw Sister Claire crawling to a jeep, which was parked in shooting range of the intruders.

I fired my pistol at the one lone gunman, standing in the doorway of the hangar across from me. Couldn't hit him with the

FBI-issued weapon. Too far to aim properly. Even so, it drew his attention away from Claire.

Cory returned.

"Ok. They know. Hopeless to light the bird. Told them they were surrounded. To give up."

Seconds later, the PA system connected on the outside of the buildings squelched.

"Who do you think you are fooling? We are loaded with nine machine guns. You have dinky pistols that can't even reach us. You may as well aim at the building, so you can claim you hit something. You cruds run for your life."

Cory asked, "Should I make another plea? A final announcement."

"Don't bother. We have Annie Oakley behind the Jeep, and I have a sniper's rifle. They will catch on quickly."

"Annie who? Who is Annie Oakley?"

"You know – out of the old west. The female, sure-shot Annie Oakley."

He didn't understand.

"You must be too young or not watch TV."

A barrage of automatic fire came from the building. Seven men ran out firing. With as many rounds as were being fired, even poor shots could get lucky. Bullets were clinging off our hiding place.

They were not aiming. Merely pulling the trigger.

Claire plugged one invader – two steps from the door. He went down. No more gun play from him.

The intruder sensed the Sister was close, and trained their volley on her position. Nonetheless, she was well secured.

From my distant location, I took aim with the sniper's rifle on the man in the center of the pack. Presumably, the leader. Head shot. All over, but the funeral.

"Not really fair," I said to myself.

I cranked another into the chamber and easily took down a third traitor. Claire shot felled a fourth. Shooting ducks like at the carnival. The attackers from the hangar had been so confident they ran right into our wheelhouse.

The trio still standing turned left. Heading directly at the Sister's hiding place. Obviously, they believed she was the easiest target. A possible escape route.

"Sister, incoming," I screamed, as I flattened another combatant.

"I have these girls," Claire said calmly. She lay prone, firing under the Jeep. The men were fleeing right into her barrage.

It was unclear whether Claire or I ventilated the sixth man, as he seemed to explode in two directions at the same time.

The seventh stopped running. Threw up his hands. Dropped the machine gun.

"I quit. I want a lawyer. I want an attorney," he screamed.

My finger pulsed. An instant later, he would have been explaining to Jesus why he was inside the aircraft facility.

"On your stomach," Claire barked. She remembered her Marine training. Did it well, I thought.

"Claire, be mindful. May be more combatants. Only seven rushed out. Said they had nine machine guns." I yelled.

"Right you are. I forgot."

Absolute silence replaced the havoc. Everyone waiting for the next hammer to drop.

"Dingbat – you on the ground – crawl over to me," Claire ordered. "Slowly, or I'll send you to hell."

He complied.

The security chief made his way to my side. He had a concerned look on his face.

"Your arm looks horrible. Needs attention. Now."

"Forgot it during the battle."

The chief added, "Only a few workers are in the plant. Most were told not to come to work today. Might be one or two more left from the Senator's group. I don't know."

Screams came from the metal building. Women and men alike – screaming. So many voices, it was hard to understand.

Finally, one clear speaker said, "We're not terrorists. We are the factory workers. Held captive. No more hostiles inside."

I called back, "Come out slowly. Hands high. Stop at the front of the hangar."

A group of 15 or possibly 20 workers cautiously made their way outside of the gigantic edifice. All obeyed. Stopped. As in an old cowboy flick – they reached for the sky...

"Okay, everyone on the ground. Face down," Claire yelled.

They followed orders. No guns in sight.

I noticed for a first time that a large contingent of security, police and military cops had joined the fray.

Stepping forward, a man with military credentials said, "We've got this."

"Brave. You show up when all the works finished," I said.

He said nothing.

The chief said, "I know him. His task force provides military security for the plants here in Palmdale."

"His security is a little underwhelming." I barked.

The officer said nothing. Gave me a dirty look.

I suddenly felt weak with nausea. I hadn't remembered my arm throbbing. Now, it was hard to think of anything else.

"Happy to hand off. Do you have enough men to secure the area?"

"Only eight. Have called for more. The police and contractor security will help," he said authoritatively. "Like you say, the work is mostly complete."

"The Sister and I will remain while you search the plant."

"If you want. Looks like your arm needs treatment."

I noticed a sergeant in police uniform had handcuffed the assailant, who had crawled near Sister Claire. Then, another official dressed in a civilian suit took the combatant into custody.

The Sister made her way to my side. She also looked concerned, noting that the left arm was covered with blood.

The individual, who handed me the sniper rifle, tapped me on my right shoulder.

"Green Beret, I'll take the rifle."

Without thinking, I returned the weapon.

"Good shooting," he said, turning and walking away.

Claire asked, "Who was that? Where did he come from? How did he know you needed a sniper's rifle?"

"Don't know."

"Too convenient for me."

"What?"

"Someone appearing with a minute's notice, who hands you exactly what you need in a combat situation, is a little too convenient for me."

The notion escaped me. I was thankful for the weapon instead of death. Even so, Claire was right. How would anyone know I was the Green Beret? Give me a replica of my exact shooting friend?

"Only the Four Star," I said. "He had said..."

"But how would he know so quickly you needed a sniper's rifle?" She asked. "We didn't tell him we were coming here."

"Told him Palmdale defense plant and protecting the new fighter. Even so, you're right. Too convenient. Something missing from the equation."

Chapter 8

CRCRCRCRCR

LONE RANGER AND TONTO

"Joseph, your arm needs a doctor, now," said Sister Claire, putting her right hand to my face. "You're white as a sheet."

"Old soldiers don't die; they just fade away."

"Corny."

"Best I could do. Feel like left-over ga-losh."

"A waterproof overshoe. That's what ga-losh is."

"See, I am so far gone. I can't talk. I meant goulash. A soup of sorts," I said. "A mishmash, potpourri or Mulligan."

"My bad," the Sister replied. "Shouldn't yank your chain when your half dead."

"More than half."

The chief was on his walkie-talkie, summoning more help and ambulances.

Claire said, "If we get stuck here, who knows who will show up. We may attract people who can't s tolerate you, Bishop. Since I met you, I've been ducking bullets all day."

"I agree. Let's go."

"You two can't leave; this is a crime scene. Espionage," said the military security cop.

"Changing your story. A minute ago..."

"I know. Orders from our commander."

'I need a hospital."

"Ambulances on the way."

"We're probably dead if we stay in the crosshairs." I said.

"Whose guns?" asked the agent.

"Don't exactly know. We're the anti-terrorist task force. Seeking the answers. This event is too bizarre to be an accident."

"I agree with you. I've been at this plant plenty over the last seven or eight years. Never seen anything closely resembling these shenanigans."

Starting to fade in-and-out, I said, "You know enough to file a classified report. Drag more national-security types out. Secure the new aircraft with a hundred men. A thousand – if necessary." I ordered.

The military cop said, "The dead guys don't seem Muslim. However, the warnings we have said they are planning calamity."

"Can't go by appearance. We need some irrefutable facts. Not mere conjecture."

"True."

Claire said, "One is in custody. Lean on him."

I am out of my mind with pain. Okay when focused on combat. However, useless palavering wasn't doing the trick. Not an antidote to agony.

I started walking to the motorized cart, saying, "I need to get some medical assistance, as well as reporting to supervisors."

The military cop said nothing.

"Can you walk, you wimp?" Questioned Claire sympathetically.

"If I'm alive, I'll crawl to the truck."

My friend, the plant's chief, asked, "What do I tell authorities?"

"The absolute truth."

"This place is almost the Alamo. Had the two of you not shown, the Muslims would have won today. When I'm asked who you are, what do I tell the boss man?"

Claire responded, "The Lone Ranger and Tonto, obviously."

Even with the seriousness of the event, the chief walked into Claire's instantaneous humor, lightening the mood.

"Right, Tonto."

Security became thick with golf carts and trucks, approaching the building from all quarters.

"Secure everyone for questioning, except those two," ordered my friend. He singled out Claire and me for release.

The military cop said nothing.

Outside, I climbed into an unattended golf cart, motioning Claire to drive.

"To the car, Tonto."

"Right you are - bleeding man."

The mood was electric. As if a nuclear bombardment had gone off at the aerospace facility. Horns were screeching, and everyone scurrying everywhere. From the heavens, God might think ants were running haplessly in all directions.

"I'm going to make a stop at the front guard shack," said Claire, unopposed. "I want to find out if anyone has been making alterations to our truck."

I was resting with my head back on the seat, bleeding all over the upholstery. I abdicated thinking. She now headed our mission.

"Hang in; I will find help. A hospital."

"I'm okay."

"Sure. You look peachy."

The golf cart purred up to the guard station. Claire circling, so he could not see her injured companion.

The man asked, "What in the hell is going on?"

"Saboteurs."

"What?"

"Anyone approach the 350 diesel truck over there, since we left it?"

"Not that I've observed. Oh, you're the two FBI types."

"Are you saying no? Conversely, are you guessing, maybe, someone did?"

"I have more important things to do than to look out for your truck, lady."

"I can see you do. Reading Playboy is vital. We will mention you to Washington. Tell them you let the spies into the plant." She lied, driving away.

The man was sickened. He believed her.

As we neared our vehicle, she said to me, "Stay where you are. I want to check out under the hood and under our ride."

"Good idea, we've had too much excitement for one day."

Claire positioned the golf cart by the right side of Duke's dully, blocking it from view of police cars, careening into the government facility. Not only did the 6-person craft provide screening, but I could easily climb aboard once the sleuthing was complete.

She pried open the hood, meticulously cared for by the trainer. No bomb. Then, Claire climbed under the beast, with her legs extending beyond the doors. Her head was fully lost from view.

"No bomb."

"They didn't have time to jimmy," I conjectured crawling into the truck. The step up into the raised vehicle was a catastrophe. I smashed my head on the back of the seat.

The Sister perceived my state. This time a compassionate nod.

"We need to abandon the pickup once we find a place to get you treated," she said.

"I'm sure Duke will appreciate our kindness. Unless I bleed all over his seats," I answered, trying to lighten the mood.

"Where to?"

"That's a humdinger."

"Yes, the choice can make us sitting ducks. Our enemy will have their radar tuned on us."

"I'm out of sorts, light headed. Let me think."

Claire said, "Don't bleed on me, wimp. A little scratch shouldn't affect a he-man like you."

"I have a doctor friend."

Claire, smiling, replied, "You have one friend. I'm amazed."

"Give me a break, Sister. Counting you, we have two loyalists."

Thinking, Sister Claire said, "No way he's treating you and not reporting to authorities."

"Wouldn't expect him to. He, however, will treat me, release me, and give us a head start to do our job. He'll take his sweet time in the notification."

"Where is this Doc."

"Can you find UCLA Medical Center?"

"You better call him - be sure he is on duty."

"Right."

I confirmed my friend, a surgeon, was working, and would wait for me to arrive. I only cursorily told him the nature of the emergency.

"I need to report." The Sister said.

"Claire, who do you contact?"

"Higher than you can reach."

"What?"

"Stratospherically high."

"I can imagine reporting to the President of the United States or The Prophet of our church. I can't think of anyone higher, other than God or Jesus Christ, of course."

"Well, leaving God out of the discussion - I'll call the Pope."

As afflicted as I was from my injury, I jolted upright by the mention of the Pope. Her having his direct line?

"You hangout with the Big Dog, huh?" I quipped. "An immense challenge to convert him."

Claire turned her head, looking me squarely in the eyes. Disbelief registered. Even while severely injured, her companion's values included bringing the Pontiff to the Heavenly Father through Mormonism. Incredible standards, the Sister thought.

The Nun redirected the conversation. "The Pope received classified information from America. He told me he had been given alarming news. His Eminence ordered me to be certain the world is not shaken by war."

"Who called the Pope?"

"Don't know!"

"Did you ask?"

"Told me the caller was confidential. He directed me to proceed as if the information is verified."

I winced as pain shot up my arm. Then, I made a face similar to the scrunched up Pug dog that Claire makes in certain situations.

"Well, we can verify the truthfulness now."

"Not even a good imitation of me." Claire stared with big eyes. Her nose tucked in a playfully crinkled expression.

The Sister added, "I'm still mystified about the coincidences at the shootout. No one in history shows up so conveniently with a sniper's rifle for an undercover FBI agent. Knowing his code name- the Green Beret."

"Once I had the weapon, they were almost sacrificial lambs," I said in agreement.

"Like road kill. Similar to suicide bombers, without the bombs. I think someone decided on killing them. Their deaths would make a bigger splash than sending us to heaven. Doesn't mean we are off the hook."

"Muslims slain in an aborted takeover of a defense plant makes great news. Perhaps, knocks the Jask nuclear attack off the front page."

"The slaughter will be reported to the world news today and tomorrow." She agreed.

"Nonetheless, the rifle saved our lives. I've seen past scenarios where the military whisked armament into the field at a minute's notice. Not unusual."

"Perhaps." The Nun was unconvinced.

"Claire, consider how fast a military cop routed to the scene. Those plants are classified havens – protected routinely. They have all types of weapons. A long range gun – no problem."

"Too convenient for me."

Claire drove out of the desert, and through the low hills. We were now descending into the San Fernando Valley. I must have passed out momentarily.

"Are you going a make the hospital before you die?" she asked.

"Sure, I'm a Boy Scout."

"You're a chameleon – always changing colors, call signs, and names."

"You can just call me the masked man – the Lone Ranger."

"You are indeed."

The Sister was quiet. Thinking.

Claire asked, "You said we now could verify that America is in danger. Right?"

I nodded and answered, "Yes, to the extent men are dying like flies. Furthermore, a United States Senator is trying to steal American military technology, and combatants are set up to die. And we are being tracked by evil. "

"What else?"

I did not answer. I was asleep or unconscious.

Chapter 9

CRCRCRCRCR

A FAITHFUL HEART

Sister Claire called Rome as she drove on the 405 freeway out of the San Fernando Valley, heading toward UCLA Medical Center.

To her surprise, she was put through to the Pope without delay. Claire took five minutes detailing the events of the day.

"Thank you, Sister. Watch over your companion. He's a worthy man. As they say, Bishops - in any faith - do no grow on trees." The Pope appreciated Claire's propensity for humor and obliged.

"Respect. The recognition of warmth, coming from the Pontiff." She knew.

He added, "This is a paramount undertaking by the two of you."

His Eminence said the words with such strength they sent shivers up her spine. The hairs on the back of her neck stood. She had never before personally experienced this phenomenon.

"For divine assistance, both of you pray; there is only one God. He will help. Everyone is at risk. The Father responds when all his children are in danger."

"One God," Sister Claire thought.

She knew Joseph's faith taught there was additional deity in heaven. Certainly, she did not have full knowledge of the beliefs of the Mormon Church. Even so, she understood LDS members believed in three heavenly beings – God the Father, his son Jesus Christ, and the Holy Ghost. Three separate - not one, as the Bible teaches.

Her brother had converted to the LDS faith, and they had numerous friendly debates - scouring the Scriptures for answers. Claire also learned Mormons, as a group, studied the gospel more than any church. They ponder the Bible and Book of Mormon daily.

"We pray to the same God," she said, with a peaceful heart.

Upon arrival at UCLA Medical, Claire gently shook Joseph hoping - no, praying - he was still alive. He had lost a lot of blood. The seat was soaked red. The sticky goo pooled under Joseph's rear end.

Specimens like Joseph don't die from a gunshot to the arm, do they.

"Honey. Not so hard," I said moaning.

Being called honey, shook her. Took her off her game.

"Joseph, Joseph.... It's Sister Claire. We are at UCLA Medical Center."

"Oh, I was dreaming. Thinking of home, my sweet wife. I apologize."

"No need," she said flushed from his words. "What doctor is providing treatment?"

"Ask for Dr. Jerry Trimbold. He's expecting me."

Naturally, as with all hospital admissions, a bunch of rigmarole ensued. That is, until Dr. Trimbold arrived. Then, magically the doors opened wide.

"Bishop," he said, looking at my blood-covered jacket.

"I'm on assignment for the US government. I've been shot in related work. I need you to help me, send me on my way, and then report the shooting to the police," I told Bishop Jerry Trimbold. I was slurring my words – drunk from pain, not alcohol.

Mormons have an unpaid clergy. Trimbold is a doctor by profession, and a Mormon Bishop of a ward different from mine. Some church goers are confused believing Mormon Bishops serve over a very large, extensive area. Instead, Mormon Bishops preside with a flock of several hundred people. Not hundreds of thousands.

"What name should I use on the admittance?"

"If it doesn't get you in trouble, agent Gene Michaels as my name. I have identification. The slightest bit of nervousness, admit me under my given name."

Dr. Trimbold summoned Sister Claire to follow.

Sister Claire entered the exam room, where my expensive suit – now in ruins – was cut from my arm. Dr. Trimbold made a preliminary examination.

"I presume you and Bishop Smith are working together," the doctor said to Claire. "He's lost a lot of blood. The injury certainly is not fatal; nonetheless, serious. It's going to take a while in surgery."

"Take care of him, Doc."

"Should we notify his wife?"

I said, "Bishop Trimbold I'm not dead quite yet. I'm right here. Nothing nefarious going on. Actually, this is Sister Claire Coogan, a Nun, sent by the Pope from Rome to help on the case. She may not appear to be a Sister. We're working undercover. So, no, leave my wife to me."

My friend nodded. Embarrassed. He had faith that Joseph was not cheating on his beautiful and loving wife. Why would he? Men die for a companion as lovely as Nancy. Joseph had everything at home.

Claire retreated to the lobby waiting area. She kept a watchful eye for predators who might be staking out hospitals. Men trying to uncover where Joseph Smith sought treatment.

No more talk. I was unceremoniously wheeled out of the room, and into a prep area. Stripped of all my clothing, and prepared for surgery.

Two-plus hours later, Dr. Trimbold emerged.

"The bullet carved a small chunk out of a bone. It took me a while to clean up the fragments. He's going to need therapy. Ultimately, he will be fine."

"When can I see him? Time is critical; a matter of national security."

"I'm staying with him until he's awake. It might be close to an hour." Answered the doctor.

"Thanks."

"Under the circumstances, you will be safer in my office."

She wondered whether all Bishops were so intuitive.

"Again, thank you. You're right."

The time went on incessantly. The day turned to evening. They were no closer to the answers. The truth was illusory.

About one hour later, Dr. Trimbold summoned Sister Claire to a private recovery room, where Joseph was groggily returning to the world.

"You okay, stranger?" Asked the Sister.

"Sister Claire, I declare."

Dr. Trimbold said, "Let me report. Your arm was impacted by the bullet. You're going to need physical therapy. You should take it easy for a couple of weeks. Is that out of possibility?"

"Bishop Trimbold, my friend, I must confess that I am more than a stockbroker. That is confidentially a front for the work as an undercover for the FBI. I'm a senior anti-terrorist investigator."

"Confidentially, back at you, I always knew there was something more going on," Bishop Trimbold confided. "Calls at hours stockbrokers are off duty. You know? You are never free."

"I can't divulge what I'm working on. Other than to say it is highly classified. Furthermore, honestly, there's more I don't have a clue about."

Looking at Sister Claire, the doctor asked, "How does she fit in?"

"This is our first day working together. Both of us were partnered by our seniors. I'm not sure we even understand why we were assigned this way. The Pope sent her. Washington commissioned me."

Claire replied, "I had a 10-minute meeting at the Vatican, with the barest of instructions, and was on an airplane to America. I met this scalawag on the steps of a Catholic church."

"Sounds like a James Patterson novel," replied the doctor.

"Reality is more painful than a book," I said.

"Where are you going tonight?"

"Don't know. We have some investigating to do before we sleep. Have a shirt I can borrow?"

His friend smiled. "Ever the optimist."

"Bishop Trimbold, how about a blessing. It will do more to heal me than your surgical skills."

The doctor now took on the role as a priesthood holder, giving a blessing to a faithful LDS member. Believers experience the power of God through blessings. For healing, the pronouncement must come from a priesthood holder who receives divine inspiration. Further the receiver must faithfully believe in God the Father and Jesus, and the power of healing. Miracles happened in the days Jesus and the apostles taught—and are not dead today.

An nonbeliever may gain comfort through kind words; however, for those without faith, there is no divine intervention.

After, Dr. Trimbold and I shook hands. For, I did have faith. And Bishop Trimbold was a worthy holder of God's Priesthood.

"If I can help you further, let me know. Here are some strong, long-lasting pills for pain and to prevent infection. Take them."

"Yes, sir. I will."

With that Dr. Trimbold took leave.

Claire said, "Bishop Trimbold is correct. We should find shelter for the night, and time for you to heal a bit."

"We have some calls to make. I need to reconnoiter with the security chief at the aircraft plant. See what else he discovered. Find where he left it with the authorities. Must report to the Four Star. Then, plot our next move."

Claire admired the intricate mind of this man. Minutes before he went through major surgery. He still was overly pale.

It was, as if, after the blessing, Joseph absorbed new strength. He was conscious only a short while. Now, he had a new mental armament.

The Nun thought the LDS blessing of peace and healing was babble, bunk or false doctrine. Nonetheless, she now observed first-hand the power exhibited through the Lord's faithful servant Joseph Smith.

Claire always had absolute faith in Jesus' healing powers while on earth. Nevertheless, for a Bishop to exude heavenly influence seemed almost bizarre. However, Joseph rose – after the blessing – as if, the healing power had come from God himself.

Joseph was looking at her strangely. The Sister realized she had zoned out. She forced herself to snap back to the instant.

"Where were you Sister?"

"Right here. With you, of course," she replied. "Where are we going to stay tonight. Am I going to meet the Mrs.?" she asked.

"Want to keep these thugs away from my family. It may be time to take our act on the road."

"Good idea."

Joseph sat up.

"Sister, why don't you get the car –I mean truck – while I figure how to escape this establishment."

"Sure."

With that, she started for the door.

"Why don't we get a taxi? Let's leave Duke's truck here. We can put the keys under the mat," she suggested.

"The taxi's a good idea. We will keep the keys. Don't want to invite danger into a friend's home."

Not grasping where my friend, Dr. Trimbold, was located in the hospital, I dialed him from my cell phone.

"This is Joseph. How much do I owe your asylum?"

"I put the charges on my account. They will give me a billing tomorrow, and then you can square up with insurance. Don't stub your toe, but you're free to go."

"Thanks, my friend."

Sister Claire had a taxi waiting at the curb.

"Where to," said the driver.

I answered, "Los Angeles International Airport, the charter side. Vance aviation."

Chapter 10

ଓଃଓଃଓଃଓଃଓଃ

WHO IS ON FIRST BASE?

"You're a barrel of fun," Claire said. "And a million surprises."

"I'm going to charter a jet," I answered. I lowered my voice, and half whispered into her ear. "We can rest on the way to the nation's capital."

"You appreciate how to impress a girl on their first date." She said "date" loud enough for the curious cabby to hear.

"First date?"

"Dating disaster." Claire had that playful twinkle in her eyed – a picture to her soul.

She noticed the taxi driver observing them. Claire intuitively knew the police or international terrorists would follow their trail.

"No freebies," she thought.

Claire squeezed my right hand, and imperceptibly motioned to the driver.

"Got you." I said nothing more.

Arriving at Vance aviation, I had a new notion. Paying the driver and thanking him, Claire and I stepped from the cab.

I speed-dialed billionaire industrialist Tyler Dovato, hoping to heck, I could reach him.

The phone rang incessantly. And went to voicemail.

"Sir, this is Bishop Joe Smith. You said, if I ever needed to charter one of your company jets, all I had to do is call you. I understand you were just being nice. However, I desperately need to get to Washington DC by private means."

I left my cell number.

Then, I dialed trainer Duke Snyder. Duke answered on the second ring.

"Hey, how you doing?"

"Your truck is at UCLA Medical Center; It may be hot. I was involved in a shooting, company related, in Palmdale."

"Figured that was you," said Duke. "The calamity is all over the news. Obvious, the Bishop and the Nun are the instigators."

"There was...."

"What can I do to help?"

"Run a tab on your time – the assistance is no freebie. I'm going to need your investigative brilliance."

"We will worry about that later. What do you need now?"

"I need private jet transportation to DC. I'm at Vance aviation. Called your friend Mr. Dovato, asking for help. Got his voice mail."

Duke Snyder said, "I'll be back to you in ten minutes."

I had barely reached the modern reception lounge at Vance before my cell phone jingled.

"Hello."

"I understand you need ferrying to Washington?" Said the deep voice on the telephone.

No introductions. No nonsense. Bottom line. No wasted talking. It was the billionaire, Mr. Dovato.

"Right. Off the books," I said.

"How many?"

"Two."

"Jet at Vance Aviation in a half-hour. Who do they ask for?

"The Cardinal."

"You must tell me the joke someday, Bishop."

With that, the phone went dead. I didn't even think to ask Dovato if he was returning my call, or if he had called at the urging of my friend Duke Snyder.

Claire and I moved, sitting down in plush seats. Within a few feet of us stood hundreds of millions of dollars of aircraft. Private and corporate.

A pretty, black flight attendant stationed behind the Vance aviation desk, called out, "Can I help you?"

I answered without a pause. As sincerely as I could muster, "I'm the Cardinal, waiting for one of your client's jets. It should be here shortly."

"Nothing on our books for any pending flight tonight," she said.

Just then, her phone rang. She picked up. Just as quickly, she stood perceptively taller. The main man talked to her – not some assistant.

"Chairman Dovato's jet will be here shortly. If you need anything?"

"No, we're fine."

Claire asked me, "What's the plan? Why are we going to Washington?"

"To catch a Senator."

"If you're fishing for a Senator, I guess you would snag him in DC," she said smiling.

I looked at my phone's contact list, trying to find the security chief's cell number. I perceived the hour was too late to reach him at the plant. I had only called him once before at home. Nonetheless, my wife always says I keep everything. Why not?

I dialed. Second ring. Keeping minutia pays off.

"Hey, this is Joseph Smith. Can you talk?"

"As long as you promise no more excitement, tonight," said the chief. "My heart won't take more."

"What else did you find out about the shenanigans being pulled by the Senator?"

"Amazingly, we found express instructions on the letterhead of the President of the United States, authorizing the instructions you heard earlier at the paint shop."

"You believe the President signed the letter?"

"No, we're positive he didn't. The Senator signed it. Several of the plant employees saw him do it. He said he had been authorized."

"What about the classified fighter in the restricted hangar?"

"National-security types roaming everywhere tonight. A termite couldn't escape."

I asked, "What did the prisoner whom we took into custody say? What is his clandestine mission? What did he say about the Senator?

"Honestly I don't know."

"Why is that?"

"No information on the prisoner since the Sister turned him over. He wasn't taken to police headquarters or anywhere else I can find."

Claire brushed against my shoulder, and I winced. Alternatively, the route of my pain possibly originated from the pronouncement about the missing spy.

"Candidly, a man who comes running out of a defense plant firing a machine gun can't be found? I saw him handcuffed. Taken away in custody."

"Well, the suit who took him away probably has a good notion. Ask him?"

"Who was he?"

The chief said, "His credentials were checked and rechecked. CIA all the way."

I said, keeping my voice friendly, "The CIA doesn't work on American soil."

"Well, then he tricked military intelligence, a captain on the local police force, and little old me. I'm the only one that's expendable."

"Any clue where they took him?"

"They told us they were taking him to the federal building in Los Angeles – or was it West Los Angeles? I checked a few minutes ago. He is not there. Never arrived. He's disappeared."

Sister Claire asked, "Any other armed foes inside the plant?"

"I bet a magician made them disappear. Am I correct, chief?" I said snidely.

"You're good. No others apprehended." The chief said he asked about the leader of the so-called Muslim offenders. "Couldn't be found. They told me."

The line went silent for a second. Then, the chief continued, "And look at it this way – you made yourself disappear. No one is concerned about the missing Muslim leader. Everyone is looking for you," he said. "No warrants for the perpetrators? Only for you!"

"Why?"

The chief said, "One wonders, right. The bad become good. The protectors become evil. Only in America."

He understood his head might be lopped off as a result of the unaccounted details.

"They know who I am?" I questioned.

"I told them you were the Lone Ranger with Tonto. As you said. Another man said you were the 'Green Beret.' Still another said you were a 'Dead Sea Crab'."

Pausing, I finally replied, "There is a message in the apparent nonsense."

"The whole thing went down like a bad movie," Claire said.

"Someone is pulling the puppet strings. I'm interested in finishing the scene. Is America still standing? Are we dead or alive?"

The chief asked, "Can't you put a lasso around the bad guys? They have your number – so you must be able to get a fix on them."

"I have about as much authority as I did when I was a kid in the principal's office. I just look like I'm in command."

Claire tugged on my right arm.

"Hold on a minute."

Claire asked, "Find out what the authorities learned about the shootings and us."

"Chief, my partner is inquiring about what the authorities were told? About the gun play in the paint shop? And the shootout at the plane's hangar?"

"I was honest. I told them that we came under fire. I explained you were FBI. You were hit. Later, you were too good for the stiffs coming out of the experimental aircraft hangar. I told them you had no alternative but to return fire or die."

"Did you...?"

"You're going to ask whether I told them your real names."

"How'd you know?"

"This is national-security stuff. I told the absolute truth. They know FBI agent Joseph Smith was here. I candidly forget who was with you."

"I can live with the truth."

"Where are you?" he asked.

"For the moment, that's classified. I'm on assignment. Chief, I will keep you informed. If you don't mind, I'll call to find out what's going on in the next few days, as well."

The chief said, "Is this call off the record?"

"No – It's official business. FBI seeking information."

"Good night, Joseph."

I hung up.

With a devious smile, Claire said, "Well, he protected the innocent one – me."

"Do you have innocence or are you innocent?" I asked.

"Bishop, that's too deep for a poor Nun from Italy."

Suddenly, I felt ill. The pain pills were making me sick to my stomach. They were driving me to find sleep. I was nearly out on my feet.

I looked at Claire. Who was uneasy.

"You need to stop. Lie down. You are going to miscalculate. Get us killed," Claire said. She has such a peaceful spirit.

"There is nowhere to lie down."

"Call your boss."

I smiled. "I thought you wanted me to stop."

She was correct. I needed answers. "I am a dead-on-my feet, one-armed agent."

I took the Sister's suggestion. Called my ultimate supervisor – the Four Star. By voice mail.

"Reporting in, sir. You recognize the voice. I'm certain you've heard the scuttlebutt from Palmdale, California. Intruders, including a United States Senator. They infiltrated the paint shop, stealing the paint which makes the B-2 invisible. More importantly, they tried to capture our new secret fighter. Sniper's rifle the difference. My understanding – the plane is surrounded by the military now."

I was having difficulty being concise. My thoughts wandering.

"Frankly, I am concerned, sir. The NSA, FBI, CIA, or the President – someone is too conveniently ahead of the power curve. We killed many combatants today. Sir, how did you know – in advance – I needed the rifle?"

I took a sip of water and another pain pill. My entire body ached. I had a high fever.

"A man with a sniper rifle was ready to hand the Green Beret the perfect weapon at the perfect time. Yes, how did they know I would be at that plant? No one ordered me to go to Palmdale. Protect the air-defense plants."

Am I that predictable? Was that the only move – the single best move — to be played in California? How did they know? How did they?

Sister Claire grabbed the phone from me. "Four Star, sir, this is Sister Claire Coogan. Your Op sucks. Idiosyncrasies too large. In reality, we're planned to be as extinct as the Snow Crab, correct?"

I took the receiver back. I made a mocking swipe at her hand.

"You don't make pronouncements against the highest ranking American officer. He saved our lives today."

Claire said, "When circumstance is piled on circumstance; then more circumstances are added they become overriding evidence."

We were fighting among ourselves over a message being left on a burner phone. It probably wouldn't come to the light of the day. Generals have a way of believing they are God. Especially, this Four Star.

Indeed, the general made all the right calls in the last few years. His military genius landed him at the White House. In fact, he might have reasoned we would find our way to Palmdale. With his military intelligence, he could deduce the fighter would come under attack.

I concluded, "In your hands – general. I will report daily. Out."

I was trembling. Not from fear. Illness had won. Putting my phone back in my pants, I remembered my official FBI cell. And I noticed a voice message was pending. My head was mush. Much like the many college kids snorting whatever. Mine was legal drugs; same effect. It took me a minute to remember the pass code.

Dialing it, I heard, "Touchdown in Palmdale. Keep on the trail. I expect more – rumors afloat. Four Star."

I had the phone ringer on silent. Was this a response to my call? Or, was the general merely giving me a report? I was buzzed with pain and medication – out on my feet.

Minutes later, a man dressed in a business suit entered Vance aviation from the flight line. I placed my hand on my gun. Claire was accurate. I was dangerous to the world. Making poor judgments.

The flight attendant from the front desk called out, "Cardinal, your charter."

Claire helped me stand. We rose slowly. The adrenaline from the day had worn off. Both of us were totally exhausted, and I was pumped with narcotics.

"I don't know about you," I said. "I can use a good back rub."

"Who are you kidding, sucker."

My armed throbbed. I should have taken even more of the pain pills while I waited for the jet, I thought. They could have carried me onto the plane.

"Maybe, I should administer those pills," she said in a concerned voice.

Claire helped me. I staggered.

"You took so much your eyes appear the same as Easter bunny. Red and pink"

"Still dreadful pain in my arm. It is on fire."

Outside, I saw the aircraft. Duke's friend, the billionaire, sent the real deal. It was large, sleek, and fit for a king. The jet had a fresh white coat of paint, with gold pin stripes flowing back to the tail. A large emblem – Dovato Enterprises lit the tail.

"This is no Piper cub," Claire agreed.

"It's a big deal jet, with air-stairs. No little Mickey Mouse two-step to the cockpit. You might have to lift me up into the plane," I said kidding.

"This is the Cardinal?" Questioned the pilot, seeing me stagger. He, no doubt, wondered why a Catholic Cardinal was high on drugs.

"Now, see what you have done to our Church's reputation," the Sister said, still a loving smile.

"I do not know what came over me when I said 'I was the Cardinal.' Was it a message from heaven that told me not to darken the name of the Mormon Church?" I paused for effect – looking to the sky.

"Real funny. Ha Ha."

However, the pilot wanted to get the show on the road. He and his attendant almost carried me aboard.

"Cardinal, the boss says we're going to DC tonight. Correct?"

"Young man, loosen your tie. Chairman Dovato and I are friends. Even so, right you are, Washington."

"Yes sir."

"No luggage? Make yourself at home."

"We're going to sleep. Keep the bumps to a minimum." I said having trouble formulating my words.

The pilot instructed the attendant to put up the equivalent of hospital bed rails to keep me in my bunk. Obvious drunks had slept aboard before. That notwithstanding, it was an air bed; I could set the perfect sleep number. I fumbled with the controls, yet in the end, let them drop.

No kneeling for prayers tonight. I wouldn't make it back in the bunk.

"Heavenly Father, thank you. Forgive my sins. In the name of Jesus...."

I was asleep.

Chapter 11

ଔଔଔଔଔ

WASHINGTON DC - EARLY

The aircraft bumped down on what I still call National Airport. Now Reagan Airport – after one of the most influential Presidents in modern times.

I was big-time groggy. Too many pain pills before takeoff from LAX. I hadn't turned over on the bunk the entire flight. Still sore, but rested.

My body recovers from injury in the same miraculous manner befitting Los Angeles Lakers basketball star Kobe Bryant. Kobe will hop off the court with what is perceived to be a broken leg. The next night he breaks a New York record pouring in 61 points.

"I can't make a lay-up, so the comparison stops strictly with recovering from an injury. Maybe, Bryant would be laid out for months if he took a couple of gunshots to his shooting arm." I mused. The torn Achilles slowed him more than previous injuries. And, then, the broken knee.

"Good morning sleepy head," said Claire.

"You get much sleep?"

"Absolutely. Great ride."

"How's the arm?"

"Much better. Not infected. I can move it. Maybe, I'll throw in 61 points today."

She looked at me as if I am crazy. "61 points?"

She paused, not understanding.

"During the night a yellow mung kept excreting from your arm. Not blood, but a yellowish, green substance. Kind of weird," she said.

"Remember the blessing. I was blessed by my faith the infection and other impurities would flow out from the body. That by faith, I would fall into a deep sleep and would be cleansed."

She peered at me wondering. "I remember."

She thought, there was an unusual transformation. A cleansing she had never before witnessed. She saw men injure and die in action. Not once had she seen yellow goo flow from a soldier's wounds.

"That's what you observed. I slept with the Angels – deep, as a child."

"You with the Angels. Hard to imagine," said the Sister poking fun at me. Even so, she did visualize. Being around a faithful Mormon man, evidencing certitude. A daily effort at righteousness. Certainly, faith.

The pilot came out of his cabin. Rubbing his right arm. The flight took a toll.

"How was the flight for you two?" he asked.

"Outstanding," reported Claire. "I can tell you the Cardinal slept well."

"And you?"

"On and off, but I am rested."

"When are you going to fly back to LA?"

I answered, "We don't know exactly. We would like to use the aircraft or another plane for refuge while we're in DC. If you can get permission?"

"That will work."

"The mission we are on is sensitive, perhaps dangerous to the plane and you. You must not leave the jet unattended at any time. Vehicles have a way of exploding. People dying."

"I'm going to fly to St. Louis. We have a hangar and hub there. The craft can be serviced. The hangar is 24/7 availability."

"How do I get to you?"

Handing me a card, the pilot pointed at a telephone number and an e-mail address.

"Either one of these numbers will direct you to me. Because the plane is in St. Louis, allow flight time. I can be at any airport here in the East shortly."

"Distance makes extraction a little problematical."

The pilot said, "We're reliable. We have a 24-hour staff and airplanes always available for executives. You've been put on our Watch Board, meaning you're priority until you release us."

"Appreciate Chairman Dovato's courtesy."

"Take your time exiting the craft. No hurry. We're going to take on fuel in any case."

"Thanks again. We'll talk to you later."

I shook hands with the pilot. Claire gently slapping him on the back with appreciation.

"What now?" Claire asked.

"Morning prayers – you want to join me?"

"You forgot the night ones, Bishop – you collapsed into sleep."

I hoped God would be merciful for my short prayer the night before. A millisecond wasn't much. I did agree. Even so, I had not forgotten.

"Truthfully, I yelled 'timber.' Then I collapsed." I laughed.

I will make amends; I promise. My prayers are somewhat conversational, talking to my Heavenly Father, whom I love. To some, my prayers are lacking in formality.

To Claire, I said, "I express gratitude for blessings received, repent for things gone wrong, and meekly ask for the assistance needed. Being particularly mortal, I require time in asking for understanding."

Kneeling, head bowed, I prayed, "We have been commanded, 'Thou shall not kill'. And yet, in the line of duty, I have. Yesterday, I did – again. I seek forgiveness. I ask for direction."

I make it clear to Heavenly Father, if I am instructed to quit my worldly FBI job, I will lay down the credentials and gun. Forthwith. No reservations.

"If I die as a result, so be it." Talking with our Father in Heaven, I remember the Disciples, who promised allegiance to Jesus to the death – then, abandoning him in our Lord's hour of need. I pray I will not be so weak; however, I know words are easy – deeds hard.

So far, I receive continuing confirmation; I am enduring the proper course.

I inquire of Heavenly Father about the apparent conflict with Islam. They claim He has told them they should destroy us. We are wicked. Muslim extremists say God gave them the instruction. They claim Divine right.

"At times, instructions from above are difficult to comprehend."

I let my Maker appreciate my difficulties. One God to whom we all pray. Mormons, Catholics, and Muslims alike ask for His help and guidance.

Some of us apparently don't listen. He gave us agency to choose from the time of Adam. He wants peace and love – not conflict. Wants us all to return to Him. After all, we are all His children. He sent his Son to light the road back to Father and forgive us of our sins.

Time after time, I receive personal inspiration to "stay the course." God has revealed to me, he will make mankind united in purpose in "His time."

Sister Claire closed her eyes during the prayer. She always feels the prompting of the Spirit when she prays. However, as Bishop Joseph Smith seeks guidance from the Father, her total being felt enlivened. Joseph's humility and seeking to God fills the cabin. The Spirit unquestionably strong in the aircraft.

She remembered, "Where two are gathered in my name," she mouthed the words – I will be there with you.

At Amen, her heart and mind were filled with peace. This was unlike any feeling she had personally witnessed before. She has prayed with a sincere heart daily, since she was a small child. Today love and answers flood her heart.

"Too many thoughts – all at once. Impossible to consider them all. A new beginning." She thought.

Claire feels she has long known a stalwart relationship with God. Even so, Joseph Smith prayed to God the Father, as if, he was in his presence. With the Almighty's arm wrapped around him.

The Bishop, still kneeling, was saying some private prayers now. His lips were moving – no words could be heard.

Claire was amazed – the Bishop talked to the Eternal Father as if speaking with his own dad. With absolute reverence and faith, with love and anticipation. With certainty—God was listening and ready to help.

"Sometimes I complain when I don't realize instant gratification. I seem to want answers immediately. Patience be-damned," she thought to herself.

Sister Claire knew all Mormons considered themselves to be missionaries. She realized some young and old LDS members went on missions to serve the Father and Jesus. Around the world. No armament. Shielded only by prayers.

This mission exceeded Claire's expectations. The ominous danger greater than she had expected. Joseph Smith looked to God and Jesus for strength, for direction, for power to do right. Not only, for salvation.

Joseph did not like killing. He abhorred it. She noticed the Bishop never shot first. Only after he was fired on.

"That will get him killed some day," she thought to herself. "Still, I certainly imagine, the quality is admired by God."

She reasoned, "He calls me 'Billy the Kid,'" because I am quick to draw my weapon and dispatch evil to hell."

Some Muslims strap bombs to their body and explode their handicraft and themselves in crowed restaurants. They believe this will open the door to Paradise.

Joseph is "living his faith," a belief that encircles his daily and hourly activities. Not a belief to pull other men down. Instead, the power to do right – treat all as equals. To lift up God's children.

"Do the right and let the consequences follow," he says.

For Sister Claire, she was lost when she left the Marines. She was seeking truth. Raised Catholic; therefore, becoming a Nun made sense.

"I was sick of killing. Thou shall not commit murder, yet I became too good at it. I saw myself as murder incorporated," she reasoned.

"Even though I pray, my life is not centered on faith," said Claire. "I have received many bizarre missions, since I've become a Nun. Probably, my superiors can see my strengths and spiritual weaknesses."

She said to herself, "Joseph puts up a spiritual veil that seems to reflect bullets. It opens the door for humanity to embrace God."

When I rose to my feet, I glimpsed her still in morning meditation. I gently put two hands on her head. I said a silent, heartfelt prayer for her. Somewhat analogous to a blessing. Asking the Father to reward her sweet spirit. To protect her and guide Sister Claire.

Certainly, the private plea – akin to a blessing – meant no disrespect to her Catholic routes. However, I discerned my companion was wavering. To some extent, lost in self-doubt.

There was a momentary pause. You could sense the Spirit, if you opened your heart. After a few seconds, she too stood. Her legs were strong and toned from years of training. Still, she faltered. Almost fell, when she rose. The blessings of the priesthood bestowed to a faithful servant.

Without comment to the blessing, Claire said, "Think we should call the Senator's office. Find if he's on the Senate floor today, or wherever. Why run around?"

I was surprised she transitioned so quickly. Without a word. No acknowledgement of the inner workings of her mind.

I nodded my head in agreement.

I called information; received his local DC number.

"Why don't you call; we might get further." I suggested.

"Sure."

Claire dialed on her Rome-issued cell phone. If someone at the Senator's office was monitoring the caller ID, they would be shocked with an area code they didn't recognize.

"FBI, who is calling?" the voice on the other end of the line said. She disconnected.

"The number was answered by the Bureau. That's outlandish. Everywhere we turn, a gatekeeper appears."

"Call back. Be insistent. Find out why the badges are answering."

"You're right. They knocked me off my game."

Sister Claire redialed.

"FBI. This is your second call. Who may I say is calling?"

"Why is the FBI monitoring the Senator's line?" asked Claire in a friendly, but formal voice.

"This call is being recorded. Who's on the line?"

"Record me all you want. I ask you a question. Why are you answering the Senator's phone?"

There was silence. Claire checked her cell. Still connected.

She said, "Answer my question, and I'll not only tell you who I am, but where I am located."

"We already know your location?"

"Well, eventually, the FBI will stop playing games and state the truth. If you're coming for me, you're wasting your time. I'm looking to meet with the Senator. I'll come to you."

"Stay where you are." The phone went dead.

I asked, "What nonsense is going on?"

"They told me to stay here – refused to answer any questions."

"Come on. We're not playing their game. Who knows to whom you were speaking?"

As Claire and I moved away from the airplane, I yelled to the pilot: "Get airborne. Now. The enemy is coming."

"It's that urgent?" asked the pilot, believing I overstated the danger.

"If you have enough fuel to make St. Louis, leave immediately."

The pilot nodded, pulling the chalks from under the tire and entering the jet, preparing for takeoff.

"Turn off your cell." I yelled. Furthermore, I also turned off mine.

"We're going dark."

We moved at double time. Left the flight line. Ran into the FBO operator, which housed commuters, rental-car companies and assorted offices.

The two of us hid out in an alcove, high above the flight line. The recess was hidden from view from below. White walls gave way to deep shadows.

A passers-by would believe the stairs led to administrative offices, which were protected by a sign that read "keep out - official airport authorities only."

"Hope no one comes out," said the Sister.

A couple of people did emerge from offices on the floor. We stood our ground looking official. No one said a word to us.

Minutes later two cars, loaded with three men in each car, roared into the terminal. They ran onto the tarmac, observing the twin taxiing away.

"She must be aboard the jet. Call the tower and abort the craft from taking off," ordered the apparent boss.

The other agent fumbled around, trying to locate the tower's number. He took precious additional minutes attempting to get through to someone in authority.

"Our government in action," I whispered.

Seconds after my cryptic remark, the Dovato jet screeched into the sky. Heading toward St. Louis.

"Call your friend and clue him, because the FBI will be waiting for the pilot in St. Louis," Claire said.

"Will short-circuit the trap before they arrive."

She nodded.

"We need to be absolutely certain these are agents and not hit-men."

Once the jet was skyward the men reentered their black nondescript cars and left. Made no inquiry. Failed to seek answers. They were certain we had flown away.

"Light weights," opined Claire. They assumed, instead of searching. Looking at their feet in despair."

"Come on. Let me rent a vehicle, and then we can head over to the Senator's office. They tried to corner us. Now, we will return the favor," I laughed.

"Under what name are you going to rent the vehicle?" Claire worried. "Don't make it easy for them to follow."

I faced Claire with a deadpan expression, pulling a Nevada driver's license and credit card for Thomas Townsgate.

I extended my hand taking Claire's unexpectedly. "Hi, I am Thomas Townsgate, nice to meet you."

Just as quickly, she punched him in the stomach.

"I'm certainly glad you chose the belly rather than my left arm for your fisticuffs."

"You haven't seen a true punch yet." She pronounced.

My belief, she is telling the truth. This Sister can bring real heat – in many ways. Slippery fast with words. A fast-draw with a pistol. And a Marine. Not to mention – a beautiful woman.

"Are you thinking I'm not acting like Nun?"

"I am extremely happy with you. You're making the mission tolerable."

"Even if you are alone. Yes, alone – with a woman other than your wife."

I said with a smile, "Maybe the Lord doesn't count being with a Nun as being alone with a woman." I wanted the words back. They had escaped before I reflected what I was saying.

I moved quickly away from her deadly arms and feet. I knew her. There would be a quick reply. Black belt stuff she learned with the Swiss Guards or Marines.

Instead, she curtseyed – very lady like. "Sticks and stones can break my bones," she said. "You get the jest – right."

Again, the leopard had clawed me, when I thought, I had scored a knockout. She was hurt, but forgave.

During our bantering, we had walked to the car-rental counter. Nothing unusual there. After renting the blue Chevy Cruise without difficulty, I rang the Senator's office once again. I did this from my day-to-day cell phone, not the throwaway.

"FBI."

"Hello, this is FBI agent Joseph Smith. To whom am I speaking?"

"Well aaaaaa.." The agent stuttered.

"Are you okay?" I said mockingly.

"Hold on, I'm transferring you." There was a short delay.

"Who's this," said a disgruntled voice. It was apparent by the clicking sounds the call had been transferred.

"Just like I told your other agent, this is undercover FBI special agent Joseph Smith. To whom am I speaking?"

"Where are you?"

"I'm here in DC – where are you?"

Silence on the line.

I repeated, "These aren't difficult questions. Who are you and where are you?

"Joseph, we need to meet."

"I agree. On the other hand, I'm not interested in being assassinated. I'm concerned about who you are, and for whom you work?" I said sternly. "Are you the good guys, or the traitors we found in Palmdale?"

"Who do you think you are talking to?"

"That's the $24 million question isn't it? Traitors are roaming our land. I find you answering the phone for a United States Senator, who is up to his eyeballs in the treason."

I wasn't pulling any punches. I might be talking to a major CIA supervisor at Langley or FBI headquarters. Just as likely, speaking to one of the terrorists. I was going to draw him out one way or the other.

The deep voice said, "One thing I can say about you Smith, you're a great shot."

"Don't you forget? With a bullet in the arm, I hit the assassins between the eyes in that Palmdale hangar. That's a short distance for me. How about you? If you're coming for me, better come hard."

"I'm talking about the hit you made last night. When you shot the Senator, from 900 yards," said the man accusingly.

"The Senator's dead?"

"As if you didn't know?"

"Hold on a second; I want to talk to my companion," I said.

"Claire, the Senator was assassinated last evening; long range rifle."

"They probably roped in the same gun you fired in Palmdale. They will want ballistics to match. Setting us up. What time and where?"

"Right."

I thought for a frantic second. I did not wear gloves in Palmdale. Someone has my fingerprints on a weapon that killed. If they fired the same weapon again, well. Proof. I turned my attention back to the telephone call.

"What time was a Senator killed, and where?"

"Good game, Smith. As if, you don't know. Attempting to fabricate an alibi."

"Get off your high-horse. What time and where?"

The antagonistic man, pausing to reflect, said, "Around 10 pm, when he came out of the diner in Alexandria, Virginia."

"Well then, whoever you are, you might say I have an airtight alibi. I was at 35,000 feet flying; traveling across the country, when the Senator was executed."

Silence.

"What's your alibi?" I asked.

The agent, somewhat apologetically, said, "We need to meet."

"I tell you what – I'm not meeting you in any dark ally. Be at FBI headquarters between 9 AM to 5 PM tomorrow. You bring your brass, and my heavy hitters will paddle along."

"A national-security nightmare exists. Need to meet somewhere today – headquarters is fine." He said.

"Not that it'll do any good – yet, what do you call yourself, today?" I asked.

"My name's the same today, tomorrow and every day. I play in the big leagues. I'm Noah Padgett. You'll find your ass is mine."

"Where is Chad Caden?" I asked, knowing my friend – the grand old man of the agency – knew everyone. Head of the anti-terrorist task force for the FBI. Chad trained approximately 60 per cent of the supervisors.

"Who in the hell do you think trained me?"

"You're out of your depth thinking you can browbeat me. Stay put, I'll show up sometime today. Call Chad. You have my cell phone number. Use it."

I hung up. Then, I turned off my phone. Making it untraceable. And impossible for him to call me.

Chapter 12

ଔଔଔଔଔଔ

THE NUN BECOMES A MODEL

"He sounds like a real darling," Claire said.

"He's a supervisor and thinks he runs the world."

"Does he? Can he bring the hammer down on you?"

I smiled, "I built up some bonus points. When he calls my friend, the chief of the FBI anti-terrorist task force, Chad Caden, he'll find I'm no marshmallow."

"What about the Four Star? How will he weight in?"

"He's reports to the President. Directly, to the President. Daily. Maybe, hourly with everything going on now. He is quite the square. Tough. Honest."

The two misfit detectives drove into Alexandria Virginia, where the Senator had been slain.

"First order of business is to check in at a local tailor shop."

Confused. Somewhat bewildered, again with the nose crunches, Claire said, "Shouldn't aesthetics come second to catching the spies?"

"Noticed when I tried to buy you some grandma clothes in California, you thought style was most important.

"Well, then, let me take you to the Goodwill." She said.

"I'm trying to bait our hook. The tailor sews for half the supervising agents at the agency. He hears more rumors and truths than a myriad of FBI types. Furthermore, he's a friend."

"How many friends do you have?"

"You'll find we Mormon folks have nothing but friends."

She studied me. Then, she observed the sly smile.

"You're still not too big for a spanking, Smith. Your arm won't take much, and you're down on the ground – out cold."

"I surrender."

I pulled up in front of a small, unobtrusive walk-up. A brownstone. No one would have suspected it as a major tailor shop.

Flower pots with bright flowers led to the double-door entry. No sign hung outside – merely, lettering on one door. Discreet. Customers all came by referral.

When the two of them walked in, a beautiful, 5'7" blonde, blue-eyed lady of about 30 years came running. Threw her arms around Joe Smith. She gave him an affectionate kiss on the lips.

"It's been too long. You don't write. You don't visit. You know; you are family. We love you," said Christina.

I saw my other friend; the thin, balding man with a measuring string around his neck. Leaning on the worktable toward the back of the room.

"Hey pops," I called affectionately.

"Too long."

"I agree. Now that I'm in California, I don't get to Virginia but once every couple of years. However, I would never breeze this way and miss family."

Actually, I was in and out of Quantico regularly for training and assessment. Even so, my trips were to the anti-terrorist team. Secret. In and then immediately out. When I came, I received instruction for an undercover assignment. No stop offs. No visits to friends in Virginia. My friend knew the pressures. The rules.

Christina, who had been studying Claire, said, "Who's this?"

"Excuse me – forgot my manners. This is Sister Claire Coogan. Sister Claire is a Catholic Nun. She's out of her Habit because she's working with me on a sensitive case."

Pops, winking at Joseph, said, "Tell me the truth Bishop, you are trying to convert her – right? Convince her it's okay to have two wives?"

"You're talking to a former Marine, watch what you say," chided Claire, playfully.

The group of friends took time to renew acquaintances. Even though thousands of miles separated them, their friendship was as fresh as yesterday.

"Pops. I came in for three reasons. Number one, to see family. Number two, to get out of this awful garb and into one of your suits. Number three, we're investigating a clandestine spy ring operating here in the United States. Possibly, FBI agents or CIA on the hook."

"They're attempting to steal secrets. Correct?" Asked the old man.

"Right," said Claire – not able to withstand the urge to interrupt.

I asked, "Did you learn about the execution of the Senator last evening?"

Christina said, "You'd have to be dead not to realize that in this town."

As pops pulled suits from his back closet, he explained the chatter among agents for the past 30 days centered on a ring of high-placed, but out-of-step government officials. They allegedly are working with the Muslims trying to bring the United States into equilibrium with other Muslim countries. Strip us of power.

"Have you heard the name of the Senator?"

Pop said, "No, a total surprise. He's been a client here for nearly two decades. A good man from my point of view. Not a traitor."

I asked, "How about an FBI type named Noah Padgett?"

"With Chad Caden retiring, Padgett is taking over part of the duties for Chad. At least, a small part of his duties. Padgett, word has it, is two-faced – knows how to work the system. He's arrogant as hell. Anyhow, if Chad picked him for anything, he's not a traitor."

"Pops, I'd agree with the last statement. Chad knows men."

The tailor took measurements, confirming his suspicions that Joseph Smith hadn't put on a pound in 10 years. Pops added a few marks. He handed two suits to Christina for slight alterations.

Claire moved over to an area and picked out several shirts and ties to go with the outfits.

"You brought your own designer?" Pops said with a gleam in his eye.

"Don't let her hear you say that. She is sensitive."

Claire said nothing. Then a face. She stayed in character.

For the next few minutes while Christina stitched alterations to the suits, Pops talked openly about Washington rumors with his friend.

"Nothing better than to take the mountains out of the landscape, when you're looking for needles in a stack of needles," I thought. Straight shooting is exactly what I needed.

Within a short time, I looked like the assistant to the President of United States.

Christina patted Joseph tenderly on the arm. "That is a nasty wound. Forget to duck?"

"As they say, you should see the other guy."

"Need to go to Forrest Lawn, for the other guy," the Sister added.

Clear to Claire, who was still standing back of the room against a wall of materials, Christina wished she could be "real family."

"She's in love with him." The Sister thought, "Easy. Quite easy to fall for this man."

"I am finally dressed to kill – as they say. More importantly, I uncovered a gold mine of information, as well."

I looked at Claire, who needed some loving hands – she still appeared disheveled.

"Pops, I now look like a million thanks to you. However, I have to outfit little orphan Annie," I said pointing at Claire. "Any suggestions."

Christina took Claire by the arm and led her upstairs. Not a word.

Half an hour later, the beautiful blonde led Claire down the stairs. Pops stared – dumbfounded.

Sister Claire Coogan was transformed into a radiant lady. Christina did magic. Claire's blue dress was cut to perfection. It fell to her waist, gathered by a matching belt, and flowed out to just above the knees.

"She looked like a beggar without funds when she arrived," said Pops.

"She is still dressed appropriately," I said. "It's merely difficult to camouflage true beauty."

In fact, Claire was now radiant. The new frock magnified her enormous eyes. Christina also did something with her hair; I knew. I couldn't explain what.

The effect breathtaking.

Pop said, "Are you really a Sister?"

No answer.

"What I want you to tell me," he asked, "Where did you hide your gun?"

Chapter 13

ରେଠାରେଠାରେ

HELL OF A SHOT

Away from my friends, I called my nemesis, Noah Padgett. We both wanted a meet for different reasons.

I said, "I did a background check on you a different way. I found out you are arrogant, a back-stabber, and two-faced – but not a spy."

"I found you belong to a cult, and lead a bunch of pansy-wipes," he responded. "The Mormons."

"That makes us quite a pair. By the way, don't look up, or I'll convert you. Conversely, we will miss you in Heaven."

"I will die first. Before I join you. I wouldn't even have lunch with such scum," said Padgett.

Claire had been listening. "I guess we know where he stands. No marriage proposals."

"At least, no poison in the food," I replied.

After pausing, Padgett asked sternly, "When can we meet?"

"How about FBI headquarters in about two hours?"

Padgett said, "You bring your friend?"

"I don't leave home without her."

"Chad Caden and Kaci Haber are going to sit in," said Padgett.

"I'm feeling safer already. Did you take everything – computers, cell phones, everything – from the Senator's office and home?"

"His office – yes. His home – no. We don't have a search warrant. Probably, no probable cause unless you can supply that," said the FBI supervisor.

"Is he married?"

"Yes."

"She's probably dead, and the house ransacked. You should get over there and knock on the door. You don't need a warrant for that," I said dryly.

Sheepishly, Padgett agreed. "Good call."

"I'm going to swing by the Senator's office. Any agents I need to get around."

Padgett said, "I'll make a call."

"Any idea who fits the sniper?"

"Hell of a shot. I really believe you pulled it off. There are not 10 men living who can make that kill."

The agent gave me the address of the restaurant where the fatal bullet had hit its target, and the location from which the sniper cut loose.

Pageant said, "Joe, keep in mind there was a 30-knot crosswind last night. Trees. Blinking lights. As I said, "Hell of a shot."

Chapter 14

ରେରେରେରେରେ

SENATOR, WHO KILLED YOU?

Green Beret sniper par excellence, Joseph Smith, knew all of America's top hitters. He also had the resumes of the world's best long range riflemen – men for whom wind and other adversity meant nothing.

"Who had gone rogue?" I wondered. It might even be a woman; nonetheless, I couldn't think of any who fit.

Answer that question and you're half way home, I thought. "That is if some helper doesn't keep hiding the adversaries whom we capture. We get a traitor who crawls to us in Palmdale. Shortly thereafter, he disappears."

The new debutante, Sister Claire, and I were backtracking to the restaurant where Noah Padgett said the Senator was gunned down.

"It's hard to think of you as a Nun in those clothes, " I told her, although I realized her true beauty was in her soul.

Sister Claire admitted, "After you're in Marine garb for a couple of years, you no longer consider yourself attractive."

I looked at her in surprised. Because I knew many military women who prided themselves on their femininity.

"Candidly, it's nice to be dressed casually. I'm not going to do anything inappropriate. Even so, it's nice to have a man stare. It's been a long while. It doesn't affect my personal values."

I said nothing. I sensed an internal struggle being waged within her. I didn't say it; however, her love of Christ shown as her true beauty.

"What is your plan at the restaurant?" She asked.

"We need to be careful that we're not next with a bullet between our ears. Someone has some serious talent. Most kills from distance are chest shots. Supreme confidence to go for the head."

The partners agreed they would drive around the route surreptitiously; being certain no sniper was looking for his next target. Further, they were going to start with the location from which the hitter fired his deadly kill.

"On with it," I instructed the Sister. "Take up a defensive posture. When you're ready, signal. I'm going to examine the spot the sniper chose for his shot."

Arriving at a juncture where Sister Claire believed she could patrol the area with a pistol, she asked to be let out.

"Give me two minutes; then park."

"Any danger, fire a warning shot in the air."

"Any stranger with a gun will find a slug in his side," she bragged.

"Be certain not to shoot the hero. That could be embarrassing."

"Hero? I haven't seen a white horse. On the other hand, are you talking about me. You notice; no one has shot little ole me."

I followed instructions. Nearly ten minutes later, I found myself at the preface from which the shooter had fired the fatal bullet.

I admired the work. The man is not only an artist with a gun, but picked a sanitary, somewhat remote location.

"The selection of site and details are a fingerprint to the sniper," I said to myself. The shot was further than I was told. More obstructions. I need to revisit the talents of my comrades in arms.

Before returning to the car, I dialed Claire. I didn't want to be the one in her cross-hairs.

"Coming out. Watch your back."

Neither of us saw any evidence of an intruder. The area was pristine – except that it had been used for murder.

"To the restaurant?" Claire asked, once we were back in the car.

"Maybe, we will make a drive-by. Don't know what we will find hiding there."

She said, "I think I should go inside. Perhaps, I can find someone who waited on the Senator. I may have a better chance."

"I want to see if there's a rear alley. Rather not expose you to the front."

Sister Claire Coogan, looking anything but a Catholic Nun, entered the restaurant through its rear door and into the kitchen. No one was in the alley.

I wasn't the only one who noticed her innate beauty. Dishes and forks were clattering when she first arrived.

However, seeing her, the noise dwindled and then stopped. Seven cooks and a chef were staring intently, and at least two of the men had their eyes focused squarely on her breasts.

Claire swished her hips over to the group, which surrounded her.

"I'm a friend of the Senator who was killed out front last night."

The chef said, "Oh, I'm so terribly sorry."

"Was there anything unusual about his visit? Anyone with him last night?"

"You might ask Nettie, his regular waitress. You'll find her out front," said the chef.

One of the other men was very uneasy. She noticed him moving from one foot to the other.

Claire asked, "I apologize; I don't know your name."

"I'm Marco."

She held out her hand. Marco eagerly took her tanned hand and shook it.

"Marco, did you hear or oversee anything?"

"I overheard the Senator upset with a legislative aide Sean Bickmore, who is a regular here."

"What did you hear?"

"Mr. Bickmore said something about news out of Los Angeles making the Senator a liability. To the cause, whatever that means?"

"Who's this Bickford fellow?"

Marco said, "His name is Bickmore. Not Bickford. He's a legislative aide to the committee on arms and warfare – something like that."

"Anything else,"

Marco was no longer looking her in the eyes, but was peering down her dress.

"Nope." He said – embarrassed, when he realized that his gaze was detected. "Apologize, ma'am. Hard not to stare – you're beautiful."

"Thank you, Marco."

Claire ventured out to the dining room and found Nettie, the waitress. She attempted to pry proprietary information from the short, matronly-looking food server. However, the waitress was not nearly as forthcoming; Claire's beauty meant nothing to her.

"We're investigating, trying to catch his killer," Claire prompted.

"The FBI doesn't need your help."

Nettie turned around and walked away. End of discussion.

Claire retraced her steps through the kitchen, waving at Marco. When she walked out the back door, I was engaged with two men.

"He looks relaxed," she thought. Nonetheless, Claire put her hand on her automatic ready to play Billy the Kid in a fast draw.

"Guys, this is my partner Claire Coogan."

"FBI, ma'am. We saw your partner hanging out. We're stationed here, investigating who shows up."

"The write-it-down crew," Claire thought. Stay out of sight and tag cars and check who came. Rookies.

Once back in the car, Claire asked whether I had found anything at all from the agents.

"No, they are dumber than a block wall."

"Apparently, too lazy to go inside and ask some questions," she said explaining.

"The restaurant is not a black hole after all. We need to find this Bickmore fellow."

Claire asked, "Are you going to share information with the brass at our meeting?"

"Are you suggesting we hide the cards from our team?"

She stared at me intently. "Yes."

Chapter 15

ରେଥରେଥରେଥରେଥରେଥ

THE QUESTION WAS WHO?

It was a sad sight to see my mentor Chad Caden. The grand old man was humped over his red walker. Stumbling, and creaking his way along the long corridor.

I almost cried when I saw him having difficulty standing upright. I tried to remember how long ago I had last seen Chad. He was then robust and every bit in control.

"More than a year," I thought embarrassed. "I've talked to him a couple of times on a personal problem. I should have kept in closer contact. He's been a great friend."

I thought, "Considering the way I have let Pops and Chad Caden down, it is telling. We get so wrapped up in our daily lives, we forget people who are important. Those who made an indelible mark on who we are."

Caden was stopping after a step or two. And then pushing forward. His red, sit down-type walker held him up. He leaned against it. His weight serving as propulsion. Pushing onward a painful step at a time.

I saw that his hands were curled – snarly looking, malformed extensions of his hands. He shuffled – instead of walking.

The FBI chief was now in his late 60s. I never believed he would retire. Even though he was well past retirement age. Now, I understood.

Caden came in from horse country to meet with Noah Padgett, Kaci Haber, the Sister and me. A short drive, but to him an eternity.

He at first resisted making the trip being ill when he received the call. Caden did everything to beg off – "set it for a different day." However, this case was the highest degree of national security. A different day was out of the question. We were already hopelessly behind the power curve.

Chad Caden never dodged responsibility – let alone a case that involved the assassination of the Senator. Once he understood my assignment, he forged ahead. Mind over the body.

Noticing me approaching, Chad stopped, waiting for me. He stood tall. As straight, that is, as a man crippled by age and Parkinson's disease could stand.

"Hello, my friend. It's been far too long," I said, hugging him tenderly.

Chad said, "Don't kiss me or something dumb. The others will get the wrong sort of idea."

He had not lost his good sense of humor. This agent was the real deal when it came to being a tactician. The country was losing its edge. You could build more drones or new-age fighters – you couldn't replace the grand old man. Too important.

"Joseph, what have you got yourself involved in?" Caden asked, with a practiced eye.

I said, "It's good to have you here boss. I'm nowhere near the top of the hill. Let's find a place to sit down. I'll explain what I know."

We walked into the secure antechamber on the 16th floor of the FBI main DC office. We were joined by Padgett, Kaci Haber, and Claire.

The final steps of Chad Caden's walk were with excruciating agony. They were evidenced on his face and by tremors in his hands.

I disbelieved a report I read earlier in the year. It said Chad is plagued with out-of-control diabetes, diabetic neuropathy, Parkinson's, and the first stages of dementia. He actually creaked as he walked. Not quite a cricket sound, but a click all the same.

Noah Padgett sat disrespectfully. The rest of us stood in recognition of the entrance of Chad Caden. A legend.

Kaci threw her arms around "the boss" and said, "Haven't seen enough of you recently, you know I love you."

"I think my wife would be jealous if we ran away together," he said. Kissing her on the cheek.

Sister Claire put out her hand saying, "I've heard great things. Let me introduce myself. I came with the Bishop, Joe Smith. I've been sent by the Vatican – the Pope – to help. My name is Sister Claire Coogan."

Chad – himself a Catholic – greeted her, shaking her hand respectfully. Looking he said, "A Nun? Really?"

"Yes. I am out of our traditional clothing."

"I'd say."

Then Chad added, "I don't know how we can lose with a Mormon Bishop and a Catholic Nun. We also have the brightest agent in service – Kaci Haber, and the disrespectful one."

Padgett's belligerent greeting did not go unnoticed.

"Joseph told me that Chad never failed to notice every detail. From the most important to the minutia," Claire thought.

"She can't stay," Padgett said pointing at the Sister. "She doesn't have Top Secret clearance. Leave – forthwith. It's my order – I have the authority."

Claire did not move.

"Padgett you amaze me," Caden said. "Doesn't the Sister have the information? She is helping you. So, you're going to have her leave. Really smart."

After the tongue lashing, we began.

"Bishop, take your time explaining about Palmdale, about escaping death at the racetrack, and then, respectfully, let Claire tell of her experience," Caden instructed. The old man took control.

It was apparent the claim he had dementia was far overblown. His mind was as sharp as a saber.

"What do you have to share agent Padgett?" I asked. I was here for answers. I was willing to share, but I didn't want to leave without knowing what the FBI brass knew.

"You don't have clearance – no need to know," said the man ruthlessly.

Caden said, "Cut the crap. You're the one we should throw on the sidewalk."

Padgett stood up as if he wanted to fight the crippled senior agent. He actually puffed his chest. Never seen that before.

However, when I stood glowering at him, Padgett thought better of it. Padgett was said to have throttled other lesser agents in order to gain stature. Nevertheless, this frump only waged war with cripples. I am way out of Padgett's league.

Two years before Chad Caden would have broken Padgett's leg with one kick. Then, knocked him to the ground with a twist of the arm.

Chad said, "You're such a pansy, Padgett. You'll fight some of the women at Quantico, but not the men."

"He's probably scared of me too," said Claire.

Padgett said nothing.

"I'm still your superior for another four months, Padgett. You were asked a question. What do you know? Share!" Ordered Chad, demanding an immediate response.

To save her comrade, senior agent Kaci Haber responded, "Joe, until you clarified the time lines – including an alibi of being in flight to Washington – we thought you might be the Senator's sniper."

Padgett said, "I'm still convinced you are the man – the shooter. You could have rigged the alibi. There's not but a handful of people living who could have made that shot. Under those conditions."

Chad said, "You saw the scene?"

"I did. Padgett is at least right about the few shooters who could have hit the Senator from there under the adverse weather."

Chad again, "You know them all. Who?"

"I'm working on it. Not only was it an improbable shot, made under horrendous conditions, but the location from which he made the kill is a signature."

Claire asked, "Do you think an American?"

"I doubt it. Other than me, maybe two other citizens could have accomplished it. I routinely speak with them. They are friends. I would say, no."

Padgett was pacing the floor. "Mr. Caden, we should have this man in an interrogation room, not in here sharing spit with him."

"Padgett, grow up. You are positioned to take over serious responsibility. You have to be worthy. You have to know right from wrong, and loyalty from non-loyalty," said the senior agent, still teaching.

Padgett said nothing.

Agent Haber, said, "We've blocked them from getting their hands on the newest offensive fighter in Palmdale. I can't promise that they have not stolen the plans."

"Who blocked them?" Claire asked. "And why don't you know?"

"The traitors have ostensible authority. They have people in the highest positions at the plant." Kaci said.

They did have control. The Bishop and this tender Sister – sent by the Pope – eliminated all, but one. He was turned over to the CIA. Afterward, he disappeared, said Chad Caden.

"How convenient. How do you explain?" Said a riled up Sister.

Kaci said nothing. Nonetheless, thought "Tender Sister?" I don't think she's quite so feeble."

Padgett strolled faster, wearing a path in the carpet. His hands were deep in his pockets. You could see his balled fists – bulging through his pants.

"Who are you reporting to?" Chad asked Joseph.

"I have to pull a Padgett. I'm sworn to secrecy. Don't bite my head off. Even though it's classified at the level of the President, I'll tell you outside," I said, waiting for the ax to fall.

"I already know," said Chad, smiling. "I was eager to see if you would buckle under the pressure. I'm the one who recommended you for the deep cover assignment."

Padgett said, "If this meeting is to crumble the beasts, why isn't his boss ordered to be here?"

"They figured you could not handle me. Why send more?" Caden responded.

No response.

I said, "Chad, I'm after the shooter. Let me think about the possibilities. Then, I'll give a list of two or three people who could have made the shot. You can interview them."

"Good enough for me," Chad replied.

"Mr. Padgett, did you find anything in the Senator's office?" I questioned.

Padgett shook his head – said nothing. He was pouting.

"So blessed mature for a supervisor," thought Claire. "What a baby."

Kaci Haber thoughtfully added, "We have the tech department going through his cell phone, computers and office phone messages. There's nothing openly apparent at first blush."

Padgett finally blessed the group with an opinion. "This Senator is a man above all reproach. He is not a traitor. If anything, he was following orders. From whom, I don't know."

"Mr. Padgett, I'm not the only one who heard his name. The chief of security at the Palmdale defense plant was there. There were a dozen men left alive in the paint hangar who will testify to his involvement." I reported

Padgett said nothing.

"They saw him forge the President signature on stationary from the White House. What does that signify to you?" said Chad.

"It's your story, you tell it," said the agent snidely.

Chad said, "Kaci when Padgett calms down clue him. Moreover, interview the chief of security at the Palmdale defense plant. He is right where action took place."

"Yes, sir."

The old-man of the agency, Chad said, "The Sister is correct. Why didn't you guys realize that these two saved our bacon in Palmdale? Rather than accusing we need to know the true facts."

Padgett said nothing – glowering.

Kaci said, "I agree sir."

Chapter 16

ལཽལཽལཽལཽལཽ

WHAT NEFARIOUS PLOT WAS IN MISSISSIPPI?

"Padgett's dangerous. He would mark you and your friend Caden for elimination, if he could get away with it," said Sister Claire, back in their car.

They were heading out from what many agents called "16 Fed," the FBI headquarters.

"He might try," I agreed. "Chad's too ill, so he isn't around much. Power gives twerps brave ideas."

The meeting had ended when it was apparent to Chad that nothing fruitful could be gained. I spoke with him for a couple of minutes outside the conference room. He said to report when I knew something. Call if I needed his help.

Upon reflection, I told Claire, "My read is that Padgett's jealous of the old-man. Although Chad looks brittle now, you met a legend. An impossible master for Noah Padgett to emulate."

Claire became the designated driver. I was resting my ailing wing at every opportunity. She drove fast and deliberate. Even though, I ignored the injury, my arm throbbed; her quick jerky turns shooting pain through my body.

"Where are we going?" she said, tired of driving aimlessly.

"Thought, you were taking me on a sightseeing tour. Good to rest."

Claire opined, "This town might be a little dangerous while we're asleep. Do you have some magical hiding place? Perhaps, the plane?"

I picked my tattered wallet, grabbing the card for the Dovato corporate pilot and dialed. I instructed him to pick us up for an overnight.

"Be at the airport in three hours." He said.

"We have some time to kill," I reported. "Let me see if Kaci Haber can give us an address on Mr. Bickmore – the Senator's aide."

"Yeah, I like to give him a piece of my mind, too."

Haber gave instructions to a fashionable, two-story home in the suburbs of Virginia. We mapped out directions and the timetable. We could lean on Bickmore and get back to the airport for our flight.

Sister Claire drove past Bickmore's home, as I said, "Duck down." Trying to hide from prying eyes. The block on which our adversary lived was tree-lined, with too many hiding places. We couldn't be certain that clandestine guards wouldn't try to pick us off.

"Marine, how do you suggest we get up that long drive, stand on an open porch, and stay alive? Might be resistance?"

Claire said laughingly, "Perhaps, we should call the Marines."

"Not a bad idea."

Instead, we parked two blocks away. We sat for a minute after she had parked. Both tired from the adrenaline rush of the day.

I believed a little levity might help. Thought I would tell a little joke I had recently heard.

So I said, "There are parades through this historic district, led by guides dressed in Colonial clothing. One of the guides fell over a tree trunk, breaking his arm."

Claire looked at me not understanding. I continued with the story. "At the hospital, as he sat in the waiting room at the emergency room, a policeman walked by. Looking at his 18th century clothing, the officer asked, 'just how long have you been waiting'?"

Claire gave a polite smile. She said nothing.

"Well, it wasn't that bad, was it?"

"Right now, I wish I had fatigues, instead of this blooming dress," she whispered, changing the subject.

"Beauty first."

Then, I put a finger to my lips, signaling her to shush. She nodded.

"I thought I heard something. I guess not," I whispered.

"All the gunmen waiting to kill us are probably snickering over your silly joke."

We existed the vehicle, only partially closing the doors. It took a quarter of an hour to make it back to Bickmore's estate, weaving in and out of shrubbery. Claire pointed to a fence across from the suspect's home.

I nodded. We moved silently.

I pulled out a wallet-type device – small, portable binoculars. With it, I could peer across the street and into Bickmore's windows.

The sister whispered, "Are you a peeping Tom – one of your four lives?

I made a funny face back at her. Signaled Claire to stay down.

"We're obviously in a surveillance mode," she said.

Another half-hour passed with no action. I was about ready to make a move on the Bickmore house. Maybe, go in a back door. A black, four-door sedan with four men inside pulled up in front of Bickmore's front drive.

"One of the cars from the early-morning roust at Reagan National Airport," I whispered.

"That's Noah Padgett," said Sister Claire quietly.

I nodded. "The bravest man in America."

"What?"

"He had to bring three additional men with him for protection. Real Brave?"

Claire said, with a cagey smile, "Well, chicken, you had to bring a Sister for your protection."

What could I say? I said nothing.

Padgett and his crew walked assuredly to the front door and knocked loudly. They weren't trying to be secretive. No shots rang out.

The front door opened, and a pleasant looking brunette, about 40, answered. "How can I help you?"

"Is Mr. Bickmore home?"

"No. Who's calling?"

"FBI, ma'am. We're calling about the Senator, who was assassinated."

"Wasn't that horrendous?"

Padgett said, "We understand your husband was a business acquaintance of the Senator. We are hoping that he might give us a list of people who knew the Senator."

Bickmore's wife answered without hesitation, "I'm sure he will be glad to help. Unfortunately, he had to travel out of state on business tonight."

Even though Claire and I were some distance from the conversation, we could hear clearly. The area was remote and soundless. No cars, no noise. The night itself was dark, moonless, without wind or competing sounds.

"Do you know where he traveled?" Padgett asked.

"He had to visit a defense plant in Mississippi," said Mrs. Bickmore obligingly.

Another agent said, "Thank you ma'am, we will follow up – if we need him in the future."

The agents left a card; brusquely returned to their vehicle, and prepared to leave.

Claire and I ducked down so the high beams of the Lincoln town car would not strike us, as the FBI agents pulled out of the driveway.

"See, when you live right, Sister Claire, you get a moonless night without any sounds. That way, you can hear a conversation at a safe distance."

"The question is, Bishop, which one of us is living right?"

Although we realized Bickmore was not at home, the two partners still scurried bush-to-bush, retreating to the car. Bickmore might not be there, but what about the assassin?

The Sister said, "Did you know? I'm a mind reader."

"Of course, Sister. And reading your mind, you're going to say that we are heading to Mississippi?"

"Kill joy."

"No Sister. It proves we're both on the same page."

"Those jerks screwed up," said Claire.

"That so?"

"Yes."

"Because they didn't ask what defense plant?"

"Bishop. You seem to read my mind."

I said, "She probably wouldn't have known anyway. They will call his secretary and delve into the information. Not so easy for us."

Chapter 17

ଔଔଔଔଔ

FLY THE FRIENDLY SKIES

"Padgett," said the FBI supervisor, answering his cell.

"This is Joseph Smith. Any update? I'm checking in. Anything new?"

"Nope, went home after you left today."

I had my phone on the speaker, so the Sister could eavesdrop. We looked at each other in astonishment.

"The liar." She mouthed

"Sister Claire and I are going out of town tonight. Afraid of the assassins lurking. I'm still working on trying to provide you with a list of shooters. Maybe, tomorrow."

"When are you returning to DC?"

"I don't have any leads here, so it depends where I determine the sniper or adversary might be."

"Give me the name. The name of any suspect. It's my job to make the arrest."

"We're both agents, sir. And in fact, I've been assigned this case – before you, I believe."

Padgett snorted visibly.

"Listen Smith, I'm going to be the station chief soon. If you know what's good for you, you will start cooperating."

"Thanks for the history lesson. And congratulations on your appointment. Hang on for the ride."

I hung up. The Sister jerkily pulled in and out of lanes driving to the airport. At times, I believed we were on a suicide mission. Candidly, however, I had to admit that she was a well-trained driver.

"It's obvious he's not going to share with us; Kaci Haber will play it straight." I said.

Claire said, "Let's give her all the information."

Almost as if making a covenant, we slapped hands. The jolt sent reverberations up my left arm, which ached.

I was being macho and not taking the pain medication as directed. Pills clouded my mind – and my judgment. However, I was now paying for soberness.

After getting a bite to eat, again Claire drove as if she was in the Indianapolis 500. We were snugly at the airport in time to see their pilot turn off the tarmac.

I touched my arm that was in pain. Claire eyeing me. We both watched as the pilot brought the aircraft to us.

"Hello again. You two have an enjoyable day?" The pilot asked.

"Eventful," answered Claire.

"Where to tonight?"

"Jim. There is some danger. That's why we sent you out of here quickly this morning."

"Yes, when I landed in St. Louis, I had three cars of FBI agents waiting for the plane." He said. His eyes wide with excitement. "They asked who was aboard on my trip to Reagan

National Airport, and I described you. I told them you were a Cardinal."

He made a face.

"They smirked at me. Said you were no Cardinal – only a damned Bishop. They wanted to know the hours you were on the jet. I told them we took off from Vance aviation and the hour we landed here this morning."

I said, "After you told them the timeline, they relaxed a bit."

"Exactly."

"Well, now we're trying to stay out of the firing line from a sniper. Wouldn't mind having us in his cross-hairs."

Jim looked at me – attempting to see if I was kidding. Seeing no laughter, he said, "Let's get the hell out of here."

"A terrific idea. Make your flight plan aloft. Perhaps, we should even change it a few times. Modifying the future is always good when you're trying to stay ahead of an assassin."

"You tell me what to do, I follow instructions."

Jim contacted the tower, making a visual flight rule take off – which technically wasn't permitted from the airport. The pilot had intentionally not told the world where he was headed.

Jim explained there was an emergency for a passenger aboard. The tower accepted the excuse.

The intercom rang, and the pilot said, "Sir, can you come up to the cockpit, so we can map out the itinerary."

I walked tentatively forward, as the plane was being bounced around at low altitude. The jet was flying northward toward the Canadian border, along the coast.

Under other circumstances, the flight to nowhere would be a vacation. The lights twinkling from below.

The pilot had made the quick departure and was staying at low altitude, flying VFR.

"Where we want to end up tonight is at Gulfport airport in Mississippi."

Jim said, "I understand you would prefer no one knowing that you are there."

"Exactly."

"It would be safest for all of us if that were the case. Preferably, when you land, we could be some other tail number. Making it impossible to track us," said Claire, poking her head in from behind.

"Wow. I try not to break any FAA guidelines. You're asking a monster," said the pilot.

Claire asked, "Do you have enough fuel to ping-pong around the East Coast like on a ferry, delivery route?"

"I do."

"That's good; take your time." She said

"We need to rest. I'd like to be at Gulfport around 6 am." I instructed.

"I don't need to divulge our passengers; however, once I file a flight plan, how are we going to keep them from knowing your ultimate destination?"

I said, "That's the most important part of the mission. Let me see if I can get you an FAA directive. You play hopscotch in the meantime."

I returned to the main cabin, and found Claire rubbing the top of her head. She apparently bumped it on the ceiling during her eavesdropping in the pilot's compartment.

"What's going on up there?" She asked.

"Trying to keep us alive. Trying to masquerade our appearance in the early a.m."

I took out the sky phone, calling Kaci Haber. From her, I obtained Chad Caden's home phone. I wished I had my friend's personal cell number with me. It was at home—my numbers I kept on my desk. I knew Kaci wouldn't share that private number with me.

I figured Chad had the pull the get any needed clearance from the FAA. I took a second before dialing to decide exactly what I was going to ask for. Then, I called.

"Chad, recognize the voice?"

"Certainly, late sleeper," said the master.

Early in Joseph Smith's training he had overslept twice and never lived it down. Chad understood exactly who was on the telephone.

"This line secure?"

"Supposed to be. However, I wouldn't whisper classified information over it."

I said, "I'm aloft. Need FAA to authorize citation jet, Zebra 9er Alpha, maintenance in St. Louis, main-base Los Angeles, reassigned call letters 70986 – landing wherever."

"You are trying to avoid being tracked?"

"Don't want a hail of bullets to greet us."

"Let me have the sky phone number. I'll call back with authorization to the pilot directly. None of this bull."

"The pilot is a nervous Nelly."

Chad said, "With you aboard I'd be nervous too." He hung up.

Time passed, about a half an hour later the sky phone rang. I did nothing. It was picked up in the cockpit.

No call to come forward was announced. I couldn't stand it any longer and moseyed with Claire to the pilot compartment.

"Jim, hear anything?"

"Yes, FAA has authorized my use of any tail number, which has been confirmed by my FBO chief officer."

"That should help?"

"I don't know who you are masked man – a Cardinal, or a Bishop, or who the hell – but you pulled a miracle," said the pilot.

"Call us the Lone Ranger and Tonto," I said smiling at my pretty companion.

"My plan now is to fly to St. Louis, land under a fictitious tail number, park in our own hangar, change planes, and take off in time to land at Gulfport in the morning."

"Great news."

"You and the Sister will sleep in the pilot's sleeping lounge. Each will have actual beds tonight. I will alert our security to possible breachers."

"How long to St. Louis?"

"Go on to sleep. I have dinner waiting for us."

Chapter 18

ଔଔଔଔଔ

SMITH, WE HAVE YOU NOW!

Giant cheeseburgers, fries and sodas never tasted so good to Sister Claire. I ate two burgers, and had three glasses of water, instead of soda.

"You Mormons don't drink coffee or soda?" the Sister asked.

"Certainly, coffee is taboo. There are no strict guidelines on caffeinated soda; however, I try to obey the spirit of the 'word of wisdom'—as well. Clearly, caffeine isn't good for you. Why would it be better for you in cola?"

"There are some medical reports out that says four cups of coffee a day helps prevent certain types of cancer," announced Claire.

"That so?"

"I have to tell you Joseph, I nearly died fright several times today. However, I haven't had so much fun in years," said the Sister still dressed more for a date than for detecting.

Her expressions were surprising to me. I wondered how the Pope took her off-the-cuff remarks. Perhaps, she cleans up her speech at the Vatican.

"Unfortunately, I'm afraid you haven't seen anything yet." I replied.

Their new friend, pilot Jim, sat as a confidante. Not really understanding anything, other than he was a target. He was in the frying pan with them.

"Whatever you do, keep the creep with the sniper rifle away from us," Jim said.

It was clear the pilot would never make it as an agent. The slightest quips about bullets or explosions and he was ready to evacuate.

After stuffing themselves, Claire and I were shown individual bunks in the pilot's sleeping compartment. There was a small divider between the two lounges. Nonetheless, the wall did not go all the way to the roof.

After wondering about the Sister and Rome, I was happy no one was taking pictures of the sleeping arrangements. Not exactly to Mormon code, for sure.

"I'll have breakfast on the plane, and have you loaded in time to make a surreptitious landing at Gulfport, Mississippi by 5:30 a.m.," Jim said. "Good night."

I waited a few minutes. Claire was already breathing deeply. Asleep. Then, I abandoned my bunk. I wasn't at all satisfied that a meager airport security guard could ward off an attack by trained guerrillas. I was positive that we faced military-trained pros.

I walked into the main hangar. I took a minute or two. I found a high vantage point from which I could see the entrance. Before I climbed up behind the jet's spare tires, I strung a rope with soda cans on the sliding hangar door.

This would be triggered by the slightest movement. Simple. However, it would work. Make a clatter if someone touched the sliding door.

Chad might call me late-sleeper, but he knew I was alerted by the slightest noise. At home, I could sleep through children or a cyclone. They are sometimes the same thing. On an assignment, the slightest breeze wakes me.

I knew if the terrorists sent an army contingent against us, I could not hold out. I reasoned it was more likely that a single assassin would come – because of the short notice.

The late night was marred by aircraft landing and taking off. Melodic sounds were almost like waves hitting a distant beach. One would escalate and take off, and then the night would return to quiet.

The makeshift alarm went off at about midnight. It would have gone unnoticed to the untrained ear. To me, it was as if the Calvary had played a trumpet.

I was awakened, gun drawn before the large door swung open. Only 10 inches at first. Enough to sound the alarm.

Just as I imagined. "One assassin. A dead man walking, as they say."

I allowed the foreign national to slip about five feet inside the door. Not too close to one of the jets. Not close enough to provide cover.

"Hit the ground. You're dead if you don't."

The man stood frozen. A professional, but in the snare. The man looked around trying to find his adversary. The building was large. Too many hiding places.

"No more warnings – drop the gun and hit the floor."

The man suddenly raised his firearm about six inches. I put three in his chest.

"You drop it, Smith,"

A burst of bullets sprayed, hitting the tires in front of me. The shooter was merely pulling on the trigger – not aiming. I saw the man kneeling next to an equipment case at the front, barely inside the hangar, near the door. He slipped in unnoticed by me.

"Drop it Smith."

More bullets sprayed, again hitting the spare tires in front of me. I picked a prodigious location. High and protected. The tires easily soaked up the rounds fired by the assailant.

The man with the automatic weapon slithered out from behind his protection, moving for a better angle.

"Lose the weapon," said Claire. "Yes, you."

The man wheeled to face the Sister.

"Too late," she said as she fired twice. I said nothing, but put two more in the man's chest.

I yelled, "Sister, take a precautionary position. I have the high ground. We don't know who is outside."

A shaken voice from inside the pilot's lounge said, "I've notified airport police, who are on their way. They're bringing the army."

Claire said, "Army – send for the Marines."

I wondered whether he had called for troops. I wouldn't put it passed him.

"He was frightened at the mention of trouble. Now trained guerrillas invaded his world."

Indeed within minutes, the police determined only two attackers had been sent. The men immobilized an airport guard by hitting him on the head. He would recover.

Claire and I moved into an interrogator mode. We needed information. These guys were not going to be whisked away. Not like the creepy-crawler in Palmdale.

"You're dying man," I said to the first assailant I had shot. "Who sent you?"

"They know your name," he threatened. "They're going to stop you."

I could tell he had only seconds before bleeding out.

"Give me a name."

"Jihad."

"From where?"

"Iran."

The man was gone. I doubted to Paradise. I knew Heaven was a matter for God – not me. In the New Testament, the Apostle Matthew said clearly, "We must not judge our fellow man." Too often I did. The Commandments say 'thou shall not kill.' Sometimes I had to – or die.

Claire said, "We gained an inch."

"At what expense? This guy was yanking our chain. He is an American. Not from Iran. He doesn't know Jihad from my middle name." I said sourly.

She thought, Joseph looks ill, extremely weary. Clear his arm is bothering him.

The Sister motioned for me to follow her back to the sleeping area, the pilot's lounge.

"Joseph, take off your shirt," Claire demanded.

She inspected my wound, and saw that I had pulled a few stitches. It wasn't bleeding badly. Even so, it needed attention.

Our pilot, shaking badly, ventured into the room. "You got shot?"

"Not today," I answered.

"Do you have a first-aid kit, and a needle and thread," she asked Jim.

"What are you going to do?"

"Sterilize the needle, sew you up. Put antibiotic on the wound. I'm also going to be sure that you take your pills as prescribed, Mister," Sister Claire said authoritatively.

"Yes ma'am."

She got to her business of tending to the wound. A paramedic from an ambulance summoned to the scene came, inspected her proficiency.

"Want a job? Your suturing is better than the original," said the paramedic, complementing her.

"What do you have on your rig for infection?"

"Not much. Let me check.

"We should have plenty from what Dr. Trimbold gave me. I have a pocket full."

"Well, start taking them."

The paramedic said he really didn't have anything aboard that would be useful, but he could get a doctor at the hospital to prescribe.

"We're not going to be here long," said the Sister. He'll be fine. He's a romantic – believes in living Prophets."

"In what?" Questioned the paramedic. "A real Bible scholar," I thought.

"Thanks," I said. "You don't believe God would leave us alone without further direction?"

"What?"

"My explanation of divine truths."

Sister Claire was keeping the mood real. We could discuss philosophy later. She changed the subject.

"They know your name. That hit-man was calling you Joseph Smith. They know where you are and who you are. That's not good."

"A tidal wave," I agreed. "We either stay in front of them, or we will drown."

"How do they know your name?"

"Perhaps, from Palmdale. Maybe, one of Padgett's men. We need to take someone alive. If we can capture Brickman – or whatever his name is – we can make him talk."

Claire said, "I don't believe in torture."

The pilot said, "I do. You capture one of these bastards, and I'll torture him for shooting up my hangar."

"How did they know you were here? We did not list you on any flight manifest. We landed with new call numbers," said the pilot with concern.

Both Claire and I laughed simultaneously. Jim's high-pitched voice was hilarious. Then, I let out a cry from the pain that shot up my arm because of his levity.

"For the next month, until my arm heals, forget laughter. I'll focus on prayer instead."

"We had better get out of here. It's not safe for us or the crew," said Claire.

"Agreed."

"Have a plan?" she asked.

"Yes, let's send Jim and his aircraft empty back to Los Angeles. That takes him out of harm's way."

"How do we get to Gulfport?"

"We don't want anyone, anywhere to know where we are going."

"Sounds good to me," said Jim. "Glad to be out of the firing line."

"Get the bird fueled and out of here," I ordered.

"Don't have to tell me twice," said Jim, departing with haste.

I told Claire to dress in a different outfit, and meet out front. She moved quickly, following instructions.

Taking off her clothes, she said, "This time you turn around Joe, or you are in for a show."

I said nothing. However, moved out of the room.

When she came out on the flight line, she saw an ambulance parked inside the hangar. I guided Claire inside, and then loaded the two dead men aboard. Swung in and closed the door.

The ambulance made its way out from the opened hangar door, moving slowly along the flight line. The firemen/paramedic maneuvered the vehicle into a visual dead zone.

The emergency vehicle was between two hangars, and another row blocked the visibility from elsewhere.

"Thanks," I said, flinging open the back door.

I instructed, "Claire hurry."

The ambulance only slowed; it did not stop. She did as she was told. Jumped out the back door. I took her hand preventing her from falling.

The ambulance then moseyed on.

"What's the plan?"

"Drawing it up on the fly," I admitted.

"Never a dull moment with you." She smiled.

I looked around, but the view was obstructed, just as it was for any person trying to see us. On the left, I saw a door. Locked – naturally.

Not for long, I knocked the lock off with one swing of the butt of my revolver.

"What are we doing, hiding out? How is that going to help?" Claire asked.

"I try not to hide. On the other hand, I try not to be visible."

She shook her head not understanding. She followed, because she would do that to the end of the earth – she trusted this man.

"Look what we've found?"

"What?" Said the Sister, looking around. All she saw was an airplane. An empty hangar.

To me, we had found gold.

"Sister, climb aboard."

She was mystified. "Aboard.... Aboard what?"

"Here, Sister," I said opening the back door of a twin-engine airplane. "This is a vintage, modified Aero Commander."

"Who gives a darn? Hiding is hiding."

"I hope it is fully fueled. Only an idiot would leave this twin empty," I said out loud.

She was sure that the pain had finally overtaken me. She climbed aboard. Certainly, no one would find them inside here. They could sleep and rest for days.

I climbed into the left pilot seat.

"Buckle in, Sister. Both tanks are full."

I exited the craft and found some old dungarees – work clothes. I pulled up the dirty over-clothing, over my suit.

Pulling a ball cap over my head, I unlocked and swung open the front doors. I kept my back to any potential onlookers.

"Heavenly Father, please, please watch over us as this maniac attempts to taxi this aircraft," said Claire. She was deadly serious. No levity. No smart remarks. She was pleading for Heavenly Father's help.

I climbed back in, locking the craft's door. I tested the craft, revving both engines slightly. They were returned to idling. I began taxi.

"St. Louis ground this is twin, Aero Cmdr. Niner, four - zero, taxing from the hangars," I said.

I had no idea where the active runway was. However, I knew I soon would find out.

"Taxing from where?"

"Twin, Aero Cmdr. taxing from the hangars."

There was silence. I knew the tower was looking for us with binoculars.

"You have the information?"

"I do; this is a repair taxi flight. I'm not familiar with your airport. Ask taxiing instructions."

Claire sat motionless, and speechless. The Sister was never wordless – until now.

"Roger, twin-commander follow the 747 which is ahead and to your right. Watch out for wake-turbulence."

The tower had found us. Now I had to find the active runway. No doubt the giant craft off to my left was a clue.

I said proficiently, "Have the traffic, will follow. Thanks for the assistance."

"Ground to Twin Commander."

"Yes sir."

"After this, check out airport procedure before climbing aboard, even if you're ferrying an airplane. Ground control out."

"You're right. Sorry."

Claire wagged a finger at me. "You get in trouble more than any man I have ever met."

Her fingers and face were devoid of color. Seeing me at the controls of an aircraft clearly spooked the, heretofore, non-intimidated, Nun.

The 747 bolted into the air. I received clearance from the tower for a departure. As professionally as I could, guided the twin onto the centerline for takeoff.

I flicked on the microphone, and said, "All passengers be certain your tray tables are up, and your seatbelts are tightly fastened. This is your pilot; we are number one for takeoff."

"You idiot," Claire shouted. "When I get my hands on you, if were alive, I'm going to kill you."

I never heard her threats as I had pushed the throttles full forward. The bird rocketing down the course, and flew grandly to the heavens.

Chapter 19

ଔଔଔଔଔଔ

CONSIDER IT PURE JOY, MY BROTHERS, WHENEVER YOU FACE TRIALS OF MANKIND.

James 1:2

"There is a small, fighter manufacturing plant at the Moss Point, Mississippi airport," I informed Claire. "Been there once as a guest of the Governor."

"You think that's where he's going?"

"Small potatoes – overall. Not like the Palmdale plant. I don't really understand how the plant would be of critical importance to national defense. They do some work. Actually send their components to Palmdale. The supplier finishes the craft there."

"How does that make any sense?" Claire asked.

"The Mississippi Governor can say he has Aerospace and jobs in his state."

Claire crossed her eye.

"I hope they don't stick."

She said, "Only in the United States would we make a part of an airplane in one state and then ship a giant part some 2,000 miles to another plant. Bizarre. That's my view."

I actually agreed. Nevertheless, said, "However, we should fly into Moss Point, unless you have a better guess. Search for Bickmore from there."

"What about the new AirBus facility being built in Mobile, Alabama, or the GE engine plant?" Claire suggested.

"The truth is we are going to have to ferret out where our adversary is visiting. Call his wife and ask her what plant. My belief is he will find us. They seem to have our itinerary, even though we've turned off our cell phones."

"I think they figured out we were using the jet. They merely tracked it. I knew it was based in St. Louis and California," she said.

"Could be."

I thought for a few minutes. I could see Claire, with head down, doing the same.

I said, "Perhaps we can have Kaci Haber or Padgett call Bickmore's wife. Ask where he is staying?"

Claire was astounded how proficiently the Bishop flew the twin aircraft. He handled air traffic communication effortlessly, as if he was a commercial pilot. What had she worried about?

She gave up her cushy seats in the main cabin. Claire was sitting in the co-pilot's chair, next to the man of many talents and mystery.

I thought it was time for a pleasure break, saying, "I think I'll call my wife from the customer's Sky-phone."

"I didn't think Bishops stole things? You've already taken the man's plane..." Claire chided.

"I wrote down the plane's metered-time, when I started taxing. I'm, also, going to keep track of the call."

"So. You can mail the man a thank-you card?"

"No. The government, the FBI, can send him a check for our commandeering of his craft. Nothing is free."

"Just keeping you honest Bishop."

I lifted the sky-phone from its cradle, and dialed.

"I'm going to wake her. She's a good egg – loves talking to me at any time of the day.""

"Such confidence," said Claire. "Sounds like you're trying to talk yourself into it."

She noticed a perplexed look come on his face as the phone continued to ring – ring after ring. No answer.

"See, you're not so charming, after all," Claire jibbed.

She stopped ragging on him when she could see that he was concerned.

"She's probably asleep – just not answering," Claire said.

"No, when I'm working, she always keeps her cell phone right with her. Even when she's in bed."

I hung up.

"I'm going to dial my cell phone's voicemail. Nobody's going to be able to track us that quick."

"Why, your voicemail?" she asked.

"My wife may have left a message. Normally, doesn't when I am working. However, who knows?"

I again lifted the sky-phone out of its cradle and dialed the voicemail. There were a number of perfunctory messages. And then the alarm.

Death Message in the Air

The voicemail message was as if a missile hit the plane. My senses were cracked into a million parts. I could barely think. It was good the plane was on autopilot, or we would have crashed.

In a vicious, demanding tone, the verbal assailant said,

"Abandon your incessant detecting and return to Los Angeles immediately. If you don't, your wife and children will be executed. We know you are headed for the St. Louis airport. We are tracking you!"

I hit the replay button and handed the sky- phone to Claire. I couldn't speak. I was barely able to motion for her to listen.

Listening to the explicit threat, Claire turned pale – nearly vomiting.

"How do you listen to the next message?" She asked.

I hadn't thought of that. My brain turned off. I couldn't reason.

Claire listened intently to the next message.

"We know you have disregarded our previous voice message. You killed more of our men in St Louis. This is our last warning, or your family will be tortured – then killed."

The voice had a foreign accent. She couldn't make it out. The accent sounded as if it came from more than one place. Odd, she thought.

She was afraid to let Joseph hear the second message. Reluctantly, she handed me the phone.

My soul was tortured. A grimace deeper than any she had seen spread over Joseph's face; even though, she had witnessed countless deaths in combat.

"Some people say they are in love," she thought. "The Smith's love was the real deal—with eternal significance," she said to herself.

Without a word, I turned the plane west, heading to California.

Claire said nothing for nearly a half an hour. Breaking her silence, she put her hand tenderly on his right arm.

"Do we have enough gas for Oxnard, California?"

"No."

Trying to engage him, but not rile him to anger, she said softly, "Let's think out loud for a minute."

"Why?"

Claire kept her hand on his arm, rubbing softly. As a Nun, she had experienced nearly catatonic parents, when they lost a child. The Nun was taught to reassure, while providing hints, which could sustain the individual.

"We need to determine how we're going to notify your family's captors. We don't want to stay mute, and have the murderous thugs carrying out the threat."

"Right. You're right."

"Better," she thought. "Three words this time − instead of one."

"Joe, how are we going to contact them? They believe there is a simple way, or they wouldn't have left such a cryptic message."

"I don't know?"

"Think."

"I should call. Have someone go by my house. See what's going on there. Perhaps, there's a message."

Color was returning to his face. Joseph Smith was a complex man; the Sister knew. Part genius, part investigator, a religious scholar and believer. However, it was apparent; he was mostly a father and a husband.

Claire said, "Call who, the police?"

"One of my counselors in the Bishopric is a deputy sheriff, and a helicopter rescue pilot. He's capable."

"You must be sure you're not sending a friend into a slaughter. Who knows what will be found in your house?"

At first, I blanched – thinking, she was saying my family was already executed. Then, I thought like a Bishop. She was trying to protect my friend in the bishopric from being slaughtered, as well.

"Roy Tanner can line up a sheriff's crew in a few minutes. They will take necessary precautions for themselves and my family."

I kept my cell phone turned on. If we were being tracked, they would know that we are headed to California.

"I'm out of range up here, but they may be able to track it."

I picked up the sky-phone and dialed Tanner. Being in the middle of the night, the call went to voicemail mail. I hung up and dialed again. On the third attempt, I reached my friend.

Brother Tanner was given the bottom line. No whipped cream, no real explanation. However, Roy Tanner knew Bishop Smith's family was in peril.

"Roy, three things – number one, watch your back; number two, if my family is there get them out alive; number three, I need some way of contacting the kidnappers."

"I understand Bishop," Roy Tanner said.

The two men, even though over a telephone, prayed together. They ask Heavenly Father for assistance and clarity of thought in the endeavor.

Off the telephone, Claire asked, "No second thoughts; you knew he would go in the middle of the night, and do what was needed."

"People say some awful things about Mormons, Sister Claire. Nevertheless, the truth is we are guided by God and Jesus Christ. We are kind, and loving people. We help each other – for that matter, we help anyone in need. "

"We Catholics do too; however, if I called a Priest in the middle of the night, I would receive many prayers, and a lot of advice. He wouldn't enter a combatant's camp," the Sister said.

"Nobody, in our church gets paid for church service. Therefore, all of us have other skills and jobs. I called a righteous man who works as a deputy sheriff."

"When we met Duke at the track, he said that you lived four lives. What's that about?"

She was engaging Joe Smith to prevent him from shutting down again. She wanted his brilliance – not his melancholy. Claire wanted him out of his shell.

"First, I am a husband and father. Next the Bishop. Then, number three, I am a stockbroker, and fourth an undercover FBI agent. I'm all of those things. I do lead four distinct lives. Sometimes, more than that."

"Does anyone in the church know that you work undercover?"

"My wife and my Stake President."

"What's a Stake President? Said Claire, still engaging him.

"Bishops report to the Stake President. For example, before a member can go to the LDS Temple, they need an approval – called a Temple recommend from the Bishop and the Stake President."

Then, Claire worried. Perhaps, the Stake President gave them up. Was the leak?

"Aren't you afraid that man will divulge your undercover work?"

"Are you afraid a Priest to whom you confide in confession will tell someone? On the other hand, how about your Argentinean Pope?"

"Well, no."

The two of them flew in silence toward the West. The mood was as dark as the night.

Approximately, an hour later the sky-phone rang. I had given the number to Tanner.

"Bishop, we took your house by force. However, it was empty. There was clearly a fight in your bedroom. Your wife and two children are gone," Tanner reported.

"What's the bottom line?"

"I brought Ventura county forensics with me. They say they discovered some blood on the sheets in the master bedroom."

I sighed deeply. Claire couldn't hear, but she could see hope. Even as brittle as Joseph is at the moment. The Sister could see the despair – the anguish.

"Forensics says there is not enough blood for them to conclude that your wife is dead. Probably injured."

"The children."

"Gone. Rooms are clean. No blood, no mess."

"What do you conclude, Roy?"

"Let me tell you."

"Please. Tell me – quickly."

I took a deep breath – hoping for the best, but fearing the worst.

"Bishop, there is a note that says they will know when you're headed back to California. Off the case, whatever that means," Tanner said.

"How will they know? Who's going to tell them?"

"I don't know," said Roy Tanner. "What case? What are they talking about?"

"There is a poster board in my study. Write in large print the following: 'Bishop Joe Smith has abandoned the case. Returning home to California'."

Roy Tanner did as instructed. He read back the note.

"Roy, call my secretary and tell him that I will be back in the office late tomorrow, or early next day. Furthermore, let every ward member know that I am available for appointments."

"You don't believe someone in the church did this? He questioned.

"Absolutely not. However, innocently, I believe I can be tracked by gossip provided through members. I am not saying that is what happened. I am covering all the bases," I said despondently.

"Bishop, we need to contact the FBI. There's been a kidnapping."

"Believe me, Roy that will be my next call."

"Do you want me to stake out your home?" Roy Tanner asked.

"No. Without an army that might be dangerous. Let the FBI tackle that. They can transfer my home phone immediately."

Tanner said, "From what I can see, you may be right."

"Roy, thanks."

"For what? It's been nothing."

With the line severed. Joseph appeared resolute – totally calm and in command. He was back being the confident, but humble and understanding man Claire knew.

"You seem to have calmed yourself. How, in the face of such pending danger and risk to family?"

Joe Smith turned and faced the Nun squarely, "Faith, sister, faith."

Chapter 20

ରେ ଜ ଜ ଜ ଜ ଜ ଜ

ANGER SWELLS ONLY
IN THE BOSOM OF FOOLS

Albert Einstein

They flew on through the night. Their plane swallowed in inclement skies. Through a stretch, they flew strictly on instruments with vision obliterated. Even though faith was in Joseph's bosom, the mood in the cabin was ominous – bleak.

I landed the twin-engine Aero Commander twice and refueled. Both looked for attackers, saw none, and retreated into the sky.

"We're being bounced around like a cork," said Claire.

"Nothing to worry about."

The Sister said, "There's plenty to worry about. With you flying, I'm not worried about falling out of the sky. However, I'm trying to figure out what the hell is going on."

"Me too. We may be flying into Hell."

"They are too well-organized and diverse to be a band of bandits."

I nodded, "Yea. Agreed. They are taking over aircraft plants, creating espionage attacks, killing United States Senators, and kidnapping families of FBI agents."

"If we can figure out the underlying mission, we're much closer to cracking them."

"Good thought."

"Unfortunately, I feel as if we're flying the wrong direction. This aggression is fueled in Washington."

I nodded. "Unfortunately, I agree. However, God and family first. Not even a close call. Our foe seems to understand me perfectly. Their understanding is part of the equation."

"I also understand. Maybe, we should divide our efforts. I should return to Washington." Said the Sister.

"Absolutely not. I learned from Jesus, we walk two-by-two. Missionaries are taught to stay together. In effect, we truly are missionaries in the fight to save our country. Perhaps, the world."

She saw a man totally concerned with her well-being – even, while the lives of his family stood in peril. Joseph was direct. He was resolute. No waiver, no room for misunderstanding. Some would not like this concrete tone.

"I was just thinking...."

"No Sister, I'm not going to lose you too."

The Sister affirmed, knowing she had lost this battle.

Probably, the Bishop was correct. The danger too abundant.

"I am so angry," she said. "This killing is senseless. I'm angry to the point I want to shoot several of them between the eyes."

"Anger is easy. It delivers absolutely nothing."

Chapter 21

ରେରେରେରେରେ

DEMOCRACY IS THE ART AND SCIENCE OF RUNNING THE CIRCUS FROM THE MONKEY CAGE

HL Mencken

When you have a Bishop and a Nun flying 2,000 miles with the oppressive pressure on each, discussion naturally gravitates between religion and duty.

"Bishop, I've noticed you been quoting from the Bible. Why aren't you expounding from the Book of Mormon?" Claire asked, trying to understand better.

"To Mormons, the Bible is the word of God and Jesus, just as other Christians believe. The Book of Mormon is an additional testament to Jesus Christ. Someday, I'll tell you of God's plan of salvation. And how the Book of Mormon was written by Prophets from 600 years before Christ's birth. How our country was selected by the hand of God in the restoration of the gospel."

Then, we were literally bounced back to reality, as the twin jolted and lost a hundred feet.

Claire asked, "Tell me. Who are the spies in Washington?"

"I believe we have to think outside the box. The answers are there. Sometimes the smallest detail uncovers the mole."

The night gave way to a new morning. There were storm clouds brewing in the West, and occasionally there was a bolt of lightning.

"I wish we saw God's hand, rather than his wrath in the skies, this morning," she thought as she tightened her seat belt.

Joseph called Chad Caden at his home, explaining the developments of the evening.

"Someone knows too much about my life. They know I will stop a mission immediately for family. Furthermore, why am I so much at the center of the terrorist's plans?" I asked.

Chad responded quietly. "I am so terribly sorry for your family. They may turn up when you are home. We desperately need you back on the job."

"Chad, I'm checking on your people. It appears this danger is emanating from Washington," I said.

"You're asking whether Kaci or Noah could be a traitor?" Caden asked.

"Claire and I have punched ideas around all night. We're not questioning Kaci."

Chad said, "Padgett is an ass – not a traitor."

"I know you old man; you have the greatest analytical mind in the business. Who is leading the upheaval? More importantly what do they hope to accomplish?"

"I don't believe the Senator was trying to overthrow the United States. Start from there," Chad advised. "He might have been misled. He was not a traitor."

"I tend to agree. Otherwise, why kill him."

"What then?"

"Our way of life might depend on finding the answer. Extremists appear to have the upper hand."

"What do you plan once you're back in California? Are you off the case?"

There was silence on my end of the sky-phone.

Chad said, "I understand, if you are resigning the case. Your family is paramount."

"Let me ask you this boss. Who's investigating at your end?"

"Depends solely on whether you're in or out of the ball game. Candidly, the FBI and agents at Langley are reticent. They'll charge into a building with a dozen shooters; however, they are not suicidal when they can't shoot at the danger."

"Meaning?"

"This is the largest, most divergent crew that we've ever seen. It's as if war has been declared. An invisible war. Even so, who are we fighting?"

"Exactly. What does the President say?"

"North Korea, Iran, Pakistan and Iraq have formed a coalition. Iran is finishing off their nuclear bomb; North Korea is building the long-range missile; and who knows what the other two are doing? Nothing good for the planet."

"What are they calling themselves?"

"Islam Against the Menace – the **IAM**, said Chad. "Candidly, I do not know the full name of the IAM. Muslims for sure.

"How cute? Do you think they were trying to get a stealth bomber, a new fighter and other secrets for their warring efforts?"

Chad, a master at military-manipulation and strategy, paused. A long pause. I could actually hear him breathing on the other end of the line.

"What doesn't figure is the Senator's involvement. Furthermore, a couple of the people you have killed are government. One was CIA and the other our agency."

"Where?"

"One of the men at the defense contractor in Palmdale was CIA, and the shooter in St. Louis was FBI. Actually, Padgett trained him."

I gulped, "Your still saying Padgett......"

"I will guarantee my life that Padgett is loyal – by the book. The fact that he has been betrayed is killing him. He doesn't get it. He fears the tentacles are too deeply rooted. He's afraid; won't admit it."

"What are the President and Secretary of State doing about the **IAM?**"

Chad said, "I am a little out of that loop. Your man, the Four Star, has the President's ear. Certainly, I don't. However, in a meeting with our director, I was told the President is trying to limit other countries from joining the IAM."

"Like, who?

"Saudi Arabia. Syria. Maybe, even China. Well, the rest of the world. The United States has been the rich – the bully for too long," Chad said.

The twin flew on with precision. Rain was pelting the skin of the Commander. The flight was not a peaceful 747 ride. Anything but.

Off the phone, I suggested that the Sister call the Vatican.

"Maybe, the Pope or others have heard of the **IAM.** We desperately need to know what they are doing."

Claire had some difficulty getting through. She ultimately was attached with a protocol Cardinal, who was Rome's answer to the CIA. A collector of data. A spy within.

"Cardinal, this is Sister Claire Coogan."

"Yes, I know you."

"I need information on something called, the **IAM**."

"First Sister, word has reached Rome that you are parading around the United States in a low-cut, stylish, gown best worn by dignitaries − not Nuns. On the other hand, even, women of the night."

I listened in. This was a slap the Sister did not deserve.

Claire was indeed a maverick. That, in part, is why she received Marine-type missions from the Pope, rather than spiritual callings.

"First, Cardinal, I am not parading. I am trying to stay alive. My more traditional garb is a bull's eye. Does the Pope instruct me to reconfigure?" Claire said, unceremoniously, without humor.

This time I put my right hand on her arm, saying, "Easy, sister. Humility."

"I am telling you."

"Cardinal," questioned Claire, "Do you have information on the **IAM** or not?"

"Sister, you know I was born in Spain. I also feel the USA has too much power, and wages war against innocent people," said the Cardinal.

"I am not receiving the assistance I need. I was appointed directly by the Pope as part of Vatican's help to the world," said Claire admonishing the Cardinal. "Do I need to talk to the Pope?"

"No. The whisperings in Rome about you, Sister, are true."

"Can we leave that for another day, Cardinal? You can't come up with anything more original than whisperings?"

The line was silent. Almost dead.

"However, to the **IAM** question," said the Cardinal in an unfriendly voice.

"Please."

"The members of the **IAM** are attempting to realign the world's power, and bring peace to all. Today, a billion Muslims are unrepresented at the seat of power. Tomorrow they may reign. Do away with the Almighty -- America First and Only," he said.

"I am on a mission from Rome, which is to stabilize the world from the harm presently underway. Perhaps, elsewhere." Claire said frostily.

"Sister, that is impossible."

"Are you telling me that the IAM is attacking the United States? Yes or No?"

"Attacking? They are organizing. They are formulating. They are seeking member nations."

"Who are the present members of the IAM?"

He laughed, "Well Saudi Arabia, Iran, Pakistan, North Korea, Syria, and Spain if I can convince them. Many more in the end. You name a country. They will be in the IAM," the Cardinal said. "Sister, God loves all people equally. Not Americans first, last and always."

He hung up the phone. Obvious, he wanted the last word.

"No wonder he is not the Pope," I replied.

"Do not get the wrong idea. Our Pope is a God fearing man. He loves everyone. He does not want a divided world. The Cardinal expresses a view widely held in most countries."

Chapter 22

CRCRCRCR

VAN NUYS AIRPORT – DAYTIME, VISIBILITY TWO MILES WITH RAIN

I requested a straight in for landing on runway 16 at Van Nuys airport. I was instructed to fly downwind because of a non-instrument rated pilot trying to make a landing. The sky was totally obscured. The approach was a challenge for an instrument rate pilot – and nowhere for a general aviation fly-about to be parading.

They were calling the weather two miles, with light rain. Wind gusts to 35 miles per hour.

"Tricky to impossible for a non-instrument pilot. He had no business in the sky today." I told Claire.

Claire asked, "Wouldn't we be best landing at Oxnard? Weather is better there. Closer to home."

"Closer to automatic gunfire too."

"Doesn't the saying go; 'I met the enemy and he is us'?"

"They've got the Army, the CIA, the FBI. I don't know who all, Sister. We have only us. We are going to avoid being shot. The best we can. They have forced me home. They know we're coming. What better excuse to hit us?"

I looked at the fuel gauge, knowing our bird was going to start gulping for fuel soon. I had weaned the gas, so that I could stubbornly prevent another landing for fuel. Not another stop, so close to home.

I turned the twin left onto the base leg, cutting the corner a little tight because of fuel concerns. Now, I was cleared to land in front of the troubled, non-instrument rated pilot. The doomed aviator was being guided to the airport by traffic control.

"Tower, twin commander turning short final for landing 16-right. Double checking, your clearance."

"Roger. Cleared to land."

I checked that my gear was down; the mixture was set to full-rich. We were ready to put the beautifully refurbished Aero Commander onto the strip.

Just going over the chain-link fence and approaching the end of the runway, the tower operator screamed.

"Tower, twin commander, watch traffic diving at the runway without clearance."

The inexperienced and panic-stricken pilot was out of control. He saw the runway and bolted air-traffic control."

I shouted back, "What? What traffic?"

Then, from the left, I picked up a flash of movement as a single-engine Cessna careened toward the pavement directly in front of me.

"Twin commander go around," ordered the tower.

The Cessna 182 collided hard with the runway. It hit the tarmac partially sideways, skidded, broke the strut, dipped, and hit its high-wing and flipped.

Joseph adroitly added power stopping his dissent. He wasn't going around. Not making another approach. To low on fuel.

Van Nuys Airport is long enough to make two landings, I thought.

I added full power, and lifted the nose slightly to clear the cart-wheeling aircraft below. However, I did not retract the flaps or the gear. I had gained flying speed, but would dump it quickly.

"Tower, twin commander landing long," I said, addressing the emergency.

The tower said nothing.

Sister Claire found herself holding her breath. As a former Marine, bullets flying are one thing. Airplanes cutting in line, and then smacking the runway, ending upside-down was quite another.

"Need more prayers to be with you Bishop."

I said nothing.

As I said, no problem, I landed the airship down the runway. Well, actually, there was plenty of perspiration running down my face. In the end, I had more than 1,000 feet left when he pulled off onto a taxi way.

"Twin commander taxiing hangars near Beach dealer," I said to ground control.

"Spectacular landing. Taxi to Beach," said the controller.

"Thanks. How's the Cessna pilot?"

"Don't know."

I knew Van Nuys Airport very well as I had taken my flight instruction here. I wanted to abandon the airplane without going through questioning. At this point, the aircraft might be listed as stolen.

"My prayers are for the pilot of that small plane," said the Sister.

"I'd run out there to assist; however, I would be in the way. I fear the pilot has life-threatening injuries."

I taxied slowly past Beech Aircraft and pulled off to the left. Finding an open spot, I guided the plane to a stop.

"Come on Sister."

Claire said nothing. She followed instructions.

The two walked away. Walked out front of the airport, clearing away from the landing strip. They strolled across the Boulevard into the Hathaway Building on the left, which bordered Van Nuys Airport.

Joseph knew the FAA had a floor in the building. A safe haven from which they could make inquiring telephone calls.

We walked into the FAA. I showed the receptionist a set of FBI credentials. Not mine, but appropriate for the situation.

"I need to borrow a phone to call the Bureau. My cell phone is out of order," I told her.

Claire and I were directed to a small office. It had a desk, with two chairs in front and one behind. The office normally was used by an FAA interviewer. Plain vanilla walls.

"Thanks. It will only be a few minutes," I said, dismissing the young lady.

"Who you calling?"

"I think we need to inquire a little before being bullish and returning to Camarillo," I told her. Without thinking, I took the seat behind the desk. The Sister sat where interviewees normally get grilled.

"This isn't like a baseball game. Warming up a relief pitcher is one thing. Letting these henchmen have time to plan our re-emergence is potential suicide," she forecasted. "They have machine guns, rather than baseball bats."

"Letting them focus their weapons on the plane as we skirt the fence at the Ventura-Oxnard airport would be worse."

I dialed Los Angeles FBI headquarters, seeking the same man who had turned me away perfunctorily at an earlier time. It might not be smart. It was necessary.

When the man came on the line, I again used my code name.

"Agent Smith, you don't need your code name anymore. Everyone, who is anyone in the universe, knows of your exploits in the last day. Everywhere you go someone ends up dead," said the bureau chief.

"It's nice to be known."

"Not when an army-sized enemy, of unknown derivation, is gunning for you."

"You're probably right."

"What do you need? Where are you? Understand your family has been kidnapped," said the chief in machine-gun style. I hadn't told anyone, except Chad Caden, about my family's disappearance.

"In Los Angeles, I need to know what the bureau is doing out here. And thanks for remembering my family."

"Chad Caden called from Washington, asking for Bureau assistance on your wife and children. The call was transferred to me."

"Thanks."

Smith learned long ago to listen – not run off at the mouth. You gain more information by listening than you do by talking.

"We received a call from someone who said they had your family. Several hours ago. Per instructions from Washington, we told the caller that you were off the case, and returning home."

"Then."

The bureau chief said, "They already knew."

"How did they know?"

"They didn't say. They said to stay out of their way, and your children will be returned home."

There was silence over the phone. Neither spoke a word. This time the bureau chief was letting Joseph Smith process information. Not talking.

"My children. My children will be returned home. What about my wife?"

The chief said, "I asked. They hung up."

"When are they going to be returned?"

"Joseph, I'm very sorry; I do not know. I've told you absolutely everything I do know."

More silence.

Joseph asked, "What are you doing out here about the case?

"The Bureau and the Army have surrounded the Palmdale defense contractors, and we have contingencies for the ones in El Segundo. No secrets are leaving California."

Joseph asked, "Have you heard of the **IAM?**"

"Of course. We have a Presidential bulletin to be on guard."

"What are we thinking about the **IAM**? How does it directly affect the United States?

Joseph was asking questions too fast to be answered.

"The scuttlebutt is that Muslim countries are trying to put themselves in an immediate position to offset the United States. We've heard the word that they might cut off all oil exports to our country."

"Wow."

"We understand that leaders of the IAM are meeting with China. Asking that country, curtail loaning money to us. Call our loans."

Joseph thought for a second. "It's kind of a reverse embargo. Stop the fuel. Stop the money. Have nuclear weapons and rockets."

"Attack us by hijacking our secrets," the bureau chief said.

"But!! How does that tie-in with what has been going on the last 24 hours here?" I asked. "Something basic is missing."

"Do not know."

"Why would they take my family? I am not Superman. I can't stop the IAM."

"Don't know" the supervisor said again. Was he listening? Or was this a recording.

"Have you dispatched any agents to my house; others working on the kidnapping?" I asked.

"Sorry. We are stretched too thin. If we had twice the number of agents, we would still be short. Protecting the 'obvious' is our first task."

"Well...."

"Local police and sheriffs will have to address your situation."

"Kidnap is a federal crime."

"Yep. However, we just don't have enough agents."

It was clear to me, I needed the assistance of the bureau. We at the FBI always say that locals just screw up an investigation for kidnapping. The FBI has anything but a perfect record.

"The locals have no chance," I said out loud.

"I know," he said. "Joseph, my orders from Washington are absolute. Defend our weapons. A life or two lost is not critical to the brass. Only the weapons."

"Sad world when hardware is more important than a man's family," I said.

"Yes."

"There was a time that protecting a man's castle – his home – was paramount."

He said, "Joseph, I have to go. Good luck. Let me know if I can help in some way."

The line went dead.

Claire said, "What an absurdity. Why volunteer a statement that you can call for help. He has just told you that he has been warned off."

Chapter 23

ೞೞೞೞೞ

A MAN BEGINS CUTTING HIS WISDOM TEETH THE FIRST TIME HE BITES OFF MORE THAN HE CAN CHEW

Herb Caen

Why are they so intent on curtailing our booming efforts?" Claire asked.

"Booming," I asked. "Blooming efforts."

The Sister – and another face. Sister Claire must have a thousand mask-like appearances to fit each particular circumstance.

She said, "What possible damage can we do? We are only two people. Why are we important?"

"You're assuming the **IAM** is behind this?"

The Sister paused, thinking.

"It's the only common denominator. Why did Rome send me here? Why did the Cardinal, so belligerently, speak for the **IAM?**"

"Last time I checked, the IAM didn't have members in the CIA or the FBI. However, agents in both organizations are involved up to their eyeballs. And there are some long riflemen too. Whoever, they are?"

"Think I should call the Pope?"

The Sister was known to me as a prankster, so I looked at her to see if she was kidding. Why would Rome have the answers? We didn't.

She wasn't pulling my leg this time.

"It wouldn't hurt." I said. "However, if I were going to call the Prophet of the Mormon Church, it would be for an update on spiritual matters. I know God is not behind this bedlam." I told her softly.

"It was all brought on by men." I added, "I don't know who. However, I can describe their lowly nature. The unrighteous two-legged ones roaming the earth. A Prophet who talks to the Almighty converses about saving souls."

She heard. Even so, looking into my eyes, she could see I was depressed. Missing on some cylinders. So Claire was immediately dialing for an update. And the Pope didn't avoid the call. Rather, embraced it.

"Your Eminence, I spoke to the Cardinal. He essentially told me to be aware of the IAM – that Muslim countries are banding together to pull down America," she reported. "Why was I sent to the United States? You were unclear other than to say you wanted me to help a friend."

The Pontiff answered, "We always help friends, just as Jesus did. Some of the time our friends turn out to be our enemies. Think of Judas."

Sister Claire was having difficulty understanding. Same as she did before leaving Rome. Was the United States considered an enemy? If so, why hadn't she been ordered back to the Vatican?

"Did you send any other servants to other places in the world to help friends on this matter? Perhaps, to countries embracing the IAM?"

Sister Claire Coogan was a brilliant interrogator. Even though she could not stand eye-to-eye with the Catholic Church's Curate, the Sister was probing respectfully.

"Naturally."

"Am I to assume that the IAM was your initial concern?"

The Pope was no slouch when it came to intelligence either. He was humble. Intelligent. Kind. He was not going to be easily influenced into an offhand response.

"Sister, you know what they say about people who assume – right?"

She was summarily rebuked for attempting to paint the Pope into answering a question he had so artfully avoided.

"We are ducking bullets, having Bishop Smith's wife and children kidnapped, and are seeking to follow your instructions. However, the road is dark. I am seeking light and clarification."

"God is the light. Please tell Bishop Smith, I am so sorry about his family. The Church wants to bring peace where there is disharmony. Sister, hear me correctly, the two of you stay the course. Pray."

"Can you tell me if we are in total darkness?"

"If I had all the answers...why would I put you at risk? If his church's President knew the evil men creating havoc, Bishop Smith would be recalled – to minister to his flock. Don't you think?"

"Certainly."

"The two of you are pure of heart. Brothers and Sisters," said the Pope. She could almost feel his kind hand on her head.

He continued, "We are aware of the intent of the IAM. We do not know what ominous response the United States will make. Further, the warning that we received did not specify the IAM as the threat to world peace."

"Then, you are saying the United States is the danger?"

There was no answer. Only a long silence.

With that, the Sister understood there would be no sun brightly shining to illuminate from Rome. Further, the line went dead.

"Well?"

"Perhaps you should call Salt Lake – talk to your Prophet," said the Sister, yanking my chain. She put her hands up, toward the heavens as to say, "Who knows?"

"Wasted call?"

"Rome received a warning from someone high up here in the states. Who I do not know. The Pope is not saying. Further, the warning was apparently not specific."

"In other words, no news?"

She continued, "I asked for light..."

I cut her off, saying, "And he said, 'Jesus is the light' – right?"

"Bishop you should become a Catholic. Maybe, even a true Cardinal. You seem to understand the Pope better than I do."

Uproar in Camarillo

Next, the Bishop called bishopric counselor Roy Tanner, deducing that his ward would be in chaos. Word circulating that his family was kidnapped.

"You're right Bishop. Everyone is clamoring, in prayer for you and your family," Tanner said.

"Any intelligence coming out of the sheriff's department? About the kidnapping or the kidnappers?"

179

"Not really. Understand the FBI has had contact with the goons. They say the children are being returned."

"What about my wife?" I asked, hoping there was some positive update.

"Don't know."

I asked if Roy Tanner knew anything else.

"I understand you instructed me to stay away from the family home. Nevertheless, we have taken refuge in the Parker home, which is across the street, kind of catty-corner from yours."

"Catty-corner?" I asked, not understanding.

"Near, adjacent. You know, the Catholic family—the Parkers?"

"What are you doing there?"

Tanner said, "We have binoculars and are surveying anyone who comes close to the house or drives by several times."

"Great thought! Has that uncovered anything?"

"Maybe. A non-distinct bluish car with government plates drove by a number of times – including twice so far today," said Roy.

"Government plates?"

"Yes. And here's what's interesting – the car has not been checked out by anyone. It's supposed to still be in the government lot."

"Interesting. More direct evidence that official Washington is involved."

"Three men inside."

I asked, "Is this a sheriff's department inquiry, or off the books?"

"Off the books. You sounded like you want them to believe you're done with the case – correct?"

"Perfect. That's best. They need to know I am not working it. I don't know why that's important to them," I replied.

"Bishop, you know we have active and retired law enforcement in our ward. They are behind you. The whole ward – whatever – you need," said Tanner.

"Roy, I'm back now. Can you line up some deputies, so when I pull into my driveway, I am somewhat protected? Not eliminated in a gangland slaying typical of the 30s."

"Absolutely."

"A couple of things."

"Yes."

"In Washington DC, the assassins engaged a highly-trained sniper. Killed a United States Senator."

Roy Tanner thought for a second and replied, "I think we had better consider that they have a hitter staked out somewhere here. They're trying to lure you home."

Tanner told me that headlines in the LA Times, and our local paper, shouted about the events at the Palmdale defense plant. Told of the murder of the US Senator in Washington. The papers and TV news says undisclosed authorities have conjectured that our country is under attack from Muslim countries.

He reported that the sheriff had been called to alert, because of the IAM. All police agencies. People are thinking war.

I said, "One more thing Roy."

"Yep."

"I am assigned on the IAM investigation with a Catholic Nun as a partner.

"A Nun?"

"I know – now you've heard everything. In the sheriff's department, you work with female deputies."

"But never a Nun."

"Don't say it that way to her, or she'll clobber you. She's a former Marine," I laughed.

"Where is she going to sleep?"

"Too dangerous to separate us, and have to guard two locations."

Roy said, "I'm sorry for being callous. I didn't think. Practicality first."

"A must under these circumstances."

"What do you mean that you have been assigned?" he inquired. Roy was in the dark about me living four lives.

"That's right. You believe me to be a simple stockbroker. Roy, my principal job is FBI – undercover, anti-terrorist task force."

"A surprise a minute. That announcement illuminates their dislike of you. I'm starting to get a better picture."

"You can't be undercover and announce it to the world."

"Guess not. I take it your no longer covert. Now everyone knows you."

"True. The Nun and I – well, without self-praise, we took out the invaders in Palmdale. We are now being hunted by the devil's henchmen."

Chapter 24

ଔଔଔଔଔଔ

GOSSIP IS THE DEVIL'S RADIO

George Harrison

"Sister, this is Camarillo," I said introducing her to our village – actually a small little town which is nestled against hills on three sides. Cooled by the ocean a few short miles away. Never too hot, or cold.

We reached the picturesque view from the grade high atop Camarillo. We traveled from the San Fernando Valley, descending into the city which had been rich farm land years before.

The air was absolutely clear, unpolluted by smog. We saw the ocean in front of us as we came down the grade.

Claire made a funny face, another of her witticism to follow. "You talk about the area's beauty as if we're about to witness the second coming. That this might be the promised land."

"You might wish."

"Meaning?"

"Our members don't gossip generally. A principle. You know, love your neighbor. Nonetheless, you are about to be involved in a hailstorm of speculation."

Claire trusted my honor. She wondered why members of the church would question my actions.

"Billy Graham is certainly not a Mormon. As a Baptist, however, he never was found anywhere, at any time, with any woman – except his wife. Hard to gossip about a non-event."

"Back there again."

"Always making fun," I said.

"We've dodged flying bullets and meandering airplanes together," she said. "Harder to face questioning eyes?"

"In emergencies, there would be no question. Nonetheless, when members see a very beautiful, single woman on the arm of their Bishop, it can raise speculation. Understand?"

"Beautiful, huh? You writing a dime-store novel? They will soon see my ire and my pistol. They will quickly understand I have come on an inspired mission – not for an inspired man. Not hanky-panky."

"I guess that sums it up."

We again discussed the homecoming relative to actual danger. We understood calling me back to Camarillo was likely part of a larger plot. Most likely, a calculated plan to net me. Then, flush the Bishop and the Nun to oblivion.

"Two sheriff deputies have already clandestinely made their way into my house – over fences – through the back door. That gives us four guns – counting ours."

"We might need more."

"I have invited my friend to spend the night.

"The more weapons on our side the merrier."

"You're right. I have an idea. I will have Roy appoint a woman deputy. She can spend the night with you."

Claire shrugged her shoulders, as if that was a bunch of nonsense.

"We can worry about etiquette another time. Let's stay alive," she said admonishing me. "The invitee might die saving your honor. Worth it to risk her?"

Sister Claire switched back into her Nun's garb. What was that, if it was not in order to respect the conservative lifestyle? To be proper. She knew I would take a ribbing in any case. Thought, she would make my existence more tolerable.

The odd couple arrived, pulling up the Smith's circular drive, flanked by colorful flowers and trees. Claire was amazed at the wash of color.

"Even the trees are flowering here," she noted.

Joseph and his wife lived in a stately single-story home on an acre lot. The 4,600 square-foot home had a brightly decorated porch with double door entry.

"This is ferry land – right out of my childhood dreams. I could see myself coming down the steps surrounded by love,"

Claire saw immediately the woman's touch in the home, as she walked through the door into a pleasant-sized vestibule with exquisite chandelier. The room was softened by personal touches, testifying to family and deep roots of love, faith and happiness.

The Smith's beliefs were captured by a gold-leaf framed painting of the Mormon Battalion at Gilder River in Arizona, a painting by George Ottingher (1833 - 1917).

Looking around the room, Claire could trace Joseph Smith's family tree back to his heir – the original LDS Prophet. A man himself martyred for his beliefs.

"Joseph Smith's kin was given the opportunity to denounce the vision of meeting Heavenly Father and Jesus. 'Say that the Book of Mormon is a lie – and live.' By a simple admission, the Prophet could have saved his life." Claire knew from history. "However, the Prophet chose death, rather than denying his vision and abandoning God's plan of salvation."

She knew Jesus had a similar opportunity to live, but stood steadfast to the eternal plan.

Claire wondered why she was becoming so sentimental. She knew there were fundamental differences which separated her beliefs from Joe Smith's faith. Some were more than mere technicalities.

"If Joseph had the same alternative – life or death – he would exercise faith to the end. She knew for certain. He would willingly die. Risk death for the country as he is doing now," she announced to herself.

Her inspection of the Smith home continued. She moved slowly, trying to understand her friend. To the left was a large, living room with a sizable fireplace and expansive mantle. A framed wedding picture outside the Salt Lake Temple centered the brick wall. Portraits of Joseph with his family were numerous.

"This home is all about love, respect, and family," Claire thought. "If anything happens to his wife and children, it will kill him. Two minutes and he will be dead."

Claire walked alone into a sizable dining room which had a hutch filled with China on one wall. And on the other, a five-foot by six-foot painting of a family standing, holding hands. They were in a color-lit setting reminding her of his front yard and porch. The home was behind the landscaped garden.

The painting was filled with brilliant colors, capturing expression and light.

"I wonder who painted it," thought Claire as she strolled to the painting – fingering it.

The painting was signed by Karl Thomas, a famous California painter, known as the painter of light. She had read that he died from an overdose of drugs and alcohol.

"Odd," she reasoned, "Because Mormons don't drink and, especially, don't overdose on drugs.

I walked into the room looking for Claire. I saw her gently touching the artwork.

"That work of art has significance to our family and friends. First off, Thomas was one of America's best artists. His vision of light is masterly. Our religion believes in home and family, and Jesus is all about grace. He brings happiness and joy."

Claire said, "That's how you knew what the Pope was saying."

"That's one of the ways – certainly not the only way. Additionally, talking about Thomas, the artwork speaks to a monumental talent lost."

Claire nodded in agreement. "Anything in excess is wrong."

"Some things in any amount do harm. How many more masterpieces would Thomas have painted, if he had found happiness? One understands the tragedy is magnified, because the artist was so endowed with the knowledge of how to portray light on a canvas. However, he didn't understand the simple way to bring the light into his own life."

I left Claire exploring. And I went to consider how to keep the edifice from being overrun by the hoodlums.

Claire saw that the home was bright and airy, with many windows. When she rejoined the sheriff's team, the deputies decided they couldn't protect the entire home. It was too large.

Therefore, they decided to arm the entry hall. Give up the rest of the home to invaders.

"With the team we have assembled, we should be able to hold this room. That is unless they send a full assault team," said Roy.

Always the Marine, Sister Claire, said, "When they come, there will be several of them – all professionals. We better make a barricade. Otherwise, they will bulldoze the front door. And gun us down."

"I agree," Joseph signaled. "Let's get the dining room table, and turn it over in here. It's made of heavy, thick-plank wood, which should provide protection."

The day droned on. Hours passed. No word. I burned up the phone lines to the FBI and sheriff's department – still nothing.

"Night will make them braver. Stay alert," I cautioned.

Roy Tanner looked confident. "We're not rookies either."

The day-long bleak skies turned to light drizzle. The clouds were low and foreboding. Still no action.

"Bring it," said the Sister.

"Watch what you are praying for Sister," said Tanner.

Then, instead of the front doors exploding and falling to the ground in splinters, as armed gunmen rushed in firing machine guns, there was a faint knock. Barely audible.

Was it? Had I really heard something?

"Did you hear that?" Sister Claire whispered.

"What?" Tanner asked, listening intently.

Again, a faint knock. A little more pronounced this time. Certainly, a knock. Then, the doorbell.

I was crouched behind the overturned dining room table. And reflexively, I started to rise. To answer the door.

Roy said, "Careful Bishop. You are in a direct line for a kill shot."

"True," I responded softly.   I moved over to the wall, approaching the front door cautiously.

Again, the bell.

"Who's there?" I questioned, crouching to one side, opposite the door with my gun extended.

"Daddy, it's me," said Kelly Smith, the five-year-old daughter of Joseph.

Crying, she said again, "Daddy, it's me. Please let us in."

I again started to stand, throwing caution to the wind. Roy, who had moved alongside, threw his arms around me – preventing me from standing.

"Bishop, be careful."

"Kelly who's with you?"

"Joe...only little Joe, daddy. No one else."

With that, I rushed to the door. And pulled my two children inside. Into my arms. Safety. I bolted the door once more.

Claire was taken by the picture of love, compassion and warmth of a father. The detective knelt on the ground, hugging his two children. Tears running down all of their faces.

"Kelly are you hurt? Are either of you injured?"

"No daddy."

Roy Tanner, who also had wet eyes, asked, "Where is your mom?"

The little girl hunched her shoulders. Made a face.

"I don't know. We haven't seen her. We don't know."

Chapter 25

ରେରେରେରେରେ

I AM GOOD, BUT NOT AN ANGEL;
I DO SIN, BUT I AM NOT THE DEVIL;
I AM JUST A SMALL GIRL
IN A BIG WORLD,
TRYING TO FIND SOMEONE TO LOVE
Marilyn Monroe

Roy Tanner's cell phone rang. The call – a report from a deputy sheriff. Looking with binoculars from across the street.

"All clear, Roy."

Tanner asked, "You looked both ways? Down the street?"

"Yea, as far as we can see. If there's a sniper hidden somewhere – well," gulped the young deputy.

I detailed the long-range shooting ability of the Washington sniper. Obviously, I had no clue that any adversary was outside. Logical, however, since they turned my children loose nearby.

They probably were trying to draw the Sister and me outside. Into the kill zone.

Police agencies searched homes. Dog teams scoured the neighborhood. Earlier, Roy Tanner took his rescue helicopter, with specialized snooping gear, low to the trees and shrubberies in the plush Camarillo suburb. No sniper.

He looked for heat signals from a prone sniper. Roy also invited the shooter to fire on the helicopter. Both activities were in vain. No shooter.

I was oblivious to the activities of my friend in the hours before the children were returned. All I could think about was kissing and hugging my two kids. And soon, my wife.

Roy Tanner said, "Joe, it appears to be all clear outside."

The Sister – still clad in her Nun's Habit – was prancing about the entry vestibule, and even into the living room. She was very excitable. I had never seen her like this.

"Where is Mrs. Smith? Where is she?" Sister Claire asked, as a litany.

The Sister's incessant moving and repetitively asking the question, "Where is Mrs. Smith?"

The mood in the house was stoic. No one knowing the next step. Roy Tanner said, "I can shoot an enemy I can see. What do we do to get Mrs. Smith back?"

I didn't see the Sister's frantic movements. I didn't hear the words of my friend. I was in a stupor.

I still clung to my children firmly. Not letting them go.

"Over my dead body will you pry my children from me," I thought. "Where is Nancy?"

I prayed. And prayed. Nevertheless, I know the unrighteous do dastardly things. The evil have free agency – just as the righteous.

I told the others, "This doesn't make any sense. Obviously, they know I'm here. Why have they returned the children and not my Nancy?"

"It's part of an overall riddle," said Claire. "Consider the puzzle," she said. "It makes perfect sense, if we can see the completed picture. The maniac behind this."

"I agree," said Roy. "We are receiving a myriad of advisories at the station; all telling us to be on the alert for Islamic terrorists. What does that mean? Why would they kidnap children? Take your wife."

"Who's sending the advisory?" Claire asked.

"Coming out of Washington."

"What department?"

"State, and even the White House," Tanner advised.

The Sister and the deputies continued to debate the state of the national emergency. I was in a frightful mood. My friends were vainly attempting to put all the odd-shaped clues together – in an order which did not exist. Or, we could not see.

"They don't fit. They just don't fit," I said.

Claire looked confused, "What doesn't fit, Bishop?"

"When working a case-scenario, I try to think of all the information as a game. Then, I try to assemble the parts. They don't fit."

"We don't have all the pieces yet," she said astutely.

Tanner's cell phone played "Take me out to the ball game," which told him that Sgt. Ray Ortega was calling.

"Yes Sergeant."

Ray listened intently.

"Bishop, Sgt. Ray Ortega reports that a brown sedan – no license plates – was seen stopping."

"Where?"

"Momentarily, at the end of the street, making a sudden U-turn and speeding away."

Silence. Everyone thinking. No one rushing outside to face the rain and a potential sniper's bullet. Was it a trap?

"Probably," surmised Claire.

Tanner's phone again. "Yes, sir." Again, he listened.

The station received a call. Anonymous. Asked if, "We are stupid or cowards?"

"That's more trace info. It's decisive information. But what?" Tanner questioned cryptically.

"We don't have x-ray vision," said Sister Claire. "I'm nearly all black with my Habit. Cover the white. I'll just crawl down there to the end of the block and report."

I knew her well enough to realize she was serious. The snide remarks, notwithstanding.

"Even if you're not riddled with bullets, Sister, you will be a drowned rat – by the time you make the end of the street. It is raining hard." Roy Tanner said.

"Take me out to the ball game" was playing again. Ortega with more news.

"We're sending four squad cars from different directions. Converging to where we spotted the unmarked sedan stop. The best we can figure there must be some message left behind. Probably, for Bishop Smith," guessed Sgt. Ray Ortega.

"Roger that," said Tanner.

We waited. Tension mounting. Even the two young children, sensed the adult's confusion. They had been through too much already. Now, forced to endure more.

The crazy situation was getting crazier. Nothing adding up. Oblivion. The mood was calamitous.

Five-minute passed. Nothing. Finally, Lt. Bob Humphreys knocked at the front door. After being cleared, the lieutenant was shown into the make-shift bunker.

"Bishop Smith and Sister, you better come with me."

"What?" I asked

No explanation. However, it wasn't a request. Neither Claire nor I requested further clarification. The lieutenant's body language said he wasn't sharing. Demanded our appearance.

We were put in the back seat of a sheriff's vehicle, which pulled out of my circular drive. Not a word. The silence roared in my head. We moved at a snail's pace to where the unmarked sedans had stopped. Rain peppered the car hard. Certainly, no longer a light mist.

Getting out of the car, Lt. Humphreys pointed. "Over there."

He didn't volunteer to follow. Humphreys emphatically pointed, but stood frozen as if a permanent marker. Frozen, the lieutenant resembled a statue found in city parks.

Sister Claire and I made our way over beyond other sheriff's vehicles. There were 8 to 10 officers hinged together. They were bonded as if carved from cement.

Lying face up on the rain-drenched planter area – between the street and the sidewalk – rested my beloved wife, Nancy Smith.

My heart stopped. So, it seemed. I staggered. Claire bracing me; otherwise, I would have fallen.

"Is she alive?" I asked prayerfully.

No one said anything.

Looking at her tortured body, the answer was obvious to all – except through my denial.

Nancy was dead. A gaping hole in her head.

A rare beauty in life, she had welts about her neck and face. Her hands were scraped and battered. She fought back. A tiger to the end.

Nancy was dressed in modest, blue sleeping attire; obviously, she was taken from her bed by her captors.

Pinned crudely to her night-clothing – near her breasts – was a note. No one found the courage to un-pin it.

No one had fortitude to come close. They stayed on the street. Seven or so feet from her. No one read the clandestine message. The deputies were stupefied, buffeted by a combination of fear and horror.

All of them had seen death before. All of them witnessed unconscionable deeds. However, to find this woman mutilated – who had given so much to the community – was beyond horrific.

I crumbled to my knees. I wept openly with my face pressed near to the curb.

"Oh my, God bless us," Sister Claire moaned.

No one moved. All wanted to run and embrace Bishop Smith. However, no one could take the first step.

The rain continued to pelt us. It gave no sign of retreating.

As I nearly collapsed in the gutter, my thoughts flashed involuntarily back to when I had first seen the lovely, blonde haired, blue-eyed lass at Loyola Law school. I was parking my car near Ninth Street in downtown Los Angeles, where the law school was located.

I returned from military duty in far-off lands. I wanted to enroll at BYU University in Utah; however, the Pentagon, Army intelligence, and the FBI had different ideas.

They enrolled me at Loyola Law School. In the library, on the second floor, I first found courage to talk with her. From then on, she became more to me than life itself.

She was funny. She was intense and soft and sweet. Incredibly smart and intuitive. I fell in love in ten minutes.

We studied together, married in our second year in a break from studying law. Graduated first and second in our class. Nancy first – me second.

That's always the way that I placed her in our relationship. Her first – me second.

She gave me an excuse for the second. "You worked full-time for the FBI and took those horrendous Army excursions when they called. I went to law school full-time in addition. Without those, you would have been first," she said gently rubbing my face after graduation.

I thought back to when Nancy and I traveled across town to Loyola Marymount main campus in West Los Angeles to obtain our cap and gown.

Coming upon a Catholic Sister, Nancy Smith – who had never been on the Loyola main camps – asked politely, "Sister, I've never been here before; I'm here to pick up my cap and gown for graduation. Where do I go?"

Of course, the Catholic Nun believed Nancy was belittling her, by pretending not to have been at Loyola and yet graduating.

"If you have nothing better to do, other than to make fun of Sisters, we shouldn't let you graduate at all," said the Nun impatiently.

Nancy Smith's sweet disposition soothed the Nun's feelings. It was only one of the million times that Nancy's kindness led to making a new friend.

Now, rain was soaking through my clothes. I was bone weary. I reached out my left hand and took my bride's mangled hand in mine.

Sister Claire finally gained composure and courage enough to move to her partner. Placing her hand gently on his wet head, she beckoned him.

"Joseph. My friend, there is nothing any of us can say or do. Her spirit is with God. You must rise... think about your children," counseled Claire.

At first, there was blinding rage and desire for instant revenge. I felt like striking anyone near me. I still knelt. Not heeding her. My intense state gave way to depression.

Sister Claire took her friend's arm in both hands. She was guiding me back to reality. To observers, Joseph Smith – the Camarillo Bishop known for providing love and kindness – staggered to his feet. He seemed semiconscious.

"There is a note," said Claire, seeing it for the first time. "Has anyone read it?"

No one spoke. An ominous silence.

As if in slow motion, I moved to my fallen wife. Tenderly put both hands on her cheeks, bending and kissing her lips softly.

"I love you. I will love you through eternity. We will meet again, my sweet girl."

Sister Claire actually turned, so Joseph's words would stay private. The conversation that he was having with Nancy was so romantically-private that the Sister felt obtrusive.

I knelt on both knees. Bent again and kissed my sweet Nancy for the last time.

"My Heavenly Father, please watch after my sweet wife. She has shown her tender love and kindness to so many in her lifetime. She is deserving of thy grace; allow her into thy kingdom. With Father, we were sealed in thy holy house, the Salt Lake Temple; married for time and eternity."

Joseph paused. To onlookers, they could almost hear a heavenly message raining down on him with greater force than that falling from the sky.

"Father, O-O thank Thee; I do understand that I have our children to watch over, and more duties to perform. Nonetheless, if it weren't for that, I would pray to be with my lovely Nancy, now.

"Again, I plead with Thee, please accept this prayer as my solemn request that Thou watch over Nancy Smith. She is a beloved daughter. I know Thou already knows and loves her; for she is a heavenly person.

"I ask in the name of Thy Son for a blessing on my children. Bless them that they will overcome this earthly and devilish disaster, and retain the lovely and kind spirit of their mother.

"Father, keep my heart from hardening. Help me to forgive those who have trespassed against my family and my country. Lighten my heart, and inspire me with direction. I ask and pray for these many blessings in the name of Thy Son Jesus Christ, Amen."

Without explanation, the rain stopped. Immediately. Not another drop fell from above. The wind became silent. Looking above, there was a break in the clouds. You could see a full moon, with stars twinkling through a mist.

Then, I un-pinned the typed note from my wife's chest. Standing, I read it silently.

"Joe Smith you are an obsessive ass. You constantly have been, and always will be. It was the greatest pleasure putting a hole in your wife's head. If I had not been otherwise directed, I would have tortured her further and raped her.

This only partially makes up for the murder of our friends in Palmdale. Suffice it to say, keep out of our way or your children will be savaged. There is a new order in the world today. And you can't stop it.

Signed,

Anything, but a friend!

Chapter 26

ଔଔଔଔଔ

THE WEAK CAN NEVER FORGIVE; FORGIVENESS IS AN ATTRIBUTE OF THE STRONG

Mahatma Gandhi

Claire respectfully covered Nancy with a blanket, as deputies carried her to an ambulance. Joseph seemed preoccupied.

"Please, come on," I called, walking toward my house. Claire followed. She wondered if allowing the sharp-shooters a clear shot was a brilliant idea. Nonetheless, Joseph was at least moving.

Walking into my house, I ignored the upturned furniture. I didn't visit with the hordes of people clamoring around.

I tapped Roy Tanner on the arm, signaling him. We walked into the master bedroom, through double doors, which were promptly closed.

"I wonder what devices they are conjuring up?" Claire said.

No one answered.

A short time later, I emerged with a small suitcase, and moved without delay into the children's bedrooms.

Claire asked Tanner, "What's going on?"

Roy shrugged.

Completing the whirling dervish, I was back in the entry hall with two suitcases.

"Claire, is there anything you're going to need for the next week? You are about the same size as Nancy. Please help yourself. We need to move."

"A washing machine and then a bath. That's what I need. Don't think we can take them along," said Claire.

To her, Joseph almost seemed himself. Reconstituted. Once again, confident. Not hunched, he was walking with vigor. It was, as if, he was endowed with renewed energy.

The Sister looked around and saw that Roy Tanner was gone. She wondered what the two of them had cooked up.

Without kicking anyone out of his house, or even considering locking up, the Bishop put his arms around his children. And meandered through a door leading to the garage.

"What about our rental car?" Claire asked.

"Let it stay."

I fastened the children into the back seat of the family sedan; returned to the house and put a small suitcase containing the children's clothes into the Cadillac.

Running back into the house, I said, "Sister, we're away."

Claire said, "Just a second." She scurried to pick up clothes in her arms. No suit case. She moved quickly and unabashedly into the master bedroom. She picked up a couple of things. Then, she gathered her own, which were piled near the upturned dining table. Her arms were full when she literally ran into the garage.

Joseph Smith was already behind the wheel. The engine running.

With that, Joseph pushed a button on his visor, and the electric garage door opener provided clearance for the elegant vehicle.

"You're not going to lock up?" She asked concerned.

"It's only a house. The things of value are in the car."

She hoped that she was included in the "things of value."

Without a word to anyone, I drove out onto the private lane and drove away.

"Where is he going?" Lt. Humphreys queried.

"Don't know – didn't say," answered a confused deputy.

Everyone initially stood around, looking at each other, not knowing what to make of the bizarre departure. Ultimately, they left the house in its upturned state.

"Where are we going?" asked Claire.

"Just for a drive."

Putting my finger to my mouth, signaling the Sister to be cautious what she said or asked.

She didn't understand. But said nothing.

She noted that Joseph held fatherly conversations with his two children. He avoided intentionally discussions of Nancy Smith when the children raised the question of where "mommy is?"

They drove into the San Fernando Valley, and turned south onto the 405 freeway, proceeding as if driving toward San Diego. Claire desperately wanted to know where they were going. Joseph made it clear he wasn't saying.

The Sister kept a watchful eye out on traffic behind. She would pretend to look and speak with the children, glancing, more particularly, at the cars behind.

She signaled Joseph by touching his right elbow, saying, "Nice to have company."

"Not all company is welcomed."

After driving a minute or two, I motioned to her.

"Sister, please climb over the seat into the back, and unfasten the children's seatbelts."

Claire wondered, "What is he planning, now?"

Nonetheless, she struggled and climbed over the seat.

"Claire, you'll find a pair of jeans and a shirt, which should fit. Get out of your Nun's garb quickly. I'm not looking."

She didn't have the slightest concern about him looking. She knew him. This instruction of changing clothes made ultimate good sense.

At least three unmarked cars were following them. She needed to be better prepared to move quickly. She was hampered by her Nun's outfit.

"What were the intentions of the men in the cars behind?" She wondered. "They certainly were up to no good. Away from his home they probably had a murderous intent."

"For that matter, who knew Joseph's game-changing plans?" She said to herself. Knowing the detective, she looked for some bizarre reaction without a moment's notice. Somehow, he would send the vehicles trailing them scurrying to catch up.

She did not finish her thought. Not quite finished pulling her red top over her head. Her bra was still showing slightly.

Without explanation, I pulled over to the center divider, separating the North and South lanes of one of the world's busiest freeways. I slammed on the brakes.

"Grab my daughter. I will gather my son. Follow me."

Driving one handed, I grabbed the children's suitcase. It was resting in the front seat, along with Claire's clothing. The left front of the car came to stop against the center divider – the vehicle was slightly out into the traffic lane.

Then, I opened my door and threw a suitcase high over the center divider.

Screaming loudly, "Roy, catch this suitcase."

Claire was moving fast. However, her sides ached from laughter at the sight of the Bishop tossing things. On the freeway, no less. It was right out of a comedy movie.

Claire grabbed his daughter, as instructed. Leaving the car, she saw Joseph with his son in one hand, and all her clothing wadded up under his other arm.

The vehicles behind started playing bumper cars. The terrorists in the unmarked sedans started weaving toward the center divider. They had followed far behind, believing they were hidden. A major mistake.

I made a beeline for the three-foot wall, dividing the traffic. By the time Claire got to the side of the car, I was already lifting my son into the arms of Roy Tanner.

And I was stepping over the concrete wall, clutching Claire's clothing. I looked down. Some of her apparel was falling to the asphalt.

I heard Claire laughing hysterically. Now, I understood. I must have been a sight. Women's shirts, dresses, and even under clothing falling. Some now hitting the deck.

Now I was on the other side of the freeway. A car was parked there with its hood up. Deputy Tanner surreptitiously stopped the vehicle, pretending car trouble.

"Come on Claire, jump the fence."

Candidly, Claire was having trouble moving quickly. The sight of me with an armful of women's clothes was too much. Tears from laughter rolled down her face.

There had been so much tension. The damn broke with the unintentional comical antics. I left a line dotted with clothing. There was a red bra on the ground near the car. White panties on the divider wall, with more falling every second.

Claire was half bent over with laughter, attempting to scurry as best she could. Seeing her made my icy tension retreat.

"Here's your daughter," she said. And then – she half-jumped and crawled over the barricade. Her red top still flapping in the breeze. No time for modesty.

They scrambled into Roy Tanner's car. He had parked the vehicle near the fence facing north, going down the hill back into the San Fernando Valley.

One of the men, who had clamored out of the lead vehicle, grimaced and fell. Following the Bishop and the Nun was difficult work, he already discovered.

Two of the scoundrel's cars collided with a white van, and were squished against the divider. Certainly, serious injuries present.

"Nice to have you back on the job, Joseph," said Claire. "Where are we going to stash the children for safety?"

"Didn't want to talk in the Cadillac for fear it might have been bugged. Who knows?"

"And now?"

Roy Tanner said, "I know the Bishop. The less I know, the less I can say – right Joe?"

I smiled. It was telling. Two friends who knew and loved each other. Willing to take risks. They were truly brothers.

"Where to?" asked Tanner.

"Whiteman Airport. You know it?"

"Freeway or surface street?"

Joe smiled slightly. For the first time since losing the love of his life, Joseph's faced evidenced a faint smile.

"You're a big boy. Just quickly. We only have about 10 minutes before they pick us up again."

Roy smiled broadly.

Then, Claire noticed a long, black leather carrying case, which was slung over Joseph's neck. It appeared the dimensions of something to carry a fishing pole. Hanging loosely, she wondered why she hadn't noticed it. And, what was it?

"Ok, I give," said the wise-cracking Nun. "You bring treats with you for a long winter."

Both men looked rightfully confused.

The Sister said, "You know – the thing slung around your neck."

The Bishop lost his smile.

"I told you that I lead four lives. Right?"

"Yes. And probably five or six lives, if we count. One of them being a miracle worker," she countered.

"Right about five lives. Wrong about the miracle part. As part of my Green Bret service, I was a long-rifle sniper. An assassin, I guess you could say. Paid by the USA to clear the way for our special forces."

No one was smiling, now.

"The case contains my sniper rifle, disassembled of course."

"Who are you planning on killing?" asked the Sister. "Maybe, it's time for me to get off the boat."

"I wish we could have all gotten off, before it sailed," I replied. "The clues are starting to mount. We have a home-grown war."

I did not explain.

"Perhaps, that is the vision of the Pope." Claire said grimacing.

"I'd rather go fishing, than hunting with a sniper rifle. The choice may not be ours. More than likely, we will need it for our existence."

Roy Tanner did not fool around. He used his siren on the freeway to extinguish traffic. He figured their window of freedom precluded more chicanery – required foot to the pedal."

Pulling into Whiteman Airport in the northeast San Fernando Valley, Roy asked, "Any further instructions or needs Bishop?"

"Stay safe. And Roy, I hate to ask."

"Anything at all, Bishop."

"My wife..."

"Yes," said Roy.

"I need to hide the kids. Will you attend to the services?"

Roy understood his friend was intentionally vague because of the children.

I said, "Nancy's spirit is already with God. Services are only for the living. To keep living, we must scramble and duck."

"Count on me."

"Thanks my friend."

"It will be done right."

"I know it will."

Claire listened intently. Saying nothing. What faith to understand that the body is really dust. The spirit departed on death. Was in Paradise.

I said, "If you're called on the carpet, place a target on my back."

"No need."

Claire and the children exited Roy's car. Joseph Smith was a trick-a-minute partner. When she saw the high winged, modified Cessna 182, she stood dumbfounded.

"What's with the big tires, and extended wings?" asked Claire.

"My reason for coming to Whiteman. This is an experimental aircraft. A fellow FBI agent and I are working on modifying it for special projects."

"What's so fabulous about the monstrosity? It's ugly."

"It will almost hover like a helicopter. It'll slow to 30 knots without stalling, and the tires will land on razor blades."

With no lost motion, the quartet loaded baggage and all. They warmed up their bird and taxied for takeoff.

She said, "Where are we going? Mars? We're really not landing on razor blades, right?"

He answered by pushing to a full throttle. The Cessna bolted down the runway, as Bishop Joe Smith told Whiteman's traffic, he was departing. He didn't say for where.

Chapter 27

ଔଔଔଔଔ

APPARENTLY, THERE IS NOTHING THAT CAN'T HAPPEN TODAY

Mark Twain

The little bird, carrying precious cargo – the two Smith children and the Nun – flew low and snug against hills.

"Okay, give. This plane isn't bugged." Said the Sister, hands-on hips.

"Only a couple of people know this plane is my diversion from reality. And one of them is my wife. So no, the plane isn't bugged."

"Yeah daddy, the lady's right. Where are we going?" Asked Joseph's daughter politely.

The Smith children did not have contact with Catholic Nun's, so they referred to Sister Claire as "Sister." Cute, thought Claire. It will be a good experience for them.

"You know Uncle Steve, the forest ranger?" Joseph asked.

The young girl looked confused. She couldn't place him. I knew that her confusion was appropriate, because Steve really wasn't her uncle. Instead, a former Green Beret. He had never seen much of her. Steve was a recluse.

"He now is more of a hermit, getting paid for working as a lookout for fires." I said looking at the Sister.

I explained, "We need somewhere safe for the children. Can't lose them."

Claire nodded in agreement. "So we are not stopping our investigation? After we get them safe?"

"Did you really believe we were abating the chase for the murderers? Who is on the chase to bring equilibrium to our land? And the world?"

"Not a chance. I knew you weren't stopping. Confirmation only."

The little Cessna was much louder than the craft that brought the two of them from the East Coast. It seemed to slug its way forward. Fighting the air. Not gliding through it.

"It bounces like a ride at the fair," said Kelly. She had a big smile on her face. Little Joe Smith wasn't so sure the plane ride was a delight.

They flew on. Both Claire and I were really too tired to talk. We were worn out. Lost sleep was only part of our agony.

I pointed to my right, "Over there is Crowley Lake. We're headed to a remote peak at Mammoth Lakes."

Finally, after flying for what seemed an eternity the Bishop came clean. "A peak," thought Claire.

"They have a landing strip there?" Said the Sister, looking bewildered.

"Not exactly."

"What?"

"The Inyo National Forest was formed about 57,000 years ago. It has a number of volcanic mountains and valleys. We're going to tiptoe down on one of the peaks."

His daughter said, "I tiptoe, daddy. I don't know about doing it on peaks."

"Well, one thing is good?" Claire said, sniping at Joseph.

"What's that?"

"Our tormentors are not going to follow us to hell."

"Once we land, you'll think you're closer to heaven, than to hell. You will look over land untouched by man."

The going was rough because the winter day had severe storm clouds. There was rain and some snow. Plenty of up and down drafts.

Instead of being afraid the children acted like they were on a Disneyland ride as the plane bucked, dipped, and climbed. Little Joe took on the excitement of his older sister.

Claire asked, "Is this bird safe for flying in snow?"

"Well I wouldn't want to tackle a blizzard. The wings will stay on. Icing is another thing."

"What a relief. I mean about the wings staying attached," Claire replied looking outside.

"I am dancing some with the mountainous terrain. Don't fret Sister. I took lessons from an Ethiopian bush pilot."

"Oh, what a relief," she said – making a face centered on fear.

"He was the real deal. Would turn off the engine and put the key in his pocket."

"Terrific. Thanks for explaining. I would have shot him," she replied.

"You learned."

Thinking of the movie "Dancing with Wolves, Claire said, ironically, "The Indians might call you Dancing with Mountains."

The children laughed. "We'll call Daddy that. Huh, daddy?"

I added, "With the skies obscure it's a bit tricky."

Joking with Claire, I said, "It really helps if I can see the peaks. We don't want a big one to jut out in front of us."

Claire responded, "Yes, that could ruin our whole year."

His daughter said, "It is fun daddy. We can almost touch the trees."

"Better if you don't," said Claire.

"Spoil sport," I said.

"How much longer?" Claire asked with a concerned expression.

"Haven't flown much in small planes, Sister?"

The Sister gave her answer as Joseph banked the Cessna hard left. He pointed at a spot on the horizon which appeared to be as long as a pencil, and straight uphill.

"There." I said pointing.

"That points us in the direction of the ranger station?" She asked frightfully.

"No, that's where we're landing."

At first, Claire believed I was getting back at her for all of her incessant jokes and wiseacre comments. Soon, she realized I was quite serious. I was lined up on the closest end of the narrow path.

"You're kidding, right?"

She saw rocks and boulders off to the right of the plane. Impossible for me to walk up the path, she thought.

"How is this Boy Scout going to land a plane there?"

At the closest end of the uphill path were large pine trees. They probably were 50 - 75 feet tall.

As we approached the landing spot, I put in full flaps. I powered back. I knew the Cessna with its modified wing did not stall until about 25 miles per hour.

"I also know that we will have wind drafts coming down the mountain.   Probably, 10 to 15 knots.   We can almost fly backwards," I said smiling. It was a rush flying my creation.

It was clear to Claire that Joseph intended to skirt over the trees, drop and stall his modified aircraft onto the closest end of the uphill, slender, none-to-straight fire break.

We were now standing still; Claire saw. Staying almost even with the trees, 15-feet below.

She thought, "If we have a down draft, now, we will be climbing down the pines."

She asked, "How long is it? The firebreak?"

"Don't know exactly."

"You've landed here before, correct?"

"Nope. On the top, by helicopter."

I wasn't kidding. My attention to detail was absolute. She knew he wouldn't endanger the precious passengers in the rear seats. That was the only encouragement.

"Snug the children's seatbelts. Yours too Sister."

They were traveling slow – very slow – being buffeted by the winds, howling around the volcanic mountain.

"Look Sister, we are really standing still. The wind is holding us even," I said. I added more power and put the nose down, and to edge forward.

"I need enough ground speed to bounce up the hill after landing."

As they approached the nearest point, the Sister realized the firebreak was merely three or four feet wider than their wings span. Claire couldn't determine the length of the plowed break. Maybe, one-half or even one-third of Whiteman Airport, she thought.

"This is amazing," I said proudly. "The winds flowing from the ridge of the mountain are holding us. I'm bringing us down almost like a helicopter."

"Why not on top, then?" Asked a pale-faced Sister.

I brought the Cessna over the tree line by, perhaps, 10 feet. I didn't want to be caught in a downdraft and become part of the scenery.

"Hold on."

She didn't need the encouragement. Claire was braced, holding her seat with her left hand, and her right hand on the ceiling. She looked back and saw complete confidence of the children, who were not alarmed. They knew their father. They had absolute trust.

The Cessna landed hard on the uphill course, bumping and leaping forward.

"Our runway looks wider than it appeared from the sky," she said. "But can we stop in 50 feet?"

"Were going up a mountain, and we're rolling at only maybe 40 miles an hour. We want to be sure we make it to the top," I said in seriousness. "Making it up the ridge is the concern. Not stopping."

As the little bird roared its way to the peak, Claire saw a bearded man standing in the middle of the firebreak, pistol drawn and aiming at them.

In alarm, I said, "The bugger better get out of the way. I can't stop until on top. Then, I have 20 feet to spare."

There were no razor blades. Nevertheless, the tires were assaulted by razor-sharp volcanic rocks. The Cessna took one more leap as it collided with and bounded over a small boulder which had not been cleared.

Steve, the former Green Beret and friend of the Bishop, dove to the right, barely escaping the blades of the craft as it passed him.

"If we hadn't collided with and been elevated sky word by the boulder, we would have severed his head," I said.

The Bishop had not exaggerated when he said he had only 20 feet at the top of the incline. However, the Cessna 182 was barely crawling. So, no problem.

The experimental aircraft was now seasoned. Claire would ask later if Joseph had designed it for such crazy events. Landing on the head of a needle?

Steve, the ranger, was back on his feet. Pistol drawn.

"Hands on your head. Out of that damned plane. You idiots," ordered the armed ranger. He wasn't kidding.

"We dropped in for dinner." I said, climbing out of the single-engine plane.

"Only one ass has that deep baritone voice, and is stupid enough to land on an uphill firebreak," said Steve, relaxing.

"I've been called that more than once recently."

"What you doing here, Bishop?"

Steve was an atheist. Nonetheless, he engendered the utmost respect for his former Green Beret sniper partner. Steve disproved of Gen. Dwight Eisenhower's statement, "You will never find an atheist in a foxhole." Joseph and Steve were in many together. Steve had never wavered, "There is no God."

"We have crawled through a thousand miles of muck together. The bravest man I ever met."

Joseph would never try to convert the ranger to Mormonism, and Steve would not condemn Joseph for good works. For faith.

"If it was anyone else attempting that landing, I would know they were crazy. I've seen you make some awesome ones in the field with guns blazing. So, this might not be that much," the weird-looking ranger said.

"I knew I had it."

"Looks like you brought me some company."

"My kids."

"This isn't Nancy, though," said Steve, looking confused.

"Meet Sister Claire Coogan, a Catholic Nun."

Steve was now impossibly perplexed.

"You drop in on a mountain, flying an experimental plane, and then tell me you've converted from Mormonism to Catholicism," he said, scratching his unkempt hair.

"Nope. I'm still going to heaven as a Mormon. Maybe, the Sister will be around at the foot of the kingdom." I said with a smile on my face. She knew I was pulling her leg. Steve looked more confused.

The explanation was as clear as mud.

"Come on, let's break bread." Steve said.

"I want to camouflage my aircraft first. We don't want any bandits dropping in on us."

Steve didn't know the mission, but he understood the seriousness in Joseph's voice. What's more, he knew his friend was working. He didn't need to be told.

"Everything was starting to make more sense."

Chapter 28

ଔଔଔଔଔଔ

EVEN RATS CAN ONLY BE KICKED AROUND FOR SO LONG, BEFORE THEY HAVE HAD ENOUGH

Joe Cowley

"Tell me," ordered the ranger. "I'm in – no matter the mission. I'm bored to hell, up here."

I laughed with my friend.

"And you've been telling me that you found heaven."

"Don't mess with me. I still can kill with one blow."

"Well, you must be a cousin to the Sister." I said.

Steve looked confused.

Steve wasn't kidding about his prowess. His muscled 6'3" frame was as hard as the boulder they collided with earlier. He weighed 275 pounds, all bulging and defined. He worked out 14 hours a day lifting weights, running and doing exercises to break up the boredom.

"The rest of the time I watch trees grow," he confessed. "Look for fires. And they are few and far between."

Claire asked, "What did you do in the military?"

"Joseph was the shooter; I broke things and people by force," he said. "Joe and I could live on the land, without anything. We could be dropped 100 miles away from the mission, and find our way – walking, crawling or pulling each other."

"He can shoot too. He's just as outstanding with a pistol or rifle," I responded.

Steve asked, "What is a Claire? How did you get mixed up with this bum?"

"Long story. I'm former Marine."

"Don't like Marines. We were special forces – not sissies."

Claire said nothing. She knew Steve was good at breaking things. She didn't want to be broken.

Steve wasn't interested in any long story. He wanted the bottom line. He wanted the mission.

"Seriously. What are you doing here?"

I told him. Bottom line. No-nonsense.

Steve asked, "Who's the enemy? Who do we target?"

"You tell us. We will both know," said the Sister. "Then – we'll take them down."

The ranger was isolated. His shift was a month on and a month off. His outpost was remote.

Steve had traded shifts so much that he had accumulated more than six months of leave. He always was working, so he had saved nearly every dollar he had earned in the decade that he had been out of the military.

"You have some significant clues. How many snipers could have made the kill in Washington? Bishop, you are one of a select number, who could have made the shot," Steve said, nodding.

He went on, making himself part of the team, whether they wanted him or not.

"Also," he said, "the biggest damn inkling comes from the note you read me. That ass hole, hates you. It has nothing to do with this situation alone. It is personal. It goes back years. Part of our special force's detachment."

I nodded, "You are right."

I guess I knew that in the back of my mind. I just did not want to admit it. Didn't want to say someone out of my past hated me so much.

"We confirm who wrote the note. We torture him. Break him in half, and have him tell us the rest."

Joseph Smith – as much as he wanted his wife's killer – wasn't in to torture. Never was. Never would be.

"Steve, the reason I'm here is to hide my children. No one is going to look for them at this remote post. I can't go until they are safe. I have lost my wife. I can't lose them too."

Stephen answered without thinking, "I'm no damn babysitter. I want in on taking these guys down."

"And what should I do with my children, hang them by their toes?"

"Nope. I have ranger Marti Hightower. She owes me. I give her every frikin' day off she wants. She loves kids. Can be trusted. She's our babysitter."

Claire said, "We know that authorities, probably federal types, are involved. Won't she melt under the pressure? Turn the kids over? Put Joseph in another compromising position?"

Steve wasn't having it.

"You might be a Nun, a former Marine. You don't know squat. Marti would die before she would compromise kids."

"Assuming you're right; she's not here. How long will it take her to get to this post? What do you have to tell her?" I asked.

Pointing at the CB radio, Steve said, "Tomorrow, next day at the outside. She has the Jeep. Must traverse up here. Five hours."

"Make the call, if you are sure." I said. My stone-looking expression told him not to be wrong.

"This is a lonely, solitary life. It's unfrequented by any, except the very few – the non-social. But our kind hang together – we are absolutely loyal to each other."

"What?" I said, not understanding.

Claire — who apparently did get Steve's off-hand remark – with an icy stare – said, "You better be right."

"Wow, Bishop, where did you find this intense bitch? She's intimidating, spine-chilling."

"Believe me, something happens to the kids, I will be more gruesome and macabre than a ghastly dream," threatened the Sister.

Steve said, "The Nun uses words I don't even understand. "Nutin's goin' to happen to the kids. Rest easy. We're family here. Plain and simple."

Steve moved to the radio.

"Personal alarm. I need relief. You there?" Asked Steve over the ranger walkie-talkie.

"Right back-at-you. U Ok?"

"Marti, need your help."

"Snow on fire trails tonight. Supposed to clear tomorrow. You okay until then? Over."

"Yep. Drive safely, comin' up. This is personal. I'll explain when ya get here," said Steve.

"I will be there late tomorrow. No worry. Whatever, you need," responded Marti. "Out."

Turning and facing the Bishop and the Nun, Steve said, "Now, let's figure, who in the hell, we are fighting. The enemy appears to be us."

I smiled...the old Steve was on the job. The Bishop said, "Exactly. Some old friends. Now our worst nightmare."

Claire looked confused, but only for an instant. "Friends who hang out in Washington, mostly," she reckoned.

"Weren't much good in the old days, either," said Steve. "Always confused right from wrong."

The Bishop, "You're correct."

The Nun, "But exactly, who are they?"

Steve said, "The Bishop remembers who hated his guts in the old days. Still does. The biggest piece of ...."

"Language, Steve."

"Sorry. Forgot your sensitive ears."

"My ears are fine. God requires better."

Steve said nothing.

"You're right about remembering yesterday in any case," I said. "He always had something to gain from his cruelty. However, what is his upside now?"

"Who?" asked Claire, realizing she missed the secret code between them.

"The director," said Steve.

"Director?" responded Claire. "Director of what?"

"Thought you hung out with brains," said Steve. "Only curves, this one."

"Hey." Said the Sister. If looks could kill – Steve would be meeting Jesus about now.

"Watch out, Steve. She will deck you," I said. "Remember, she wasn't with us. She doesn't know all the riff-raft from the old days. She doesn't know the director."

Without a word, Claire landed a straight right to Steve's temple. He might be 275 pounds of pure muscle. Tagged squarely by a toned, athletic, former Marine, Steve was momentarily staggered.

"My God." He said.

"I thought you didn't believe in God?" Claire responded, attempting to teach.

"That really hurt."

"Warned you."

"Obviously, not in time. Thought, she was a Nun?" Steve said.

I said, "Didn't say she was a saint. Only a Nun."

"Hey, watch it! I can deck a Bishop too."

"I apologize."

Claire said, "I asked civilly enough, who in the heck is the director?"

Chapter 29

೧೩೧೩೧೩೧೩೧೩೧೩

CRAMPED CORNERS

Claire and I were beyond tired. The ordeal the children faced took a toll on them. Nonetheless, it was somewhat astonishing how resilient children are. They asked several times when they would see mom again. They believed she was on an outing, a vacation.

I said nothing.

The ranger station was small for three adults and two children. There were only two bunks. We gave them to the children. They fell quickly asleep.

There was only one large room, plus a small bathroom with shower. Windows 360 degrees. Walkways all the way around on the outside. However, even in inclement weather, while protected inside their shelter, the rangers needed to view of the forests beyond.

Steve said, "Sorry Sister, we don't have separate rooms here."

"We will manage."

Steve and I started to reminisce about our special forces days. How much our lives had changed.

Steve said, "I miss those days. I am lost. Like to train – running, pull-ups, etc. I never have a call to use my conditioning any longer. Not doing any damn good. I'm dead here."

Claire wanted clarity too – a mission with clear boundaries. Her mind floated to her friend, Joseph Smith. She believed the Bishop required separation. Distance from a day claiming his wife. Joseph had no time to grieve. Further, he had to hang on to a rocky exterior – instead of tears – for the sake of the children. Joseph couldn't let go and break down. There was the turmoil ahead.

"A time for quiet divergence," she believed.

The good-old boys were talking about military. About death. About untold hardship. Friendship based on war. She wanted the two in present times.

"The two of you were talking about 10 or 15 years ago. Want to think back a 100 years?" the Sister asked.

"Wasn't alive," said Steve.

"Cream puff," challenged Claire.

"What about 100 years ago?" I asked.

Claire had recently studied the year 1912 for the Vatican. A report on comparisons. How things changed. She remembered some off-the-wall statistics.

"Only eight per cent of the homes had telephones." She said.

"Fine with me," chirped Steve. "Telephones are only a distraction."

The Sister continued, "Only 8,500 cars with 150 miles of paved roads."

"None up here. Again. Fine with me."

Claire's noticed the change in the tenor of the room, relaxing everyone. Getting the Bishop's mind off of death.

"We're into it now." Steve interrupted again.

She went on. "The average wage was 24 cents per hour."

Steve said, "That's about what I make up here per hour." He was kidding, but his toil was long for what he earned.

"Well, the average US worker made $200 to $400 per annum."

"Well, I guess I do better than that." Steve said.

"Ninety per cent of all doctors had no college education – went to so-called medical schools," Claire opined.

"Me neither. No college," said Steve. "Maybe, I'll become a doctor."

Both Claire and I laughed at him. I realized what she was doing. I greatly appreciated her kindness. It was working. Claire was many things. Funny, bright, intuitive and loving.

"Sugar, I believe, cost four cents a pound and eggs only 15 cents a dozen."

I asked, "How many stars did the flag have?"

"Ten, I believe," said Steve.

Claire looked at him in astonishment. "I don't remember exactly. I would guess 44 or 45."

"No way," said Steve. "Impossible."

I said, "45."

Steve looked down, deflated.

Claire said, "Here are some things I find most interesting. Two out of 10 adults could read or write, and only six per cent ever graduated from high school."

"Now you're nothing if you don't have a Master's Degree," I said.

Claire yawned.

"Me too. I am exhausted. I'm done." I said.

"May I say the prayers tonight," Claire asked. "I know it's Steve's abode. His right to choose."

Steve looked at me. As if saying, "She doesn't know I don't pray – right?

"Sure. Sister, make yourself at home." Steve instructed.

"Heavenly Father, accept our good Sister Nancy Smith into your arms tonight. The name of our religions may divide us, but our faith in thy son Jesus Christ and his atonement binds us as one.

"I do not know Father, but it is possible we are fighting for the right to pray – in our own way – as we desire. A fight to be free. Hear our prayer and preserve our freedoms. Father, freedoms are becoming fewer each year.

"Preserve our rights and religious freedom. Tolerance. Love. Respect." She paused. "Amen."

"Amen," I said. Privately, I added in prayer, "With only the barest of a clue, Sister Claire Coogan received understanding that Steve did not pray. She included him in a special way. Watch over this Sister as we root out cruelty and evil. In the name of Jesus Christ, Amen."

Steve – without bowing his head, closing his eyes, or participating in the prayer at all – said, "Thank you Sister. That was nice. You are right. We are losing our liberty. Every day, another freedom disappears."

We rested on blankets. More over us. Snow was on the ground outside, making a perfect white blanket. It was cold. I looked at the Sister. She was already asleep. A cartoonist would draw "zzzzs" from her mouth, as she snored slightly.

Her pretty face rested on a hand that she used for a pillow. Her hair was tossed to one side. Even with closed eyes, God painted a beautiful picture on her face.

I put my head down, knowing I would be minutes behind her. I first talked to my wife. I often did that when I was away from her. I could not explain. However, in some ways I felt closer to her tonight than ever.

"I love you," I said softly. My life had come to a stop when my precious Nancy was stripped from me.

This perky Nun, sent by the Vatican, hurled me back to life.

"Her witticism-a-minute personality and insightful mind cut away the dagger put in my soul. Claire has true love. A passion not killed by menace, the vile or depraved men." I said softly to myself.

Chapter 30

ଔଔଔଔଔ

PINNACLE OUTLOOK - MID-DAY

The rain and snow continued throughout the night. Today was nearly a replay of yesterday's inclemency.

Admittedly, I was still depressed. My asserting that I knew Nancy was with Jesus was fine. "But who was with me."

Selfish – I know.

"My children. My faith. Sister Claire Coogan. My work. My ward. All still here." I knew. "Balanced against the devil at work in his playground on earth."

I had to kick myself – to jump start my life.

The children took to the rustic mountain escape. They played without the burden of knowing their mother was dead. I would give the kids time to mourn when we could be alone as a family.

The Bishop and the Nun were restless. They knew an ominous plan was afloat in America. And they were stifled not by threats, but by locale.

"I don't care what you say; Marti will be here. The slush and snow might slow her down, but she'll come," promised Steve.

"I just don't see how," said Claire. "The conditions are horrific."

Steve said, "What in the hell, I want to know is how we're going to get out of here?"

"Work turning the plane around. For takeoff," I said.

Claire looked out the window again. Her gaze took her down the slope from which they had come.

"There is a good foot of new snow. Two or three feet of the white stuff in some places. No way. The plane will get stuck or flip over."

"I agree," said Steve. "Will take the Jeep when Marti gets here."

I countered, "If you guys like driving, go ahead. I'm flying out."

"How?" Steve was ready for a good fight, but not for suicide.

"We're going to clear the 20 feet of flat land. Do what we can down to the boulder."

"How far do you need to go for takeoff? It's not a copter."

"Get it up to 25 knots with full flaps, we can lift off. Remember, clear the snow, and the topography falls off beneath us. Going over a cliff. We can almost point the nose downhill and pick up speed."

"Still have to get those big, honker tires off the ground."

Claire said, "Well, the question is if Marti makes it. Impossible, I'd say."

Conditions seem to be getting worse, and temperatures falling to zero. We would have ice instead of snow. The late-afternoon sun was obscured by overcast skies.

The trio trying to figure out a new plan. Even Steve was beginning to believe that Marti would be stalled by the falling snow.

The door to the lookout was flung open. And in walked Marti Hightower. She had on snow shoes-bundled in heavy clothing.

"We had given up on you," said Steve. "I kept telling these two you would make it. The conditions worsened."

"I had to abandon the Jeep about 45 minutes ago. The roadway is too treacherous – icy. In parts, I couldn't even tell where the road was. You said trouble, so here I am."

Introductions were short, because it was now or never for flying today. Marti agreed wholeheartedly that she would watch the Smith children. They seem to take immediate kinship with the 35-year-old ranger.

"Help us Marti. We have to clear the flat area and turn the plane around," said Steve.

I said, "I'll turn the plane around and get it de-iced. If you guys can start clearing the way."

"We have that stack of 2 x 10 planks. We are going to use for more decking. If we put two together – for each wheel – it should make a good takeoff point," said Marti.

I signaled approval to Steve, who walked with Marti Hightower to get the planks. He took her hand. It was clear they had more than a working relationship.

The combination of talents cleared the aircraft and made the site ready.

"Got an idea," said Steve, dragging a fire hose to the edge of the embankment. "Marti, turn it on full blast."

The flow of water almost sent Steve to his knees. He regained balance as he shot water cascading 50 feet down the embankment. Soon, there was no snow to the boulder. Only water running down the hillside.

"The Cessna's ready. Warmed. With what we've done, I'm confident we don't need to dump any fuel. As they say, it's downhill from here," I joked.

My heart was still frozen from the death of my beloved wife. Even so, like the down slope of the mountain, I felt stirrings from the companions around me.

Unabashedly, Steve kissed Marty and hugged her. The kiss was returned with fervor.

"Yes, they were more than merely rangers," I knew for certain.

Joseph took each of his kids in his arms and hugged and kissed them.

"I'll be back for you two charmers in a day or two. You be good for Marti. I don't want to go. I must."

They said in unison, "We will dad. Love you." They ran off playing hide-and-seek. How fast kids recover.

Steve came out from the watchtower carrying his sniper's rifle and ammunition.

"No more weight," I warned.

"When you're heading for war, you go prepared."

Everyone strapped in; I lowered the flaps to full. Then, holding the brakes firmly, I put the power to the firewall.

The Cessna wined from the urgency. I waited while the prop cleared the last trace of winter snow from the plane. I had the craft so wound up – brakes fastened tight – that the small airship almost lifted straight off the ground.

"Say a prayer, Sister. Here we go."

Claire did not need instructions. Her hands were together; eyes closed. She was praying not only for them, but for the two little Angels left behind with Marti.

The Cessna 182-modified bolted toward the edge of the cliff, lifted slightly, settled back to the ground and jetted downward.

"Please, Heavenly Father, help us lift this plane skyward," I said to myself.

Before tumbling into the boulder, the Cessna 182 cleared the mountain's landscape. Barely. However, the landscape was all downhill from there, and the modified plane needed no more divine assistance. It flew.

"I'm gaining cruise speed, by aiming at those trees at the foot of the hill," I said, as I removed degrees of flaps.

The little Cessna stayed in the air – screamed over the snow-laden trees, and flew into the dense weather.

Chapter 31

ଔଔଔଔଔ

PLAYING HOPSCOTCH WITH THE CLOUDS

"We have a nightmare before us," I almost cried aloud. "We need to borrow an aircraft and create a strategic plan. Get our butts back to Washington DC. That's where the monster is hiding."

"Is that all?" Retorted Claire.

"If you can find the Bishop Airport, we can steal a plane there," said Steve.

Claire asked, "What do you mean? If you can find the Bishop Airport? You can't find it? Is there really an airport nearby?"

"Sure."

"All I see is grey-white clouds, enveloping us. Nothing else."

"Seriously. There is an airport. The Bishop airport. Out there – somewhere." Steve said sarcastically.

"Oh, I forgot to mention when I was listing problems, that we're flying into nearly zero visibility." I said.

Steve added, "You can convert me now, Bishop. Have your Jesus be a beacon."

"Jesus is always the light; however, he expects better than our stupidity."

Dropping to lower altitudes – as the mountain gave way to a valley – we found that we sank below the major portions of the clouds. And only slightly above the trees. In and out of clouds. However, flying away from the mountain.

"I'll skim the tree tops. We are traveling slow – 30 knots. Should be able to spot the landing strip."

Claire opined, "If you are heading the correct direction. As I hear it, Mormons are hopelessly lost." Claire's bazooka wit was ever present. I had learned she only focused humor on friends.

"Hallelujah, there it is," Steve said pointing. "I thought it was 20\80 we wouldn't make it."

"Was it 80 per cent we would find the airport," Claire asked.

"Nope."

"Oh."

"I'll fly the plane, you masterminds figure out a plan."

Claire said, as if rehearsing, "Who's the director?"

"That's a good place to start," said the bulky ranger. "The director holds a little position as head man for the Central Intelligence Agency."

"Doesn't make any sense," Claire argued.

"To know the man is to hate him," said Steve.

"Disliking a man is one thing. Thinking he's in command of a treasonous plan is quite another," she responded.

Steve said, "He's the primary candidate for the author of the note. Every step of your partner's career, CIA director Aaron Bramwell has been there to object."

"Why?"

"Jealousy. Joe Smith did it better. Everything better. It infuriated Bramwell. In the field, Joseph would always have to walk behind him. Otherwise, Joe would be dead. Bramwell would've shot him in the back."

"Come on, Joseph, tell me the truth." Claire distinctly disbelieved the characterization.

"Steve might be exaggerating a trifle. Not much."

"Have the Bishop tell you one other individual who hates him."

"Well? Not so much."

"Also, the man has to be in a position to command. A foot soldier didn't make the order. Decide to kill her. Leave that bastardly note."

Joseph Smith did not clarify. He was devoted entirely to keeping the Cessna 182-modified about 25 feet above tree tops. Any unexpected obstacle could snag them.

"I'm lined up for landing. Snow flurries. Very strong cross wind – off our right wing. Maybe, 30 knots."

Within seconds, I had the landing lights on. Closed in on the Bishop Airport. Luckily, at the lower altitude, vision was better; even if, the wind was worse. I was crabbed into the wind – flying sideways. Now conditions have given way to light sprinkles.

Claire and Steve were still dissecting the mission, and the inevitable probability that the head of the CIA was part of the undertakings.

"Well, assuming I agree with your scenario about Bramwell, who is the sniper?" Asked the Nun.

"If I didn't know better, I would think Joe made the shot. None superior to him." Steve said.

"FBI's Padgett thinks the same thing."

Just as the plane was about to skip down on the snow laden landing strip, I kicked the nose straight – pointing it straight on the runaway. I had flown the entirety of final flying sideways to the strip. Otherwise, the wind would have pushed us far off the intended spot.

However, if I had not made the last second adjustment, we would have flipped. Similar to the small bird that crashed at Van Nuys airport.

I was now significantly more relaxed as our small craft was on the ground. Taxing, I was looking for an airplane to steal. Well, borrow.

"Have been considering those who could have made the kill." I said.

I added, "At first, I rejected all the candidates. Because I didn't believe any of us would shoot a sitting United States Senator."

"You change your mind?" Claire questioned.

"If you add the director to the scenario, men in uniform follow orders. More evidence that brass is involved."

"Well, don't keep us in the dark." Asked Steve.

"Who made the shot?" Claire added.

I asked, "What do you think, Steve?"

"I think – what I think – we'd better take him out, before he gets us." Steve answered. "What makes the two of you believe there is only one shooter?"

Chapter 32

WHILE SEEKING REVENGE, DIG TWO GRAVES – ONE FOR YOURSELF

Douglas Horton

An elderly guard – shriveled by the passage of time, and by years out in the sun – pushed slowly forward, holding an old and rusted cane. He stopped and waived the cane, greeting the aircraft.

"You boys a bit crazy. Flying near the widow-maker in zero visibility," said the man with a slow-stuttering drawl.

"Harry, I'm Steve. You know me – I'm a ranger with your niece Marti."

A flicker of recognition.

"Oh, right, yes Steve. What are you doing out on a day like this – flying? Just checked the cross-wind meter. It reads 30 to 50 knots – gusting." Said the old-timer, trying to put a cogent sentence together.

"The rangers are sending us back East on business; Marti is at the pinnacle overlook."

Harry, trying to stay up with the conversation, said, "Yes, Marti. How is she?"

"Harry, you saw her yesterday. She brought you food, remember?"

The slumped-over man was in his late 80s. He was retained by the flight service for overnight watch duty. He had Alzheimer's. The job was as much a favor to him as obtaining real service. However, he knew how to pump fuel. His years of experience made tying down aircraft securely an art. Instinct – not current intelligence. He could hardly walk.

"Harry, what's in the big hangar?"

"We have a King Air 200. Sleek as hell."

Steve looked at me to see if it was something I could fly.

"No time in that version. I flew the King Air 90, a bit. They purr like a kitten."

The guard looked perplexed. He knew these were not the pilots who brought the vacationers for skiing. On the other hand, Steve was family. Wasn't he?

"Was Steve married to Marti?"

Harry couldn't remember. He knew when he thought of his beloved niece, he always pictured her together with him. When Marti would take him to the pinnacle, Steve was there. They must be family, he concluded.

"Harry, we're going to need fuel in the Beech 200," said Steve.

Harry said, "Steve, is it okay?"

"Absolutely."

"You'll have to taxi her over near the pumps. That's the only place I have the fuel for that beast."

30,000 Feet - over the Rockies

The ceiling below the clouds was minimal. However, visibility to the end of the runway was okay. After fueling, we piled in. Guns and all.

Steve raided the lounge and packed the plane with food, water and sodas.

Takeoff was uneventful. The King Air was heavier than Joseph's Cessna, and the cross wind had abated to some extent. Climbing to altitude was vital. We didn't want to dart into some low-lying obstacle. Like a mountain.

"This baby is like a hotel room," said Claire.

"Flies similar to a commercial passenger jet. All the bells and whistles. Program your course and watch the miles fly by," I said drowsily.

"Don't fall asleep."

"No chance. Got enough while we were at the lookout."

"What's our speed?"

"We're cruising over 400 mph with winds aloft. We should experience a tail wind, across the country."

Claire asked, "When does that put us into DC?"

Steve retired to the back of the plane. He lowered the seat and fell fast asleep. No concerns to the world. He was back on a mission. Purring.

"The minute Steve awakes we had better do some pre-mission planning. This beast carves up the miles quickly."

Claire returned to the plush cabin area. She was going to get some quick shut-eye, as well.

I was almost robotic. I could go for days. Sleep 20 minutes and work the next 23 to 24 hours. After the mission, I would crash for days. My mind worked similar to a computer. Details flashed around, with puzzle pieces finding their home on the game board.

I dialed a cell number reserved for emergency contact with the Four Star – my ultimate boss. He was a friend of sorts. Not close, but there when I needed him. Like giving me a sniper's rifle at the instant, I needed it in Palmdale.

"Hard to really get to know. However, the Four Star always had my back. That made him a friend. Because sometimes assignments got crazy."

Chad Caden would always be my confessor and sounding board. Nonetheless, I was now assigned to the anti-terrorist division – attached to the White House. Under Four-Star general Brighton Mills. Like it or not.

"Brite," – as he was called by Joseph – was a career Air Force pilot, turning to a quasi-spook/politician in his closing days of his career. He was at the right hand of the President.

The line rang, rang and rang some more. The phone did not go to voice mail. I had hours to fly. I wasn't giving up.

After incessant ringing, the general finally answered. Perturbed.

"This better be good, Green Beret."

"Well hello to you too, Four Star."

"Your report."

"I truly called for information. However, I am re-engaging, after losing my wife to marauders. My children are secure."

The general was always business. "Sorry about Mrs. Smith."

"I don't have all the pieces. Many are in my wheelhouse."

"Your conclusions?"

"No real conclusions, sir. Nonetheless, the danger appears to be from at home. Not from abroad. I know everyone is talking about the IAM. The Muslims. However, they didn't kill my wife."

"Is that right?" he said, disbelieving.

"I am confident of that sir."

"Well, the papers and news anchors are saying we are being attacked. Our intel at the White House says the IAM is about to nuke us. You are smarter than everyone else? "

"Certainly can't say that, sir. My troubles appear to be more local. Only you, Smith, would see a plot by loyal Americans."

We both paused. Not liking the tone of the conversation.

He added, "I heard reports you chickened – flew home to California. Gave up. Quit the mission. Why should I trust you now? Believe your insanity."

"I had to try to save my family, sir."

"How did that work out?" the general said coldly. "This is war. You don't abandon a mission for anyone. Got it?"

"I do. Sir."

"I believe you are out-of-bounds," said the Four Star, who was a life-long golfer.

"General, if you know the goal of my mission, tell me. Tired of games. I would like to know what I am dying for."

"All I can tell you, the President doesn't know. Other than what I have reported. It is clear the IAM is planning to hit us one way or another. I had dinner last night with the President. He is hardly sleeping with everything going on in the Middle East, and at home. We are about to be over run."

"Does the President have any suspects at home?"

"No. In fact, you haven't convinced me there is any. Other than the Muslims."

"Don't we need to discern who the players are?"

"Probably the names of the Muslim infiltrators. The delay in your working the case will make it impossible for you to catch up," said the Four Star. "You are too far behind the power curve."

"Anyone, in Washington that I should watch out for, be afraid of?"

The general said, "Focus on the threat from abroad, the Muslims. We are under an attack."

The line went dead.

"Is the old man losing it? Alternatively, – with half the world aligned against us – are the IAM countries truly attacking. Could they have hundreds of boots on the ground in the United States?"

The plane was flying itself. Above 30,000 feet, at levels assigned by FAA trackers. I received advisories when traffic was in the air corridor, or if he needed to make alterations to flight levels.

I was not letting moss grow under my feet; I picked up the sky phone and dialed – almost immediately after being hung up on by the Four Star.

"Caden, here," the phone was answered. It was a late at night. Yet, Chad was alert and working. "Who's on the line?"

"Joseph Smith, Sir."

"My son, I am so terribly, terribly sorry for your loss. This is a nasty business. And under these circumstances, sometimes we forget pure love. Focus solely on our country at risk."

"Thank you sir."

"Where are you?"

"On-the-job."

"Never had any doubt. Kids – secure?"

"Hidden in the belly of the earth."

"What do you need?"

"I've been out of the loop for a day. I need a news report on what's going on in the world, and most importantly in our case here at home."

"At home, FBI and military are being warned off. Highest level. No one knows who's behind the assault. It's unlike ever before. They say the IAM network. Don't really know."

The old-man of the FBI continued, "The FBI director has said to leave it to the military, and the military says the FBI will mop up."

"Leave what to the military? What's the objective? What's the oppressor's plan?" I asked.

Chad said, "Yesterday, North Korea fired a test missile which landed only 250 miles off the coast of Seattle. The test was made with the approval of China."

"Say what? They fired on us?"

The grand old man never missed his cadence or raised his voice.

"They say it was only a test. No nuclear or other device on board. It flopped into the ocean – sank to the bottom. Furthermore, the North Koreans contend they didn't believe the rocket would fly that far."

"They don't have an abort mechanism," I asked unconvinced.

"The bottom line: the North Koreans will momentarily be able to fire a nuclear weapon at us. What's more, their new alliance – with the **IAM** – incorporates all the Islamic/Muslim states. And more."

"You're telling me China is against us?"

"Don't become an alarmist."

"With news like this, and things at home, it's hard not to be alarmed."

Chad said, "China's merely trying to walk the middle thin-line. Russia as well."

"I guess I can see that."

"Keep in mind, everyone believes the USA is broke. Out of money. Dependent on China for loans. And the Middle East for fuel. Cut those off and its lights go out in America."

I questioned, "Is that the plan?"

"It certainly is the plan of the IAM; however, why would leaders at home want to subscribe to that music? It doesn't make sense."

Chad Caden heard rumors of the clandestine note pinned to Nancy Smith's clothing. He wanted me to read the message to him.

I folded the note away neatly. Privately. I put it in my shirt pocket when I walked away from the crime scene in Camarillo. I showed it to no one.

"Authorities have looked for the note. To no avail." He said. He asked if he could hear it. The request was an order – however, he made it with kindness.

I read, with my voice breaking, the message. To my mentor and friend. There was a heavy pause after I completed my recital.

"I can only think of one person who would have been in a position to have authorized the hit, and cruel enough to pen the note," said Chad.

He paused. Not wanting to make the admission.

"Aaron Bramwell." He finally said.

"Yes, sir. The director."

"Why would the CIA director be targeting Americans? Why would Bramwell be behind a terrorist plot at home?"

"Don't know, sir. Do you have any other suspect who could have authorized my wife's execution? Have been the author of the note?"

"Not with the wording. Not with the hatred."

"Agreed. He's been out of his mind for twenty years. Keeps it from his superiors."

"You're heading to Washington, aren't you? I know you Green Beret. You're a man of allegiance to the country – to honor."

"I have allegiance to fulfill my mission by eradicating the dogs that are screwing with us."

"Revenge derives more revenge."

"I believe in Christ, I don't have time for revenge. God deemed that America is a very special place. Jesus embraced our founding fathers. As long as I'm alive, the USA is going to stand tall. The traitors are going down."

There was silence on the phone. Both men thinking.

"Are you still there, son?" Asked the FBI leader.

"Yes."

"Believe the President is involved?"

"No."

"Why?"

I was now in an area of national security, and right to know. There was a conflict. I had no authorization to tell him about the Four Star, or our conversation.

Chad said, "Your hesitancy tells me the person to whom you report has not authorized his name being bandied about."

As always, the old man knew. Without being told, he just knew.

"You're right. It's classified. And unfortunately, my friend, you don't have a right to know. If I determine there is a breach of peace at that end, you will be my first call."

"Higher than my level of security. I can guess the rest."

"Sir, I figured as much."

"We must maintain order. Faith, honor, respect are always foundations for our way of life," he said.

I started hearing Chad talking platitudes more often these days. He knew his friend was closer to the end of his life, than the beginning. Certainly, however, that didn't make him wrong.

"Keep the light on," I said. "I'm headed your way."

Chapter 33

CRCRCRCRCR

BURNING UP THE PHONE LINES

I knew our flight to Washington DC was going to be the only time to think deeply – to realize the goal of our ultimate target. Once in the center of political and physical danger, we would be called upon for action.

"Why is North Korea risking annihilation by firing missiles at the United States? Why is China openly supporting the **IAM**?

I knew our country had been weakened by political blunders. However, I also know that we could pulverize by bombs of mass destruction any country – including China.

"Why then?"

So again, I picked up the phone, and dialed.

There were numerous clicks, which singled the routing of the call. It was forwarded. Away from my friend's home. To where, I wondered.

"Hello, this is Pentland."

"Hi, how are you Bri?" I asked one of America's top active snipers, Brian Pentland.

"Joseph Smith – America's most-wanted man? Surprised you would be calling me."

"Me, the most wanted?"

"Yep - you!"

Brian Pentland's tone was sharp and hostile. I have long respected him. He became one of the top world snipers in Iraq and Afghanistan. Younger than me. A great shot. I always considered him a close friend.

"Bri what makes me a target?"

"Word is you are a traitor. I've had you in my cross-hairs twice. I didn't take the shot, out of the past friendship."

"Why didn't you pick up the phone? Ask if I am a traitor?"

"Orders, Joe. Orders."

"Who told you I was a traitor?" Who gave you my number? Told you to execute me?"

There was silence.

"Classified."

"Were you involved in killing Nancy?"

This time Pentland was eager to answer. No hesitation.

"How can you ask me that? I know you wouldn't take a shot against Betty – what makes you think that orders or not I would execute Nancy?"

"Doesn't it tell you something that orders were given to kill her. To disgrace her? To leave her in the street? In the rain!!"

The silence was deafening. Brian Pentland didn't want to be in this discussion.

"Joe?"

"Yes."

"Why don't you turn yourself in? I'll have to take the shot the next time," said Pentland remorsefully.

"Who told you to kill me, Brian? I'm on the job for the FBI. anti-terrorist task force. The White House. I'm looking for the traitors."

"Classified, Joe. My orders are from as high as God."

Brian Pentland knew that Joseph Smith was a devout Mormon. Knew he was a Bishop. He knew Joseph Smith believed that closest to God was the Prophet in Salt Lake City.

"Brian, the orders came from the director? Right?"

"If they did – you know – you are dead."

"Why would the director of the CIA be attacking Americans? Why kill a United States Senator?"

Silence on the other end of the line.

"Brian, it took me a few hours to figure out who could make the shot on the Senator. Your work. Right?"

No hesitation. "The dude was selling us out."

I disengaged the autopilot, descending to much lower flying altitude. I did not notify the IFR flight authorities. I headed for the deck.

"Brian, you know me. I'm willing to die before I sell out my country. Regardless of orders, you know the truthfulness of my declaration," I told the sniper.

"That's why I didn't take the kill shot. I just could not believe it."

"You're on the wrong side, my friend. Orders or not – someone's trying to take away our freedom. Our country," I told him sincerely.

"Bishop, I follow orders. Proper orders. The next time you're in my cross-hairs I will take the shot."

"Brian, you don't have proper orders. Call the President. Ask him as commander-in-chief whether he condones such a subscription?"

"I did; told that's who gave the order?"

"Who told you that – the Prince of fairyland?"

"Orders are orders. See you flying over Kansas – heading east."

I expected from the tone of the conversation that I was being tracked. I was now dropping below 10,000 feet.

"You guys going to shoot missiles at me?"

"I'm not. The Air Force might scramble a couple of jets to intercept."

I turned off my transponder, hoping I could evade interception. Brian had notified me the track was complete. I would have a little time before the Air Force would react once orders were given.

Again, for the moment, he saved me.

"Have to leave you now Brian. I need to turn off your tracking. Consider that you are on the wrong team – my friend."

"Maybe it's you who should call the President."

"I work at the pleasure of the President," I responded.

"Looks like you have been fired. Certainly, you are out of his pleasure. Out in the cold."

Without saying more, I turned off the connection and all radio contact. Hard to make a King Air 200 as small as a Piper Cub. Right now – I felt like I was flying a plane the size of Rhode Island. However, I did as much as I could to elude tracking.

"Fall out of the sky," I had been trained. "To the hard deck. Sit right on top of a truck."

Brian Pentland's statements made no sense. I had spoken to the President's right-hand man – not an hour before. He seemed pissed that I had disked the FBI assignment for a few hours – to save my children. He expected I would stay the course.

"Brian had not denied his order to kill the Senator came from the director. Aaron Bramwell."

Pentland was an intuitive officer. No one's fool. I respected him. The man was a leader—a good one. A better sniper.

"He wouldn't go on a mission to kill me halfcocked," I said to myself. "The director had a grudge. No doubt. But not Brian. We barbequed. Our kids played together – when we were not working."

I thought, "Brian has it wrong. The President of the United States is a great man. He's not pulling the ticket on Americans. Not having us running around after each other with sniper rifles."

The President would vomit at what had been done to my wife, Nancy. Wouldn't tolerate the note.

Chapter 34

ଔଔଔଔଔ

THE KING AIR TRACKED FOR THE KILL?

I didn't want to mess with the fly-boys. If they were sent. They would find me. They would lick their chops. I would look like a slow-moving blimp to them. However, I didn't have a lot of choice.

"Now or never," I said to no one. My buddies – Claire and Steve – were asleep.

My craft descended rapidly. I was now creeping down to 500 feet off the deck. Moreover, I turned north. Deviating from my original course, I hoped the move would confuse, whoever was attempting to track us.

"I am certain the trace came from Washington. Not from an actual lock on my craft. They expected my call – and traced it. That might make it easier to avoid. The trace probably from the CIA. They would not have the immediate resources of the Air Force. They would have to pull a few strings.

"That string pulling would take time – unless the CIA truly had been ordered by the President. It was our only hope."

"What?" Said the Sister, who was shaken awake by my antics. "Are we being shot at?"

"Not yet."

"What do you mean? Not yet?"

"My fingers were caught in the cookie jar."

I explained briefly my discussions with Brian, and that he had warned that a lock on our cell communication had been made.

"I've turned off all avionics. We're down at flight level 400 feet."

"Isn't that dangerous?"

"You think?? Nonetheless, were over Kansas – flat as a pancake. I'm tracking north. Trying to alleviate detection."

"Some of Kansas isn't so flat."

"It is tonight." I laughed. "Better be, or we will make a large crater."

"Will it work?"

"Not for long. Maybe, we can make a landing strip. Sit down."

Sister Claire retreated to the right seat in the cabin. Even in the most stressful circumstances, she had a peaceful spirit about her.

She said, "Just another adventure." Then, she smiled warmly.

This circumstance, I knew, had significant risks. Flying a Cessna 150 at low altitude is one thing. Flying a King Air 200 at 400 feet is ultimate suicide.

"I can't believe Steve," said Claire.

"Why?"

"All the maneuvering you're doing hasn't changed his snoring at all."

I laughed.

"I don't know about the snoring, but I know that we're all trained to get sleep when we could," I told her.

We were in a remote area, and I eased the King Air up to 750 feet and pulled back on the throttle. I was scouring charts of Kansas.

"What are you doing?" Claire asked with genuine interest, rather than fear.

"Trying to find a place to set this sucker down."

The search of the maps revealed Blosser Municipal airport with a 3,600-foot asphalt strip. It was primarily used for general aviation.

"Claire, anywhere we go, there will be significant risk."

"Joe, use your best judgment. I have faith we have protection from above."

"Blosser has only a few multi-engine airplanes. And according to the information, I find a small percentage of military on the field. Whatever that means."

"How many ultra-lights?" She quipped.

"There are a couple. You want to borrow one of those for our trip cross country?"

Claire again smiled easily.

I lined up the King Air for landing on runway 35, which I found was the active. The weather was crystal clear, so finding the field had been easy.

"We might be flying into a trap. If they are tracking us, police or military will be waiting for us."

Claire asked, "Should we just fly on to Washington?"

"No, in this bird we're sitting ducks. I can't turn on the transponder. I can't field calls from traffic control."

"Well then, say a prayer."

"Get sleeping beauty up. Tell Steve to prepare the guns and be ready to move."

I knew the operational limits at Blosser, but I had no choice but to land. So we did.

Chapter 35

ଓଓଓଓଓ

A RANGER IN A RANGER

Blosser, in the middle of the night, was deserted and dark. After an almost crash landing, I taxied over to the private tie downs.

I remember the old pilot's lingo, "Any landing you can walk away from is a good one." Well, then, this one must be terrific. The wheels were still on the plane.

Steve poked his head into the cockpit, as I was cutting the engines. With the practiced eye, the ranger evaluated.

"It looks deserted. If we don't flee the area, we will be tattooed by cops shortly," he said wisely.

"I parked the King Air, obscured by a tall hangar."

"If you think no one's going to notice a multi-million dollar aircraft parked here, you are insane," he said. "Are we borrowing another plane?"

We were bolting from the expensive twin-engine. Carrying an armload of weapons. Little else. Claire's dresses were a donation to the jet's owner.

"They're going to expect us to steal another aircraft, once they find the King Air. Too risky an approach," I said. "Let's see if we can locate a car or truck to borrow. Topeka isn't too far away."

Claire suggested, "I've got a Vatican credit card. We can use obscurely. Why don't we charter a plane in Topeka, under assumed names?"

"You're going to have to provide the charter company with identification," said Steve.

"So I will. The charter company isn't looking to reject paying customers," said the Sister.

Steve pointed. "Look. There is an old Ford Ranger. A forest ranger escaping capture by capturing a stolen Ford Ranger."

He thought it funny. Almost made him a comedian. Ready for television. I was sad at the disappointment of taking another man's vehicle. Nonetheless, there was little choice.

"What,?" Said the Sister looking at him cross-eyed. They were becoming friends.

"Thought I was dumb. I can make jokes too."

"Yeah, that was a humdinger." She said. Making a face.

He swatted at her playfully.

I said nothing – still saddened by the prospect of confiscating the small truck.

The vehicle was parked off the side of the road, outside the airport. The Sister was limping. Her spirit was willing, but her feet were sore.

Steve was enjoying the excitement of the mission. I was nervous. I knew we didn't have much time to disappear.

We sat close together in the Ford Ranger we borrowed. It was old, beat up on the outside, but ran as if a mechanic owned it.

The shift lever was between Claire's legs. Of course, Steve noticed. He said nothing.

We sat scrunched together. Our ranger was a very large man. Three of us were too many for this small vehicle.

"I think we have until early morning before someone's notices the truck is gone," said Steve.

I asked, "Sister, having any luck on our ferry to Washington?" She was telephoning while we were on the move.

Putting down her cell phone, she said, "Easy as pie."

"I'm concerned about them tracking your cell phone number."

"First off, I gave them a direct line which will send them to the Vatican. Rome will back us. Second, like you, I have more than one line on my phone," said the Sister engagingly.

It took some time making the loop to Topeka. We encountered no one chasing us. The night was quiet. The weather much better than California.

On the ride to Topeka, Steve was energized. It was as if someone had put new batteries in him. Claire and I were nervous. Steve was ready for real action. Been sitting on a mountain top for too long.

Our guns were stowed in the small cargo space behind the front passenger seats. We didn't want to put them outside in the truck bed. We were afraid someone would spot the guns. Call the police.

Driving conditions were good. A large moon lit the sky.

Pulling into the Topeka Air charter service, Steve said he would find a wrap for the weapons. Claire left the small truck, walking confidently inside. Sister Claire Coogan made easy work of the bashful young man who willingly took her credit card.

Steve returned with a tarp and wrapped the weapons. They were heavy; yet, he carried them without difficulty.

I knew they were not leaving without me. So, I went to ditch the stolen truck. I took my time finding a secure hiding spot.

"Sister," said Steve. "You know style. Strictly, first class." He was pointing at the chartered airplane.

"He's right. This is better than anything we've flown in. Kudos."

The three of us were seated in the back of the plush jet, which would wing us to Washington.

"Won't they ask questions, when they find the truck," asked Steve. "The authorities will soon find the charter service."

I told him, "They might when they find it."

"Where did you stash the Ford?" Steve asked.

"I put it in a deserted metal building on the other side of the airport. It might be days or weeks before the driver gets it back."

They looked at me curiously. I only was gone a short time. I said, "I double-timed it back to the charter service."

The Sister said, "You didn't look like you even went for a walk."

Looking at Steve, I said, "Now you know who is really in shape."

"Ha," he said. "I'll take you on – any time."

On this occasion, I was sleeping soundly in a split second. I said nothing.

I woke briefly during the flight. A bump or something. I thought how wonderful it was not to be driving the plane. A slogan came into my head. "...and leave the driving to us."

In my sleepy state, I couldn't remember. "Oh, yeah, Go Greyhound and leave the driving to us."

Well, I certainly was thankful that someone else was piloting. I love flying. On a mission, it is comforting to have restful periods. This assignment had found me behind the throttles too often.

The Sister started off across the aisle from me. By flights end she fell asleep. And she was slumped over, her head resting on my shoulder.

"Wakeee, Wakeee," said Steve.

Claire woke first, with a start. She realized she was resting on my shoulder. Embarrassed, she quickly sat up.

Steve rubbed two fingers together, as if saying naughty, naughty.

I woke up, rubbing my face. I shook my right arm. It went dead on me. Why I wondered?

Turning to Sister Claire, I said, "Sister, you have a red face. What's going on?"

Claire shook her head innocently. Made a nonchalant face.

Steve said nothing.

Chapter 36

ରେ ରେ ରେ ରେ ରେ

ONE VALLIANT FRIEND DEAD

The pilot made a perfect landing on the strip in Charlottesville, Virginia.

I was surprised when I looked outside. I was not where I expected. This was all new to me. I have never been here before.

"Why did we fly to this location?" I asked, looking around.

"Better chance they won't be looking for us," said Claire.

"Masterful job, even if you are Catholic," I kidded her. Now, I was returning her jocularity. One day soon, we might debate God's magnificent plan without bullets flying nearby.

Steve said, "I'll get the car. They won't be looking for me."

"No. If they suspect your identity, the children will be at risk. Claire, let's charge the Hertz car to the Vatican."

We did. Again, smooth as silk. The Sister had a knack of getting her way. Beauty always opens doors. Go to the car rental service that has a man. With Claire, that made rental child's play.

Once situated in a new Chevrolet Suburban, we drove toward our destiny in Washington.

I had picked up a New York Times, and I scanned it for the latest national and world news. A story concluded the reports out of China were bleak; the US debt to the Chinese was in danger of being called. They don't want our debt. No more loans to the bankrupt nation.

"What then?" I wondered.

What's more, many other nations were supporting the Muslim/Islamic **IAM** stance. A greater headache for the President. No relief for us.

Steve said, "Says here this is the best time to drub America. Let me read: 'the United States has been exerting its will on the world for decades. If the imperials don't get their way, they send a drone or nuclear bomb'."

I asked, "Then, you conclude our troubles are with the **IAM**?"

"I am merely reading. Joseph. You know I'm better at resolving a problem militarily than I am figuring out political issues."

Claire said, "It's a little too neat."

"Very much so. I don't think that's the end game."

I headed the Suburban toward the capital. Claire had not listed me as an additional driver, but I had the wheel. We all knew our direction.

"Certainly, we need to have a heart-to-heart conversation with the director," the Sister summarized.

"We've got the entire military establishment looking for us. The director is one of the most powerful men in the world. How do you envision we're going to chat with him?"

Steve shook his head.

"Why don't we invite him to Quantico?" Claire asked.

"I'm not going to that meeting," said Steve.

I thought for a minute, knowing her suggestion was absolutely the safest meeting place. However, our arrest was certain.

"Why don't I go in? Meet with the director at Quantico." I volunteered.

Claire shook her head vigorously.

"You go. I go too. We're a team. Period."

Steve added, "You don't expect him to confess?"

"No. Surely not."

"Well, when he doesn't break down and cry like a baby, you are going to be in chains. They will trust him; take his word. And slam you in a cell. Life without a pardon. Treason." Steve said.

I nodded in agreement. "On second thought, my idea stinks. Perhaps, Chad Caden can meet him somewhere."

Steve said, "All you're doing is throwing an anchor around Caden. He'll sink like a load of rocks."

"Right. You're right. See, you are not bad at deducing."

Steve said, "Yeah, I know crap when I see it. However, I can't come up with the right plan."

"We have to do something to draw him out." Claire said.

"The slug will meet us anywhere. He'll have Pentland and other shooters waiting on us. I can see his smug grin," Steve answered.

I knew that Brian would take the shot, and that the CIA director would authorize many more guns.

Claire slapped her hands emphatically.

"Come on, think."

Steve questioned, "Who do we have as allies?"

I answered, "Beyond the three of us, Caden, Kaci Haber, and a few who have not been tainted from the old days."

"Let's find a secure line where we can make uninterrupted calls. Let's call out the troops."

"Steve, how are you going to know those we call aren't setting is up?" Claire asked.

He answered, "How did you know to fly to the pinnacle – to me?"

"With you, never a question."

"Then let's call the ones that are 'never a question'."

We found refuge in a Mormon church outside of Washington DC from which we could make phone calls. We were only calling six individuals who made the 'never a question' list.

Two of the selected were out of the country. Two others declined the invitation to help because of directives from kingpins in the government.

"They will keep our invite to themselves. They both said they had declined service against us, when they were invited. Yes. The director." I reported.

Harry Ayres and Terri Bolan said they had heard the scuttlebutt about me being a spy, but didn't believe it. They agreed to 'man up,' embrace the old days.

"Then, there were the five," said Claire.

"Against an Army," I added.

Steve said, "Don't forget the CIA, the FBI, Air Force and the Navy. Have I left anybody out?"

"No. I think that about covers it. Oh, yes, the Marines."

We settled on a location for the trap at a walk-up law office of a former US attorney. He was a conservative, government-sensitive individual who could be trusted by both sides. Well, maybe, their team more trusted than ours.

"Well, somewhat trusted by us." Said Claire.

Chad Caden made the invitation to director Bramwell, indicating that I would be present for a briefing on the **IAM** fiasco. Chad attempted to set the meeting with an hour's notice.

"I need more time to prepare," said the director.

"Prepare what?"

The director said, "Thanks for the meeting, Chad. Now, stay out of it."

"If that's what you want."

"Yes. Go fishing."

When I returned the call to Caden at the appointed time, he announced deftly that I was walking into a trap. The director's trap – not ours.

"The building's exterior will be loaded with snipers. You don't have a chance. There is even a question, whether the director will show up. More probably, his henchmen will make the visit."

"He'll show," I predicted.

I called Langley announcing myself. Bramwell didn't come on the line; however, a well-placed assistant did.

"I need to meet with the director. I know that Caden has set up a meet. I'm not going to show until the director is present. He doesn't show; I will be long gone..."

"You can't make threats like that. It's a federal offense," I was told.

"He doesn't show – neither do I."

Then, I hung up. Not time for them to get a trace.

Logistics were our only major advantage. We set the location for the meet. We could pick the perfect gun placements.

Claire said, "Won't they just outgun us? Have 10 times the shooters, we have?"

"Don't think so. Bramwell isn't going to want to have a bloodbath on an Alexandria, Virginia street. He'll be selective. Certainly, Pentland will be here."

"Are you better than he is?"

"That's a question we both have asked for a decade."

Steve conjectured, "Bramwell's team will look for the same kill-spots that we select. If we're alert, we will take them out before the confrontation."

"Don't under-estimate Brian Pentland."

"I know; you're right."

Harry Ayers called us, saying he was stationed in the second-floor office, across the street from where the director would come for the meet. Harry was a former Green Beret sniper. Good-but not great. He made costly mistakes. Hit what he shot at. Sometimes, however, his mistakes cost American lives.

"Harry," I said quietly on the secure talkie.

"Yep."

"We have only a sparse amount of time left before..."

"Damn. Leave me. I am secure."

Terri Bolan was better with conventional automatics and taking down subjects. At war, she was no lady. Like Steve, she preferred breaking things – people too. She was placed inside the law office. Terri would restrain the former US attorney. Terri would hogtie him, if necessary.

"When I am done, he will pee his pants. Afterwards, he will ask for a Silver Star for bravery when he tells the story," she laughed.

The law office was a key spot in the plan to capture the director. We had no idea how many men the director would try to bring with him inside the law office.

We knew Bramwell was a conceded—thought he was better than the world around him. Always over-valued his personal opinion. We believed this might give us a crucial advantage inside the law suite.

Sister Claire would join Terri Bolan to sequester Bramwell, and any others, who might wander that way. There was still a chance, he wouldn't show. Alternatively, he could merely send snipers and gunmen.

"He will think he can eliminate us while we walk up to the law offices."

We were taking a significant risk. I knew it. What other plan has a chance. We needed the intel. The director was giving the orders. Shut him down, and perhaps the internal war would be over.

Both Steve and I took locations high, atop the buildings, at a preferred angle across the street.

"Claire," I said. "Don't underestimate Bramwell. He's a coward – unless he can grasp the upper hand. Then, he's ruthless."

"I know the kind."

"He might send one or 10 other people inside. My reason for believing he will come alone is his arrogance. He will believe we will be cut down outside. He will want to gloat. Be operationally in charge."

The Sister could be the kindest, warmest, and sometimes seemingly the frailest of women. Underneath, the veneer was the heart of a Marine. Vigilant. Tough. Quick-thinking.

"I'll take him down. He's never had such a headache."

The law office was bolted down. The metal back door was bolted and blocked. The only way encroachers would find access was by sending a SWAT team. We believed the director would not want to announce Swat's presence to the international press.

"He can't say the IAM did it," Steve said.

Approximately, one hour before the meeting, I saw a glimpse of an attacker, dressed in military garb, coming out onto our roof. No contest. I saw him. Before he saw me. He didn't expect us to be there. One smashing blow from the butt of the sniper rifle put him to sleep.

I tied him and gagged him firmly. He was out of action. Steve, the barbarian, was still sleuthing for more targets. We wanted to be certain that we had a tactical strength on our building.

"Keep the heat across the street. Then you can shoot the bastards," said Steve. He was in his element.

Steve 'The Magnificent' – as we called him in the service – worked his magic clearing the roof tops on our side of the divide. Undetected. I looked, but never caught a glimpse of him. He was truly a 275-pound ghost.

There was no subterfuge in the director's appearance. He showed up in a black, Mercedes limousine. He thought he had the ultimate upper hand.

"He expects me to cower undercover until after he arrives."

I told him I wouldn't come until I could "verify his appearance." He knows me to be a man of my word. That's what he expects. I considered him an enemy, so he couldn't go by old times when we were on the same side.

He showed his power blatantly, stepping head-high and walking pompously up the steps to the law firm. The ultimate ass.

"Come in," invited Claire.

"You must be the Nun," said the director differentially. He did not expect to see her there. Even so, he wasn't overly alarmed.

She was early. Very early. He expected to see her dead on the street with her companion, the Bishop.

That's all he would remember for some time. It was lights out. Sister Claire did not play around. She didn't give him a chance to assess the situation. She cold-cocked him, tying him up – feet and hands tied behind.

His driver waited in the car. A mistake. He brought no other interlopers. A bigger error.

"Let's move," said Terri Bolan.

She pointed a finger at the former US attorney, warning, "Stay tied down. Call anybody for 15 minutes and I'll set off the plastic explosives I planted; go outside my snipers will cut you down."

This was all banter. Bolan wanted him to stay out of the tussle.

Claire followed the plan without exception. She sent me a text message to a secure phone.

"We have the director. We're on the move."

The attorney sat tied to the conference table shaking – agreeing readily not to move for half an hour. He was no fool.

For the first time, Steve showed himself. He took down another vulture. "Roof secured," he said.

Not a second later, I saw the glint of a scope from across the street. High atop a building, three doors down from the law office. The sniper was panning, looking for prey. He spotted movement on our rooftop.

"It's Brian," I said to myself. "He's in a bad spot, because his vantage point is 10 feet below us. We have the catbird location."

"I desperately didn't want to take that shot." He was a friend. Under orders, I knew. Yes, he would put one right between my eyes – given the chance.

"If I have the chance. Well. After all, I did not want to kill a close friend. What I wanted was 10 minutes alone with Bramwell," I thought.

I said to myself, "Keep vigilant. Pentland will make the shot this time."

Steve nodded, moving away.

I spotted two more military types on the roof across from us, and figured there could be more. We all held our positions, waiting for an all clear from the Sister.

"Can't move off the roof until then."

The Law Office

Inside, amazingly – with little effort – the ladies picked up the director by his arms and his legs. Because his arms were placed behind him, they were wrenched from their sockets. However, he was still out cold. They carried him out of the back door. A sack of potatoes. No ceremony. Not a word.

The Sister and the other former marine, Col. Terri Bolan, treated Bramwell like cargo. Bolan lifted him. She had experience with prisoners in combat. Put him over her shoulders.

Reaching a low fence, Bolan rested the director on the top. He folded in two. His head over the fence, with his feet on Bolan's side.

The ladies climbed over. They were in a back yard, which was located on the street removed from the ruckus. Watching for intruders, Claire helped Bolan pick up the director.

"Give the slug to me," she ordered. She unceremoniously flung him over her shoulder. Claire guarded the two of them with a shot gun as they moved to security.

Bolan carried him through a passageway from the house behind the law office; they made it to the Suburban which was parked in a neighbor's driveway. As the Bishop and Nun had predicted, they encountered no one.

Joseph and Steve stayed hidden. A shot rang out from a sniper's rifle from across the street – not from Pentland.

The breaking of glass told me that Harry Ayers had come under fire. He probably was exposed. Harry always did move too much. He kept trying to improve his position – ultimately giving himself away.

It had been a while since I had fired on a live target. That said, I felt comfortable. The commandments are paramount in my mind, but when fired upon I returned the volley to protect comrades.

I squeezed, placing a round in the sniper's right arm. And just as quickly, another in his left arm before he could react. Harry's attacker was under control.

"Not so rusty after all," I mused.

Immediately, a barrage came from the location where Brian Pentland had stationed himself. He was below and off to my right.

As I predicted, my position was pristine. I had the optimum cover. His shot banked harmlessly off the fireplace stack covering me.

I yelled to my friend.

"Bri retreat, I've secured high ground. Seven of us were here hours before you," I lied. "All of your men are dead if you stay. We already have Bramwell. If you don't believe me, call him. He won't answer."

More shots rang out. I returned fire hitting another CIA-type in the leg-sending him sprawling. At this range, I could be selective where I aimed.

"Like in an arcade. Position is everything."

Because of our elevated position, and the chimney, I could peak between the mortars and see my longtime friend, Brian Pentland. We were now pitted against one another. Meet somewhere else and we would hug.

"Have a beer," he would offer. Knowing I would not.

There was a round, quarter-size metal piece above his head. It numbered an electrical device of some sort behind him. It was no more than four inches from his head.

"Brian, watch this," I yelled, squeezing off a shot. My bullet hit the disc – dead center. "Like sniper practice. It brings back memories of tactics on the range. Right Bri?"

I said, "That could have been your head. I have you in my cross-hairs. I've chosen the metal marker. The next one won't miss. I can see right into your hiding place."

I heard a laugh, from across the street. Leave it to Pentland. "I had you two times in my sites. Not one."

I added, "This is a turkey shoot, Bri. You saved me when you failed to take me out. Now buddy, I returned the favor. Retreat or die."

Brian screamed from across the roof top, "Can we take the two wounded?"

"Of course. Leave the rifles. Secure your men. Two of yours are down over there. Many others tied up over here."

"Should I come over there now? Retrieve my men. Perhaps, we can arm wrestle."

"I would wait five minutes, unless you want to be ventilated," I responded.

Then, I yelled, as if talking to our men, "Guys, hold your fire, unless fired upon."

Brian answered, "Sorry Joe; my hitter tapped Harry Ayers in the head. I saw him go down. He's dead."

"Dead."

"Yes."

"You sure."

"How did you recruit him? Who else is on your team?"

There was no more shooting. No more talk either. Brian Pentland and two other men picked up their wounded and retreated, as I ordered.

An incoming text from Claire told me they had the director. They were secure in the car. Driving to a pre-arranged location to pick us up.

"Five minutes. Steve and I will be with you in five minutes," I texted to her.

Next, I called Ayers. No answer.

I did not know where Steve had been hiding. In fact, he crawled around our roof. He tackled and tied up five so-called sniper professionals. Once Steve got you in his claws, it was lights out.

I rang his phone.

"With you Green Beret." He hung up.

We didn't wait around for their troops to re-engage. We half-crawled along the roof. By rope, we repelled down the backside of the building to the ground. I covered Steve until he was below. Then with armament, he protected me.

This was a time-tested procedure, which had saved our lives in the field many times before. Then, we marched to the reunion with the Sister and Terri Bolan. Our comrades stationed the Chevy suburban three blocks removed from the festivities.

And, most importantly, they had the director.

Chapter 37

ଔଔଔଔଔ

A POIGNANT ARGUMENT FOR WAR

We waited five minutes. Harry Ayers did not show. I screamed in a clear brash voice – calling for our friend. The yell was loud enough to restore hearing to the deaf – but not to a man felled by the director's hit squad.

"Dangerous," Steve called, trying to silence my yelling. "He's a soldier. Understood the risks."

"What if you were injured."

"Leave me. However, he isn't injured. He's with your Angels."

Prior to the outset, we had agreed there would be no delay in the departure. I felt totally responsible. I encouraged him to come.

"Too risky for all."

I called Ayers on his cell phone another time as we neared the car. The walkie-talkie phone broadcast my message. If he were alive to receive it, he would answer.

No Harry.

"Where's Harry," asked Bolan. Not knowing. The ladies had turned off their talkies.

"Dead," I answered. "Brian reported one of his men took Harry out."

The Sister started to get out of the vehicle. She was going after Harry, regardless of the potential danger to her.

"We don't leave anyone behind." She said with a sharp voice.

I grabbed her shoulder, restraining her.

"Brian is not a liar. Harry is dead."

"We have to retrieve him."

"Brian Pentland is Harry's friend, as well. I could hear his stress. When things settle, he will see to him. We leave now, or we will be in body bags ourselves."

Claire didn't like it; however, she knew my words were true. Furthermore, we were in combat in America – for America. Not in some foreign land. Harry served his country again with honor.

I switched on my phone and dialed Brian.

"Pentland," Brian answered.

"This is Joseph. Was it worth it?"

"Orders, Joe."

"Ask the President – the commander-in-chief. Watch after Harry."

"I will. I promise. He was a very good friend. This is a nasty business. I'm glad we both got off the roofs today. Thanks Joseph – you could have tapped me."

"No Brian, I could not. We are family. As married, as you are with your wife. We are bound together by ties stronger than a wedding band. By honor. By miles of mud." I said.

"Be careful, Joseph. You better kill Bramwell, or he will cut off your balls. He's the man. Don't know if it goes higher." Said a remorseful Brian Pentland. "However, Joseph – in this case Bramwell is correct about the Muslims."

I switched off the phone.

Bramwell's Inquisition

Director Bramwell awoke slowly. His face was swollen. Claire had knocked a tooth loose.

He was moaning, "My arms...my arms. Oh, my leg."

A cursory examination showed that an arm had been wrenched from the socket. He was in acute pain.

Bolan said, "Turn up the radio. Drown out the rat."

She knew Bramwell from our days in the service. The hatred was real. When she had been asked to go with us, she asked, "When we get the creep, I get to kick him."

The director was the perfect candidate for the CIA. He was cold-blooded. Absolutely heartless. No character.

"Well, no character with honor. A strange combination." Said Steve.

Sister Claire showed heart. She climbed over the seat; into the back where he was crying – crying a mournful country song.

"That's not appropriate," said Sister Claire.

Col. Bolan said, "Shoot the bastard. Put him out of his misery."

"Got to put his arm back in the sockets," said the Sister. "This is cruel."

I agreed.

"Hold him," I asked. I grabbed his left arm and flexed it quickly. He screamed.

"Back. It's back in the socket," Claire announced.

Bramwell was out again.

"At least, the crying has stopped," said Terri Bolan.

The Sister said, "Bishop. You're a good man, for helping this poisonous snake." She spoke with extreme formality. "Impossibly kind to the man, who ordered your wife tortured and killed."

"Silly," said Bolan. "By tomorrow you will regret the decision. He is the devil...pure evil."

I looked to see what I could do to give him relief from the pain in his leg.

"I don't see an injury. None that I can view."

"It may be his soul weeping," suggested the Sister.

I certainly did not like the man. I did not fathom his cruelty. Even so, I wasn't going to commit the same heinous act on him that he had ordered.

"It would be easier to practice cruelty. Walk with the devil." However, I smiled. A robust, strong one.

I thought to myself; Sister Claire's influence was rubbing off on me.

"Who knows − without you Claire, I might be a rouge."

The Nun looked at me with confusion.

I knew it was not so. I laughed again. I was dedicated as poet Robert Frost said, "Walking the road less traveled by." A little melodramatic. I also knew. However, it was true.

Back to reality. We were driving around city streets with the director of the CIA in the back of our car. It was no stretch of the imagination to understand we were officially Number One on the hit parade. If they wanted us dead before we grabbed Bramwell, now they wanted to barbeque us.

"Where are we going?" asked Bolan.

I knew Alexandria, Virginia well. I had been a government witness in a spy trial in the township some years before. I directed Terri Bolan to a remote parking garage. Traffic was light.

"Top floor. It's outdoors. No one goes all the way up," I instructed. We did. So we could be alone with Bramwell. The elevation and the outdoors would drown his pathetic crying.

Parked securely at the far end of the rooftop hangout. Steve would call out if anyone was venturing to the rooftop.

I slapped Bramwell on the face smartly. It took a couple more slaps to revive him.

Claire said, "Bramwell is going to have a 'time out' in the hospital when this is over." Always a quipster.

I nodded. He wasn't faking. The ladies did a number on him. I wondered whether Terri Bolan had delighted in treating him so roughly. She would like to kill him. Bolan's feelings were always clear.

I did not know the entire story between Bramwell and Bolan. However, I did know the director. The treacheries he routinely dished out.

"I wouldn't ask Terri. I knew she had her reasons for true hatred."

It took some time to get the director to the point where he could sit up. More time to where he could be questioned.

"Listen, director," Claire said. "I don't want to hurt you more than you already are. However, some of my colleagues will delight in seeing you tortured. You know Terri Bolan? Right?"

He looked at Bolan in certifiable fear. He actually shook when he saw her.

"You're going to get life in prison for this kidnap and torture," he agonized.

"You are going to die if you don't cooperate," Bolan said. "You think you hurt now. Wait 'til I pull your arm out of the socket again," she threatened. Bolan was serious.

"Remember my wife," I asked Bramwell.

"And you are a Bishop?" he cried. "How do you live with yourself."

"Priceless – Bramwell." I said.

"I want you Smith. You in my grips." Bramwell screamed, spitting blood.

"Remember thug, you told them to torture my wife, kill her and then had the temerity to pin a note to her breasts. I don't have a great deal of sympathy for you."

He moaned, but wisely said nothing.

"Director, make it easy – save your own life. Answer a few polite questions. And we will drop you off at the hospital," Claire said softly.

"Not answering anything."

"Bramwell, I know you. You are and always have been gutless – a screaming chicken," I said quietly.

"Claire, give me his arm," Terri Bolan screamed at him. "Let me wrench it out of his socket again." She wasn't fooling around. Bramwell knew too well that Terri Bolan was not blustering.

"No, please Joseph – God no. Don't let her."

"I am not God; however, you are on the right track when you say your prayers," I answered.

"Joseph. Please Joseph. Take me to the hospital."

"Director, what is going on? Why are you working with our enemies? Against America?"

He moaned, noticeably. He was in agony. Without touching him, he was tortured.

"I'm not. We are under attack from everywhere abroad. We are at war already; even if, the shooting has not sounded. In a week or two, North Korea or Iran will nuke us. Plain and simple."

Bramwell's declaration was almost a pronouncement of war. Clearly, some would consider him a lunatic. Others might say he was a clairvoyant. A Savior of sorts in his own right.

"A pre-emptive strike stands in the way of them over running us. Billions of them. If we don't wipe them out, while we have the chance, we will be a third-world country. We have to stop them now," screamed Bramwell in an agonized voice.

"What evidence? Show me the evidence," I pleaded.

"China is cutting off loans. They want their money. The **IAM** is preparing to nuke us. Shot a missile at us just the other day. A few feet more and it would have taken out part of Seattle."

The director was incoherent. "We need to take out China too while we have the chance. They have a billion people, but ..."

"Director. Are you planning on bombing all the IAM countries? I protested.

"Smith you were always such a purist. A sissy, so-called Priest. Can't see the requisite direction the we must take. Now! Immediately! Wipe them out."

"You are mad."

"Joseph, you are the dangerous one. The Muslims have all the oil. China has all the money. The Chinese and Muslims are ants. They will crawl over us and sting us. Now you can see why the brass decided to kill you."

I asked, "Who is 'we?' You said, 'we'—we must take."

Bramwell stopped his moaning. Lifted his head and looked me directly in the eyes.

"Well, for one, asshole. I have. You have done it this time. You have kidnapped the director of the CIA. You are dead."

He might well be right. However, the insane man painted the picture. Not a Renoir, but a masterpiece of cryptic nightmare. He – together with some other unknown rats – decided to genocide an entire religion. Then, pick on China – a country we called friends.

"How about Canada?" I asked sarcastically.

"If they embrace the IAM – yes." Said Bramwell.

"Worse than Hitler. Crazier than all the despots, who came before him," I theorized.

"Not so crazy at all," said Terri Bolan. "I despise the man. I want to kill him. However, he is correct. Islam wants all of us dead. They will keep coming until they kill us or put all Americans in chains."

Claire asked, "What has the man planned?"

"I don't know. He was mostly out-of-it." Steve said.

"He is behind this skullduggery. Even so, he said the 'brass ordered' – who are the brass?"

"Why would he order the torture and killing of your wife?" The Nun asked.

Bolan said, "That question I can answer. He has killed innocents his entire life. Tried to kill me once. Raped me. Then tried to kill me. A friend saved me. He wanted to hang me by my breasts. He's a sadist."

The director was revived enough to question again. Barely. He was in and out of consciousness.

I asked, "Director. Are you the brains behind this insanity?"

"Wouldn't you like to know? You can't stop it. Too much tooth paste has come out of the tube. Them or us. Bottom line. The IAM wants our hide."

"Who is calling the shots? You have used Sister Claire and me. Had us traveling around the country—saying that we are in cahoots with the IAM."

Bramwell made a twisted face of genuine evil. It was a true picture to his soul.

"What's more, that was the best part," he said with delight. "Better than killing your wimp of a wife. You got America believing that Muslims are here in the United States attacking us. Palmdale was classic. You killed American citizens under orders to take you into custody. They were guarding a plane. Stupid."

"I was told the troops were Muslim invaders." I protested.

"Well, the way it has played is that the good guys were protecting the defense plants. The Muslims – you and your bitch girlfriend, the Sister – shot the hell out of American agents. We even got your rifle. Used it to assassinate the United States Senator."

He gave a loud, tortured laugh.

"Explain that dummy – at your trial. Unless, we cut you to pieces before that," he crowed.

Bramwell might be crazy. Nonetheless, he was a strategic nightmare. A planner. Just right for the crazies at the CIA. Claire and I had helped advance his sinister plot.

"You are dead. You and the silly Nun are dead. You merely haven't fallen over yet."

He was out again. This time I could not revive him.

"He's dying. We are killing him," said Claire. "He may be garbage, but we can't take his life."

"Why not. Do the world a favor," said Bolan.

I also knew that unless we got him to the hospital, NOW – he was going to die. The Sister was right. Even though, it is also true that we were putting our necks in a noose by letting him go. His testimony alone might get us a death sentence.

"You are right, Sister."

Bolan said, "He believes he is aiding the United States. He is the head of the CIA. True, he is a piece of shit. He knows the truth – knows those religious zealots will evaporate America. If not stopped now – it is a case of them or us."

"Really?" Said Claire. "Killing a billion people is your idea of justice?"

Back in the car, Steve agreed. "It's apparent Bramwell believes it's now or never. It's like Bramwell is encouraging the President to attack all the Muslim people before they hit us. Forget negotiations."

"Apparently, the Bishop and the Nun have been flying around the country, and the CIA tells the world our exploits are the work of Muslim extremists. Helping to sell his cause," I told Steve.

Then, Steve had a rare moment. A sense of humor. "You both are under arrest. Stick up your hands."

Sister Claire didn't realize he was kidding. She took him in a headlock. Steve actually flipped her over the seat and caught her. Laughing.

She wasn't amused. However, Claire realized he was so strong – she would leave the bear alone. No punches to the arm.

The tense situation was anything, but funny. I remembered the nuclear explosion in Jask, which was also, no doubt, the strategy of the CIA. Start a war now. While we can win.

"We might have already nuked them once," Claire agreed.

"I still think we should throw him on the side of the road," said Terri Bolan. "Right or not. He is not worth a dime."

I returned to the front seat. Started the car. And took off for the hospital to save him. Sister Claire pulled Bramwell close, comforting him. Compassion for a man, who had none.

"Easy, director. We're on the way to the hospital."

Bramwell was out. He didn't hear the too-kind words from the Sister.

I repeated his admonitions to my peers. "Clearly – as whacked as Aaron Bramwell is – some of his points have merit. There are a billion Muslims. Many of them would like us dead."

"Now or never. Is he correct? Playing God is never the path." I said.

I remembered from history lessons the suggestion that the President had allowed Pearl Harbor to be attacked. This before we entered World War II. Some said he needed all citizens to support the war. Let a few die to save the country. Otherwise, mothers would not send their sons to die on foreign soils.

"Was this another case where the President was salting the mine? Did the President believe we were headed to war? Was he drumming up universal support? Was the IAM about to attack us?

My stomach was twisted in knots. Who sent me—the LDS Bishop and the Catholic Nun on the mission in the first place? Was the President behind the misery? How had the Pope been tricked?

"Was the Four-Star General wrong when he said our President is a man of peace? That the leader of the free world is trying to reconcile with foreign leaders. Had the President – who is Catholic – consulted with the Pope? Had he asked for help? If so, why?" I asked.

"Certainly, he is a good man. He wouldn't order my wife killed. I wasn't seeing the entire picture." I said to myself.

"Is the **IAM** going to nuke us?" asked Steve. "If yes, that is a game changer."

Claire said, "I do not believe the IAM has a nuke. Certainly, they can't deliver it. They don't have a rocket that will carry the payload over here."

Bolan said, "Maybe, not today. The point is that they will shortly. Tomorrow or the next day."

"So we should kill billions of innocents today?" I asked her.

"To protect my children, perhaps." She answered.

The woman, who came on the mission because of so much hatred for Aaron Bramwell, had now accepted his point of view.

"It really is not that surprising that Hitler got so many Germans behind him. Sell an untruth and watch them march. People are truly gutless," I said somewhat disappointed. "This crazy bugger who ordered the slaying of my wife has nearly convinced a combat soldier to nuke the Muslim world."

Bolan said nothing.

I was driving fast, so I could not see her facial response. Words were not quick in coming.

"Yes. If we have incontrovertible evidence that the IAM is going to war with us, we should attack first. Why have Americans killed innocently?" Bolan said sincerely. She finally gave a military decree.

"All-out attack. Fire nukes from the subs, aircraft carriers, and send the supersonic bombers to the Middle East?" I asked.

"Yes."

It appeared, she had made the argument for the Bramwell group. He was in a position to tilt the scales. However, he did not control the nukes. There was the Congress and the President.

"Hopefully they are more cautious. Demand absolute proof. Ask for inspection of nuke sites in IAM countries," Claire responded.

Steve asked, "Do we have the bombers, ships, subs and drones that can carry enough payload to get the job done? To wipe them off the face of the earth."

I asked, "Steve, is that what you want?"

"No. Absolutely not."

"Only one question," Claire asked.

"What is that?"

"How does killing us with sniper's rifles from roof tops in Alexandria, Virginia, help defeat the Muslims?" Asked Sister Claire Coogan.

I did not answer.

Chapter 38

CROROROROR

BIRDS OF A FEATHER

There wasn't a word in the car – other than the moans from Bramwell. The short drive for medical assistance was made in silence.

"I am out," said Terri Bolan, without explanation when we reached the hospital. "No more for me."

I pulled up to the side of the hospital. Away from cameras and people. She calmly opened the car door and walked. Not one more word. Gone.

"Help me Steve. Let's get the director out of the car. We'll prop him against the wall. After, I will call nurses for assistance. We can't be seen," I said.

"Sure."

Steve and I worked as an oiled machine. No wasted motion. The director was picked up as easily as we could, and placed against the hospital wall. He never moved. Only grunts and louder moans.

Claire called the hospital. And delivered clear instructions where we put him.

"He is the director of the CIA. Give him priority service." She argued for his life. No qualms. No misunderstanding.

Once he was propped, I took out the note that was placed on my wife's chest.

"You probably want this back, director," I said – folding it unceremoniously in his pocket.

"Shooting him probably would have felt better, Bishop," observed Steve.

"Nope, the realization that the Bishop knows Bramwell ordered the killing is better medicine," observed Claire.

Back in the car, Steve looked in the direction that Terri Bolan had walked. She was gone. Out of sight.

"What's up with Terri?" he inquired.

"I am not certain."

Claire said, "I think the director's response shook her up. She's wondering if she's on the right side."

"Could be," I agreed.

We drove out of Alexandria moving at the speed limit.

"If anything," Steve said, "Her leaving our party makes us look much less noticeable. They will be looking for an army. Not three of us."

Claire with a wry smile said, "But what are the three of us going to do against an Army?"

"Maybe, that's why Terri fled the coop," said Steve.

"No. Terri is brave to the death. She may believe in the director's theory. His notion that we should kill them before the IAM takes an opportunity to destroy life in the United States," I said on reflection.

I added, "Steve, we need to ditch the car. Can't count on Terri. She may spill about what we're driving."

"Others may have seen it behind the law offices, or near the scene of the shootout," Steve agreed.

Claire busily communicated with the hospital. She wanted assurance the director had been recovered. Was receiving first-class treatment.

"They have him. Asked who I was," she said. "I hung up."

Steve and I worked mentally on finding a new vehicle.

A thunderbolt struck me. I knew where the director parked his off-duty vehicle. He was fastidious – washing the car so much that the paint wore down to the primer. The obsession was a legion. Everyone knew it.

"Let's borrow Bramwell's car," I reported.

"Dangerous?" Steve said.

I didn't wait for approval, turning left and then left again. We were approximately six or seven miles from the pickup point.

As I drove through town, an additional precaution hit me. I pulled up in front of a cell phone store.

"They might recognize me, Steve. Buy five new, burner phones."

Sister Claire jumped out of the car, about the same time as the ranger. She went another direction.

Steve didn't break stride, but yelled back, "Is she abandoning ship too?"

"No." I said, with conviction.

I had no idea where she was going. I knew, however, that someone who wears a Nun's habit, runs through crowded streets, jumps over fences, knocks the CIA directors unconscious, and faces death unrelentingly is not about to abandon a friend.

"Furthermore, she was the one going back for Harry Ayres, at the shootout. Dead or alive. She hardly knew Ayres. The bottom line – I haven't a clue where she was going.   She would be back. I guarantee," I said to myself.

In five minutes, both were back in the car. Steve had seven phones, and Claire had an assortment of wigs and hair extensions.

"I'll change everyone's appearance," she laughed.

"I'm wearing no damn wig. I will die first," cringed Steve.

"You might." I said.

Steve added, "Seven phones were all they had. I would have bought more."

The New Acquisition

Arriving at Bramwell's remote parking lot, Steve moved first. "I'll handle this."

"Ranger, you can't drive out the front door."

"Not an idiot."

Claire and I drove around the block. And found Steve driving the freshly polished Lincoln town car over the sidewalk.

"He thinks he has a Humvee," Claire said.

"He would drive it up the side of the building, if that is needed."

His diversion was flawless. He went out the back of the parking structure, where no one would consider that a $60-thousand automobile would be driven.

Once back on the asphalt, Steve signaled for us to follow. We did. We drove for fifteen minutes. We found a secure location for Claire's Rome rental car.

"Lose the Suburban," instructed Steve from a rolled down window. "My turn to drive."

"I remember the last time you drove."

"Bishop, we made it out, didn't we?"

"I wet my pants, however."

"You're not afraid of land-mines, enemy fire or...."

Claire was unreasonably quiet. I thought she might be tired because of all the excitement.

Then, with an amused smile, she said, "This is what we do. First, drive me, so I can rent another car on a different credit card."

I am sure I was the one looking confused now.

"Ok. So...you are great with credit cards. We already have a car," I said.

"Yeah. One that will be missed shortly. Then, there will be an all-points bulletin. They no doubt have a tracker on Bramwell's car. Don't you think?"

I look sheepishly at her.

"You're right."

"But the diversion of taking the car will send the CIA a false clue." She smiled. "They will look for us near where we abandon his car."

She was like the cat that ate the birdie.

"But I did enjoy the shenanigans of Steve stealing the director's auto. Priceless. You two were so cute," Claire laughed. "In the final analysis, the ruse will send our detractors on an end run. If you don't mind a football analogy." She winked.

I said nothing. She was on the mark.

We looked up car rentals and found one some distance away. She had me park down the street. Claire hoofed it into the rental yard.

Shortly, she left the lot with a white Chevy Malibu. She still was smiling – almost laughing.

"So, what's that funny," I asked her, after we parked the Bramwell car in a rarely used, back alley.

"Let's call everyone and tell them that we stole Bramwell's car. That we are driving it through the gates at the White House. We plan, if necessary, to take the unorthodox action to bring this Opp to a conclusion."

I still knew I was missing something.

"What we will do is give everyone a slightly different picture of where we are and what we are going to do. Then, the winner loses," she said.

I got it. We tell Padgett one story, call Terri Bolan and tell her another, and down the line. Whoever shows up to pluck our feathers is the enemy. No risk. High reward.

We were now following what I named Operation Claire. We started to drive to a secure location; from which, we could sleuth the possible Bramwell accomplices.

The ranger was a little behind the power curve. He was the best when it came to executing a plan. Not so outstanding at making them.

"I think Terri left us because she couldn't see us taking that piece of scum – the director – to the hospital." Steve said.

I thought, we had already covered this issue. I said nothing.

Claire asked, "Aren't you afraid she will tell the authorities that Steve is involved? That will endanger the children."

"She's not doing that," Steve said.

I agreed. "Not the type. She would die first. She will take a vacation."

"Padgett is somehow tied in with Bramwell; I think," said Claire.

Steve added, "Two strange birds. Likely, they would flock together."

Chapter 39

অ্যঅ্যঅ্যঅ্যঅ্য

EVERYONE BUILDING
MARBLES FOR WAR

I called the Four Star to no avail. The phone rang incessantly. I tried Chad Caden; however, the line was picked up by Kaci Haber.

"Where's Chad?"

"Is this Joseph?" Kaci asked.

"Kaci? Where's Chad?"

There was silence.

"Joseph, I closed the door here at Langley. Chad's gone to the White House. You're being hunted as America's number one most wanted. As a Muslim spy. Please. Come on in."

I thought for a second, before responding. "I never have abandoned a mission in my life."

"The mission is dead. You will be too if you don't stop. Please come to Langley."

"I've called my assigning officer, but can't reach him. I have no instructions to call off my actions. It's the same as it was when we first met. Do you know exactly what is going on?"

"No. Other than we're hunting you!"

'Where's Padgett?"

Kaci said, "A... here at Langley. You understand. I am not at FBI headquarters. I've been ordered here with the CIA."

"Why?"

"Top Secret."

"Come on Kaci. Tell, something."

"You took out the director; furthermore, shot several military officers; China has refused any additional loans; and Saudi Arabia has said 'no more fuel.' Is that enough? Oh, and I forgot. Your fingerprint is on the trigger of the gun that killed the Senator."

"Say what? I assassinated the Senator?" I queried. I already knew that was the CIA hoax. I wasn't admitting it – no matter what.

Kaci said unbelieving, "Same rifle that killed the men in Palmdale. I don't believe it. However, how do you explain the facts?"

"What a patsy. A fool. They hand me a gun. Allegedly, to protect a war plane. After, they retrieve the weapon. Ship it to Washington to assassinate the Senator." I said to myself.

I said, "Find out when I can call Caden. In fact, I will call back in an hour."

Kaci said, "You might be dead in half the time."

"Rather dead than see America shriveled up."

"If you are alive, call back. Joseph – turn yourself in. We won't shoot you."

"Kaci. I'm not so certain."

We both had spoken in clipped conversation, so the time on the phone was hopefully untraceable. Kaci still believed. If she was on our side, so was Chad.

Better said – as long as Chad Caden believed in me, I was okay with Kaci and many others in the FBI.

I searched for the same burner phone I had used to call Brian Pentland. Perhaps, I could wheedle something out of him. That is, of course, if he knew anything other than his own name. I dialed.

"Joseph, you're a gutsy bastard, if nothing else," said Brian.

"Can't enjoy your pearls of wisdom for long Bri. Have you spoken to the President?"

He answered, "I verified my mission. You're wanted 'dead' – not alive. Dead."

"Dead or alive?"

"No. Like Osama bin Laden – dead only."

"Never been so important. I must be getting close to the nerve center."

I almost could see him nodding.

"Exactly."

"I'll keep in touch. If you know anything, call this number and leave a message. I am not a spy." I told him.

"You are not. I know. But I have..."

I cut him off, "I know you have orders."

I hung up. A lot of information. Only a few seconds on the cell phone. Brian Pentland was telling me, indirectly, that the order had come from above.

"What's above the CIA director?" I knew. I just didn't want to say it.

Claire said, "The President."

We pulled over at a burger joint, because we hadn't eaten in a long while. Steve was unilaterally going for a gluttonous feast. Might be his last, he deduced.

I thought about the President. He was the first elected Hispanic to the highest office. And he had moved into the White House only a few months before.

If it had been Barack Obama still in the Oval Office, I might have thought of all the jokes about him being a Muslim. Perhaps, I could make a case for nonsense. But, then again, why would he want to nuke all the Muslims?

"But the new President? A Republican? A Hispanic? I found the suggestion implausible. I didn't believe it," I said out loud.

"Who else? He's the only one it could be," Claire announced. "I don't like it. It's him."

I rolled the information over-and-over in my mind. The campaign where camouflaged-conservatives had retaken the highest office. They had promised the American public "peace, prosperity, and apple pie."

Men were still out of work. Families were without food. The Democrats ruled with the national debt expanding beyond imagination. Everyone knew the balloon had to explode.

The poor and unemployed did not riot. They switched parties.

In truth, there was a strong, militant faction which had funded the parade to the Presidency. They wanted to cut the frivolous spending on the poor, and increase mechanization for the military.

The President was a smart, caring man – who sees the party from kinder, gentler days.

I tuned in a talk radio station in Washington DC.

"Why do you want to listen to that crap?" Asked Steve.

"We're substantially behind the power curve."

Claire asked, "What are you thinking, Joe?"

"Bramwell was following orders. Someone's orders. Brian Pentland is a good American and taking instruction from above. Whose orders? Why?"

"Maybe, he is following his own orders. Like the Senator – signing a blank check. Falsely giving orders from above?"

"Doubt it," I said.

Claire asked, "You're thinking world events are dictating American policy?"

"Do you think our government wants me dead because China needs the United States to repay the loan? Would the President set us up to be killed? Leave us out in the cold? How does that compute?"

"It doesn't."

"There's a missing link. There has been one from the beginning."

"We thought it was Bramwell." Claire said.

"I still do. You suckers turned him loose," Steve poked at us. "He played possum. He is already back at Langley. Now the spooks will hunt us down."

"Could be," said Claire. "However, he was truly hurt."

Talk radio was abuzz about the failed North Korean missile strike, which landed miles from our shore. Other commentators were saying that America is so weak that China wants its money. Without the Chinese, we can't buy fuel and essential products.

Tom Fool, as I jokingly referred to the announcer, said, "Now the IAM and the Saudis say no more oil."

The caller said, "So, Tom, what's your move?"

Then, the great-dummy aligned himself unknowingly with the director, "I would nuke all of them. Kill them Muslims. Make the land over there not habitable. We can still get their oil for free."

One of the most knowledgeable talk radio commentators on a different station said the strife was a combination of the **IAM**, North Korea, Syria, and other Muslim countries pulling together.

"But if they don't sell their damned oil to us, it will rot in the ground."

Another caller theorized that the compact of nearly 20 nations, including China, posed a substantial military and economic threat to the United States.

Steve was a great hand with a rifle, or looking for a forest fires at a ranger station. He was no strategist. He was becoming riled.

"We going to sit here all day? Just waiting for them to hunt us down?" He was tired of waiting. He would run in circles, rather than sit still.

I told him, "Better than colliding with their snipers."

Claire finally picked up one of the burner phones and called Rome. Since it was not a number her clergy recognized, it took some time to get through to the Pope.

"We are sitting ducks over here. We need some definition as to our task," she said politely. "They say they want the Bishop Dead, only dead."

Claire listened intently. Nodding her head, she said, "Certainly." She nodded again, and another time.

Off the phone, Claire said, "The Vatican's extremely concerned about a nuclear war. We are fearful that millions – if not billions – will die. Afraid the USA will fire on the Muslims."

I noticed that she had joined with Rome by saying, "**We** are afraid."

"Claire, who is going to start firing Nukes? Why does the Vatican believe there's going to be a nuclear war?" I asked.

I had never seen her so deflated. Even when my wife had died, she was attempting to comfort me. There was warmth and a hopeful belief. Now, there was only grave concern.

She put her head in her hands. Down on her lap. Claire was normally a ray of light – a fresh air. The call has made her despondent.

"Rumblings on both sides of the pond. Our Cardinals throughout the world are reporting strong evidence the world's powers will throw down with nuclear mite," she said in a whisper.

I asked, "Do they believe countries, including North Korea and the IAM, have nuclear capabilities?"

She nodded somberly.

"Yes - absolutely."

Chapter 40

ରେରେରେରେର

FAITH

"Bishop, how do you do it?" Claire asked.

"Do what?"

"Your wife is killed. They torture her. They mock you. You are on a bended knee for five minutes. Then, you are back hatching another plan to save the country. How?"

"I believe wholeheartedly in divine goodness and intervention."

"I do, also. But, still..."

"Mormons know America was established by the power of the Father. Our founders were spiritual leaders. Our constitution was inspired by Heavenly Father and Jesus." I announced sincerely.

I added, "It serves a greater purpose than setting up a stable government, under which freedom will prevail. A land prepared, through the Constitution, for the restoration of the gospel. That's how I get up and march on."

"You really have faith that God imbued the framers of the Constitution."

I answered, "Absolutely. That is why countries try so hard to disrupt America and the Constitution. Their efforts are truly the devil's work."

"All Mormons feel the same?" Claire asked.

"Yes; although – probably – not as fervently as I do."

Claire had a sober expression. I guessed she was wondering whether I had gone off my noodle. Lost my mind.

"Life on earth is a significant test for the hereafter. I know I will live again with my mother and father, all of my relatives and those who followed Christ. Yes, be with Nancy. Forever."

"You're talking about mankind having belief in Jesus. Christ taking upon himself the sins of mankind. Dying so we might live. I get it. Your belief in being with your wife again subdues revenge."

"Yes."

I nodded my head. Mormons are missionary minded people. I wanted to spend the next many days talking to her about heavenly matters other than war, nuclear attacks and those chasing us. It would have to wait for tomorrow. If there will be a tomorrow.

"On Claire, I had never seen the pure and innocent look that I beheld on her face at that moment. She had quit being a Marine because she believed in charity, love, and grace. Not killing. The pure love of Christ was written on her beautiful face."

Claire believed in a world united in doing good. Saving the starving and dying children in Africa. The Muslims, the Catholics and the Mormons. Protestants and Jews. She accepted the orders from the Pope. Came home to the United States for the good of all.

She believed in Jesus Christ. Believed his words as recorded by Apostle Paul "that her sins were forgiven, and she would be with God in Heaven." She did her best to evidence the love of Christ by works that she provided to humanity.

In my view, she believed much more than some so-called religious people, who claim that have faith but go to church twice a year.

Steve finally chipped in, "Are you two going to pray yourselves to death."

I said nothing.

"We need to figure out where we go from here." He said firmly. "Now. Not in the hereafter."

Claire said, "We will. Be patient. Joe will find a hole in this misery."

Steve said nothing.

"If he fails," Claire said, "I will slap him silly."

Chapter 41

ଔଔଔଔଔ

WHEN DOES A LIE,
BECOME THE TRUTH?

I tried unsuccessfully several more times to talk to the Four Star. Was he intentionally avoiding me? Too busy for me? Ultimately, I left a message for him.

A message of sincere concern. I included within the message what I had learned from Kaci and Pentland. I was wanted "dead." I told him so. I asked, "Why Four Star – why does the CIA want me dead – when I am doing the country's work?"

I asked Steve and Claire, "Is the President preventing the old man from calling me?"

I knew the general monitored the number sparingly – only when he got ready. He had told me a number of times, "I am God when it comes to you."

Furthermore, the Four Star had direct and hourly contact with the President. If something was underway at the White House, I deduced he would know. He had the most insight.

Nevertheless, he was the person – other than the President – who was most busy.

Steve said, "This group doesn't make life easy."

"Hey, Steve, hold it together," I said, with a smile. I had on a 'smiley face' – as children would say – even though, I did not feel like exuding one.

Claire certainly was not smiling. She was in the dumps.

Not being able to get a hold of the Four Star, I tried to re-contact Chad Caden. As I promised.

The phone rang and was picked up on its first ring. I reasoned the FBI and CIA probably had ears listening. Padgett, maybe?

"This is Joseph Smith for Chad Caden," I said.

"One minute please."

I hung up. It was clear to me the agency was in a delay mode. They wanted to get a trace. I waited five minutes. Then, I reinitiated the call.

"Look, I'm not staying on the line for trace. I want Chad Caden now. No delays."

A beleaguered and stressed Kaci Haber came on the line.

"Joseph?"

"Yes, where is Caden?"

"Still at the White House."

"Kaci, not nice to trace friends."

"Orders."

"Tell Noah Padgett, I'll talk to him later. Chad would not order a trace."

I hung up.

"Do you think your friend is really at the White House?"

"Absolutely. Otherwise, he would've taken the phone. He's a straight shooter. Even if he has orders to tell us to drop-dead, he would have talked to me," I responded strongly.

My conviction was only half banter. Perhaps, my friend Chad was in trouble over me. They might have concluded he set up the director.

Steve wondered, "Still asking if we're waiting to be captured? We just sit here like idiots."

I started feeling a prompting from within that we were in danger. Over the years, I had learned to follow inner signs. They did not lead me astray.

Steve had faith in continual action. Not in God. He had been telling us to move for nearly an hour.

"Drive Steve."

"Where?"

As we negotiated the busy streets, I had a strong impression where to go. The concept would be impossible to explain to nonbelievers. I long ago understood the clear prompting that some call the subconscious. To me the Holy Ghost. Instruction about "right" or "wrong," if one actually listens.

Since I had been a Bishop, there had been much clear direction. Mostly, for ward members. However, in unusual situations, I received direction from above for me. Uncanny things.

Claire looked at me with an understanding smile.

"Bishop?" She said knowingly.

"Yes."

"Where are we going?"

"We are headed the correct direction. I'll know the exact spot when I see it."

"You're not suddenly Brigham Young are you? Heading us to Salt Lake," kidded Claire. "No handcarts for me, Bishop."

Steve looked hopelessly confused. "You two," he said, shaking his head at both Claire and me.

The Surprise Guest

As we drove, I had an idea. I had Claire dial information for the popular talk radio show of Thad Diamond.

He is highly entertaining, controversial, and listened to by everyone in Washington. From the bum on the street to the President, Thad Diamond had an immense following.

Calling in, I explained to the operator that I was America's number one "most-wanted" FBI agent, Joseph Smith. Some called me the assassin. I had the verifying information for the producer.

I am the type guest radio hosts dream about. There was no delay.

"This is Thad. You're on the air."

"Hi, Thad. This is FBI agent Joseph Smith. I understand the FBI wants me DEAD – not alive."

"Is that right?"

"As I understand it."

"Why?"

"Well, I don't know Thad. I suspect one of your listeners – perhaps, a United States Senator, maybe, even the President, can answer that for us."

The commentator was openly excited. He had never had someone open up with such controversial frankness.

"Is this classified?"

"I don't know Thad; I can't get anybody to talk to me. They've killed my wife; they sent snipers at me, and I'm told America is at risk for a nuclear confrontation. What do you think?"

"Is this really Joseph Smith?"

"Certainly. Have someone call the FBI. Ask for Kaci Haber. Have her tune you in. She can tell you that I'm Joseph Smith.

Alternatively, get the President on the line. He can verify my identity."

"Well," said the host. No words for once.

"Thad, I'm looking for answers. For our country. For democracy. What's going on?"

"You're the FBI – don't you know?"

"I'm out in the cold. I don't have the answers. However, before we get sucked into something beyond comprehension, I hope someone can give us all the straight answers."

"Yeah..."

"That's enough for now Thad. I'm sure some of your listeners will be able to answer frankly."

I hung up. There was bedlam on the radio as they tried to sort out the information. The broadcaster promised calls to the FBI, the White House, and the CIA. He said he would attempt to have a comment from a Senator.

He said, "What we do know is that North Korean spies momentarily captured CIA chief Bramwell."

Obviously a lie. Since we had accomplished the act. I wondered who released that piece of misinformation?

Thad continued, "Bramwell later was reported in a Beltway hospital. Further, there have been reports of Muslim and Islamic attacks on defense plants. They're attempting to obtain our most classified aircraft. They are shooting missiles at us," reported the talk show dignitary. For once, he was trying to give an accurate account.

Diamond reported that the Congress and US Senate have been closed sessions on the Hill. The talk show host added that both the anti-terrorist's task force of the FBI and the CIA have been in day-long meetings with the President."

Good. Now we gained some information. The FBI's top anti-terrorist guy, Chad Caden, might actually be at the White House.

Thad went on expounding and recapping from data released to him. A parade of facts and lies—released by the FBI.

"Our last guest—Joseph Smith—is an FBI spy. So the agency claims. He's on the run. He is pretending not to know why—says 'he's out in the cold.' Yet, why wouldn't he know his fate, since he was the person who executed a sitting United States Senator?"

I thought, another lie. A gigantic whopper this time."

I knew from the broadcast that the FBI, CIA or the President had released information aimed at my heart. Had I been in the web from the outset? A sacrificial lamb?

I flashed back to the start of the mission—they killed my partner with a bomb in Santa Monica. Shortly, after I met Claire. I was the chosen scapegoat from the initial blowing up of my car.

"The Santa Monica fool," said Claire, winking. "I knew I shouldn't have trusted you. If I were smart, I would have gone inside the Catholic church there in Santa Monica and prayed."

I knew she was jerking my chain; however, if she had visited the priest in Santa Monica instead of starting on this clandestine mission, she would not be in trouble.

"I played my role to perfection. Muslims were accused for havoc at the race track. Later, for killings at the defense plant. I had been stupefying in my role. I had run around the country playing directly into Bramwell's plot."

It now was evident the military, and the agencies were targeting me.

"It's all wrong," cried Claire. "All lies."

"Not all. They put some truth in a hat, shook it up with lies, and dispersed it. Tell a lie enough times, and it becomes the truth. All the pieces are present. Just mixed up."

"I'd rather run through a brick wall. Don't like figuring out crap," said Steve, looking tense.

"We confirmed some important facets. Caden is no doubt at the White House. People in high places are giving the American people misinformation for a reason.

"Probably, trying to justify a nuclear event. Furthermore, wanting us dead is part of the plot," I told my peers.

"How does killing us help them succeed?" Claire queried, getting back to investigator mode.

"If we are IAM spies, killing us proves that Muslims are attacking America, for example. If we are alive, we can talk. They don't want the truth. They want misinformation."

"They want the lie to become the truth," said Steve. Finally, he got it.

She nodded her head. "DEAD – we are evidence of the plot. We ran around the United States confirming the attack by the IAM."

"Afraid so," I confirmed.

Chapter 42

ଯେଯେଯେଯେଯେ

UNCERTAINTY

The most senior US Senator, together with the Speaker of the House of the Representatives, appeared at a joint news conference within an hour of the broadcast.

Clearly, the conference was called to put out the fire started when I dropped my bomb on the Diamond show.

"We are urging patience. There has been a cry for a declaration of war, or in the alternative, an embargo against the countries that have infiltrated the United States," said the Senator.

"We see no proof – no reason for immediate alarm. The White House is urging calm. We are in negotiations."

The confab was on the steps to the Capital building. The day was beautiful. Everyone would agree. Temperatures – mid-70 degrees, a slight breeze. However, no one was taking about the weather.

Journalists were screaming, "What about the missile?"

"What about the sniper; the killing of a US Senator."

Some of the screams were obscenities. Journalists were mocking the leaders for inaction.

311

The declaration from the Senator was meant to calm. It had the opposite effect.

If it was possible to build a bomb shelter in a day, contractors could have sold many millions. It brought back the days that President John F. Kennedy had a standoff with the Soviets.

A tanker floating toward a line drawn in the sea. A possible nuclear war with the Russians. We were there again. Possible war with the world.

"This time we might be an under-dog against the world. Hitler had aspirations of dictating to everyone. He died in a bunker," I said.

Claire responded, "He didn't have 10,000 nuclear warheads."

There was no comment from the White House. The President said nothing.

As hard as I tried to drive Chad Caden or the Four Star into a conference call, I had no success. Every time I called the FBI, I got the runaround.

I am an anti-terrorist task force FBI agent assigned to the White House, yet no one at the agency will talk with me.

"Strange. Impossible to explain."

Claire said, "Maybe not if the President believes we assassinated a sitting US Senator."

"Claire, you really think he is out of the loop with the Four Star joined to his hip?"

We were in a parking structure in Maryland, across from Alexandria, Virginia. Close to where we had our showdown with the director. My inclination was to stay in sight of Washington, but not too near.

"See, but not be seen." Claire said.

"But who will we be confronting? And more importantly, why?" I asked.

The newscast ended with the hordes screaming for answers. Still, the President said nothing.

Intervention By An Inspired Nun

Once coming out of her doldrums, Sister Claire was deep in thought. She looked through her iPhone contacts, saying, "No... No. No... Well, maybe... No... No, absolutely NO... Perhaps...."

I was working with a collection of throwaway phones, and Claire had an encrypted iPhone, with all the luxuries of home.

Sister Claire dialed. "Cardinal, excuse my interruption and interference with your prayers and your day. This is Sister Claire Coogan, who..."

"I know who you are," the Cardinal said.

"Cardinal, my apologies. The reason for my call is to avert world calamity. I'm in the United States on a mission for the Vatican."

"I'm one of five Cardinals who consulted with the Pope. I told him you might be able to find traction in the United States – stop the unthinkable," said the soft-spoken religious leader.

"I need your input from your region."

"Sister, pray. We are expecting drones and missiles carrying nuclear warheads to be rained from the sky. Here, leaders are rounding up people who they say are American spies. Innocent men and women are being jailed. Or worse."

"How do we get through this – a path for both sides?"

"This is long in coming. I see no escape," the Cardinal said.

"Do you see the United States as the aggressor?"

"Yes, Americans will pompously pound their chest. And say they are the world's most powerful. Fire death at the IAM, North

Korea, Pakistan and any other country that steps out of line. Even, possibly, China. That is not God's way."

"So it's all on us over here?"

"No, there is treachery everywhere. I am near the seat of conflict. In the North, they conspire with Iran, Pakistan and others," he said. "They are tired of being ruthlessly ruled."

As she listened, I tried to interrupt. I wanted to know with whom she was talking. And where?

The Cardinal said, "Sister, is there any way you can get the superpower to step down? To show restraint?"

"Will try."

"I understand you are working with a Mormon Bishop?"

"I am." She said.

"Remind him the Bible is all about wars. It's time for the Lord's message of love to rule."

"Cardinal, I believe we've had enough conflict."

"What really matters, Sister, is allegiance to God. All the conflicts will be resolved in Heaven. We don't need to put each other in Hell here on Earth."

"Do you know whether any of the adversaries in the IAM, including North Korea, Iran, Pakistan, or China have a nuclear weapon?"

"Confidentially, they do. Many."

"Cardinal I hope to see you in Rome. Unaffected by war or innuendo."

"Amen to that Sister. Pray."

Off the phone, I pressed Claire for any insight she may have gained from the call.

"Two things, the IAM have nuclear weapons. They are willing to use them in defense. They may hit the US offensively, as well." She said.

"A weapon – they have one warhead. They'd better have many. Otherwise, they will be annihilated. The United States has enough in its arsenal to wipe all the Muslim countries off the map."

Claire said, "The question is who will fire first. It's like teenage kids playing 'chicken' with their cars."

I thought for a second, internalizing her comments. Serious information from the Cardinal.

"Who Sister? Who was the mystery guest-on the line?"

"Micholas the 94 years old, South Korean Cardinal. He served as Archbishop of Seoul until retirement. If you call his life a retirement."

And my Nun friend had him on speed dial. I couldn't even reach my superiors.

Micholas was an educated man. The Cardinal studied chemical engineering at the Seoul National University. This man may have insight when it came to bombs. He wasn't a radical. Although very strong.

"Well, what do you think my good Sister?"

"Similar to your trust of Chad Caden, I trust my friend the Cardinal. He's close to the action. He is not seen by those around him as a threat. Although a Catholic, people know his heart is pure," she replied.

"So?"

"I believe the Pope was correct in sending me here to stop the nuclear attack."

I winked at her. "No doubt, you're the 'Live Wire' we need – if we're to stop the insanity."

"You must connect with either the Four Star, or Chad Caden. No one else is close enough to the President," she reasoned. "Can you call the President direct?

"No, you may be able to call the Pope or the Cardinals on a second's notice. I don't have the President on my speed dial. As to the Four Star and Chad, you know I have tried. Should I send up smoke signals?"

A news bulletin was broadcast from the American Broadcast affiliate: "The armed forces' and both houses of Congress are meeting to determine whether a declaration of war should be voted, and against whom."

The tone was grim.

The Vice President of United States, who serves as Senate pro tem, sent the short handwritten note for broadcast.

"The President prays for calm; your leaders are at work determining the best course of action."

"What a drip," said Steve. "A trained monkey would have told us more."

We stayed stationary, so we couldn't be spotted from the sky. Claire was next to me in the front seat, with Steve sprawled out amidst the guns and armament in the rear.

"One thing's for certain."

"What's that Bishop?" Steve asked.

"It appears, you were sent into the field as sacrificial lambs to stir up anger and animosity. To be blamed by everyone, including the Muslims and the North Koreans. And I was crazy enough to buy in with you."

Claire was nodding. She agreed.

"We need to react with vigor," I said. I thought to myself, what does that mean? Lame."

I turned and looked at the Sister. She was smiling gently, making mocking clapping sounds with her hands.

"Running for President? Preparing stump speeches?"

Chapter 43

ଔଔଔଔଔଔ

WAITING FOR ANNIHILATION

I tried the Bureau, and no one picked up in the anti-terrorist task force offices. Strange. I checked the number on my cell. I dialed correctly. The number was the direct line to Caden and the task force. Very strange.

"I've been locked out."

"Worst news," Steve said. "We are the hunted."

"Morbid," said Claire.

"No. Truthful," replied Steve.

I dialed Chad Caden's home telephone number; even though, I knew where he was. And he was certainly not at home.

On the third ring, Chad's wife of 40 years answered.

"Hello," she said in a husky voice. Toni invariably spoke with hoarse, raspy tones. When her kids were young, they always had to do a double-take to know if mom was mad at them.

"Hi Toni,"

There was a gap in the conversation as the now great-grandmother of five was considering who was on the line.

"Toni, this is Joseph Smith. Chad's friend."

"Joseph you don't need to tell me who you are. It's been awhile. I just was trying to recognize the voice."

She was friendly. There was no difference in how she treated me. She either didn't know of the conflict, or still believed me to be an innocent. To the Caden's loyalty was loyalty. No exceptions.

"The true behavior of Christian people," I thought; I knew she was a Catholic – not a Mormon. Claire and Toni – similar qualities. To her, it didn't matter. Friends are friends for life—the faithful will be together in the hereafter.

"I'm trying to reach Chad. Do you have his private cell phone number? I have it on another phone that I'm not carrying right now," I explained.

"No explanations necessary. Chad always wants to hear from you, Joseph."

Without any trepidation, Toni gave me the cell phone number.

"Does he keep it on, when he's in meetings?"

There was a chuckle. "You know our great love story. He puts it on vibrate. Chad searched for a phone with a super-duper vibrator, so when I call it gets him excited, he says." I could tell she was smiling.

She might be a grandmother and even great-grandmother, but Toni had a love as fresh as springtime. They would march off to heaven holding hands – in love.

I said, "We've got to get together, but I need to run. I need Chad."

"Me too. Always."

I waited for her to hang up the phone – heard her singing an old Judy Garland tune.

Claire asked, "Did you get it?"

I nodded enthusiastically as I dialed. I hoped he wouldn't notice the number wasn't from home. I was afraid he would duck the call.

However, on the fourth ring, Chad answered, "Baby, I'm in some tough stuff right now – can it wait?"

I responded with a light jovial tone. "No honey, heat-seeking missiles are coming my way."

Chad continued the conversation as if he was whispering to his wife.

"Can't talk right now, will you be home in a half an hour?"

"If I leave the light on are you going to trace my signal and send the big bad wolf?" I asked.

"I die without you to honey. If you're going to be at home in about a half an hour, I'll take a short break and call you."

"In the interim, think how we will be able to help. How we can stop a world war."

"I love you too honey," the head of the FBI's anti-terrorism task force said. Then, the phone went dead.

I told my comrades that we had a life-altering decision to make. When you know an enemy is chasing you, it is basic training to turn off all ways of being tracked.

We knew the life-saving rule. The FBI, the CIA, and the military want us dead. Who else? We knew for certain killer eyes were searching for us. Probably, even voice-recognition software on the net.

However, we did have the new burner phones that Steve had picked up. They might not have those numbers – yet. Maybe? A gamble leaving an open line.

"I don't see we have any alternative. Leave the phone on."

Steve was looking at his watch, and told me to turn off the phone.

"He said half an hour – plain and simple."

"You are saying to turn off the phone – turn it back on in about 30 minutes."

"Chad made it clear the call would come in thirty minutes. Not before. Not a call back in five or ten minutes."

"Chad was punctual. Prided himself on keeping appointments – on time."

"Turn it on with five minutes to spare. Certainly, that reduces our risk a little," Steve conjectured.

Claire said, "A little. Not much. And you don't want to miss the call."

Steve suggested, "We could drive around. During the conversation, drive aimlessly. And then throw the cell phone in a vehicle going some other direction. When we are finished."

"Old school."

"Why's that?"

Claire touched me softly on my right arm. When I looked in her eyes, I saw faith. A belief we would get it right. Something more – a love of sorts.

"Relax." She warned.

I turned off the phone.

The time passed slowly. I remembered back to my first date with my wife. The clock actually seemed to go backward.

"In love and war," I thought.

I thought, perhaps, I should attempt to report to the Four-Star General in the interim. Give him a chance to alter my mission, or scrap it all together. Give him a chance to determine my path before resorting to orders from a different person.

I tried futilely to no avail. This seemed like my 500th attempt to reach him.

"Joseph, you are concerned about going out of the chain of command. So, try him again." The Sister suggested.

I did. I dialed from one of Steve's new burner phones. The line sort of hiccupped, and then nothing.

Claire said, "What's happening?"

"The phone went dead instead of connecting. A poor connection. I'll try again."

I dialed the Four Star once more.

This time there was a recording, "The number you have called is no longer in service. If you feel you have reached this recording in error, please dial again."

I must have had a curious expression on my face. Claire said immediately, "What's wrong?"

I redialed the number. I handed the phone to the Sister. The message droned on as before: "The number you have called is no longer in service."

I hung up

Claire said, "We are being played."

"You think?" I responded angrily. "The question is who are all the players on their team?"

"Yep. I know we're being axed. Has the President cut off the communication? Stopped Caden from talking to you. And the Four Star?" Claire answered in a freakish voice.

"Now, we know why they want us dead, for certain. Run around the country stirring the pot. They claim the **IAM** is involved in espionage," I said bitterly.

"Who are they? The President?" asked Steve. "Must be the head honcho. He has the killer-box."

"Be cool," said Claire. "We don't have all the answers."

I said, "If we wait much longer getting them, we'll be dead – and a world war will be raging."

My mood was dark. We, as Mormons, are taught to forgive our enemy. To release one's anger – even if someone maims your wife.

I looked the other way when I had Bramwell in my grips. I did him no harm. I took him to ultimate safety. Questioned him almost too politely.

"It's hard to keep the Commandments. Hard to love your enemy. Especially, 70x7 times as in Revelation."

I looked to my right, not understanding the silence from Claire. She had her hands together; face bowed in prayer. I heard her say "Amen."

My respect for her grew with each adversity. The greater the wrong, the closer she was with the Almighty.

"This is bleeping ...; I mean double-dipped," screamed Steve, breaking the spirituality of the moment. At least, he made it only "R" rated, instead of "X."

My military friend found his peace in the jungles or looking over treetops near Mammoth. I never heard him pray. The antonym to the Sister. Sad.

"Time. Time to reengage our phone," said Steve caustically.

"I turned it on a minute ago," I responded.

"Trying to give them more time to zap us," he said..

I said nothing. What was there to say? Either Chad Caden would call, or helicopters with special forces would circle above us.

We waited well past the appointed time. No call. The fear was palpable. We understood if no call came, there was no hiding place for us on earth.

Steve might make it back to Mammoth, but would have to explain the missing King Air 200 – the one we borrowed. I would die as the sniper who killed the Senator. Murderer of supposed innocents in Palmdale.

"Maybe, they will link you to firing the killer nukes. Say you are responsible for erasing the city of Jask," said Claire, her eyes twinkling.

"Say I'm the devil."

She said smartly, "Well, I have wondered. Thinking back – the first time I saw you – I believed you to be the devil."

How would Claire get out of the country and back to Rome? Would they accept a Nun, who would be categorized as a spy?

"Well, I have nowhere to run. I can stand at the Lincoln Monument with my sniper rifle pointed at the sky. Be target practice for our troops, and absorb the multitude of bullets fired in anger."

"I have never been a defeatist," I thought. "With the gospel as a foundation, my nature is one of continual optimism, loyalty, and a new tomorrow."

Claire said, "The phone will ring."

"Or, we have each other for a short while." I said.

"No, forever. We are family, Joseph."

Chapter 44

ભ૪ભ૪ભ૪ભ૪ભ૪

THE PROPITIOUS SMILES OF HEAVEN CAN NEVER BE EXPECTED FROM A NATION THAT DISREGARDS THE ETERNAL RULES OF ORDER AND RIGHT, WHICH HEAVEN ITSELF HAS ORDAINED.

GEORGE WASHINGTON, First Inaugural Address

The phone rang.

Forty minutes – but it rang.

"With all of us nearly bumping our heads on the vehicle's ceiling in excitement, the damned phone rang," said Steve.

Chad was whispering. I couldn't understand him. His voice was too faint.

"Sir, this is Green Beret. You're unintelligible."

There was silence on the other end of the line. It was muffled. I listened intently, holding the cell away from my ear, so Claire could hear.

"Green Beret."

Still muffled, but the connection was better.

"Sir."

"Bottom lines: Congress has voted against calling a state of war."

"Phenomenal," I thought.

Communications were again muffled.

However, we all pumped our fists in the air. Hearing that our legislators maintained their sanity – denying global warfare. No nukes would drop.

"Joe, I must speak in clipped conversation."

I said nothing.

"The Four Star and the military have overpowered the secret service agents here at the White House. They have the President. The Four Star has taken the football."

The phone connection was broken. We had information, but not instructions. Taken the President where? In this fewest possible words, Caden had told me that the military had the potential of sending a nuclear strike.

There was a coup.

Veto the Congress. Start World War III. Alternatively, possibly obliterate the IAM – the Muslims. Who else?

"Is he going to call back?" Steve inquired.

I nodded. "If he can."

Claire conjectured, "Sounds like a full-blown coup is underway."

"From the latest information. I guess the military demands a declaration of war. They are going to precipitate it," I said.

Steve conjectured, "Some of the military. Not all. Illegal orders are not enforceable."

"When the nukes fall, people won't be counting votes." I told him.

I thought, now my uneducated friend was a military lawyer.

"That's absolutely why the Four Star had us running around the country. Our suspicions are confirmed. He was trying to whip up anger at the Muslims, so Congress would act his way," Claire groaned.

"Absolutely. He ordered my FBI partner blown up in my car; tried to kill us at the race track," I agreed. "Every step I reported to him. He had our play-book."

I was calm now. Inner peace. I was always more somber once I had a target.

The phone jingled again.

"Joseph, I hid my phone. We were searched, but not very well, obviously. And then locked here in the Oval Office. The doors are locked. Desk phone ripped out. We're being guarded by a military contingent. They are outside the doors. Standing sentry.

"I'm sitting under the President's desk in the Oval," said Chad.

I snickered. I could see this vigilant man – who could hardly walk – knelt beneath the desk of the President.

"Eyes in the back of your head, Chad. Don't get caught."

"Quiet. Let me talk uninterrupted. The President has been secreted away from the White House at gunpoint. The Four Star and two other high-ranking military officers plan to unleash a nuclear strike from Air Force One."

"Why there?"

"Plausible denial."

I looked at Claire. She actually had her mouth wide open.

I covered the phone, saying to Claire, "Catching flies."

She wacked my sore arm. I groaned, but she wasn't sympathetic.

Chad continued. "Make it look like the President condoned the air strike. They are going to unleash hell on all Muslim countries. Wipe them out."

I had questions, but I was ordered not to speak. Was there more? What should be done?

"Where are you?" Chad asked.

"We're about three or four minutes from Andrews Air Force Base. We are five minutes from everything in the beltway. We're in a parking structure – hiding like kids. While you are manning up."

"Joe, consider this a priority one order, the Four Star cannot be allowed to take off in Air Force One."

"How?"

"Bishop, rely on all your resources. If Air Force One is allowed to take off from Andrews, America's nuclear arsenal will pulverize innocent Muslims. It will render Saudi Arabia, North Korea, Iran, and Pakistan, Syria, others uninhabitable."

"Hold on," I said. "Steve, front seat, please. Drive to Andrews Air Force Base," I said. We were going to be scrunched together.

I knew the Presidential helicopter would land there by Air Force One. It would not take long in arriving. I certainly didn't know what was going on at the White House – outside of the oval office. More secret service agents might have to be corralled. It could take some time.

"There's no way to stop him," screamed Steve in hysteria. Out of control.

I asked Claire to calm Steve. Keep him from driving off the road.

Chad said, "What are you going to do?"

"Chad, I've been on Air Force One only once. Remember, there's a building on the far side of the field."

Chad raised his voice slightly. "What in the hell good is that going to do?"

"There's no way through the perimeter closest to Air Force One." I answered with some agitation in my voice. "Impossible. The only possible penetration is across the field."

Steve was driving feverishly. He heard my words. I selected him to drive, because I knew his instincts would take over. He would listen to what I was saying to Chad Caden. Then, without instructions, he would guide the car to the needed destination.

"Too far — way too far," said Chad, which came through clearly on the speaker of my cell phone. "Know you are good – but no one makes that shot," said Chad in a voice far calmer than I felt. And he was hiding under a desk.

"Chad, who's in the Oval Office with you?"

"Four secret service agents who were overpowered..."

"Sir, hand the phone to the agent who knows the far side of Andrews best."

I could only hear hushed discussions. I knew the old man was precise, and would deliver the best intelligence.

"This is secret service agent Rankin. Mr. Caden says you need information regarding the layout on the other side..."

I cut him off. No time for politeness.

"I need a building. At the end of the runway, directly across the field from Air Force One. I need an elevated spot. A building -- from which to fire a kill shot," I said.

The secret agent paused for only an instant.

"Sir, when you get to the far end you will see some houses. It's an area called Flower Village. Pull in. You will see a building in the rear. Other side of a fence. You'll have to fight through the trees. I don't know if the building is high enough. I know it's too far. No one can make a shot from there. Hopeless."

I asked, "Why isn't it secured – protected?"

"We're not concerned. You'd need a missile to hit Air Force One from there. Additionally, there is a high, protective fence that is normally closed."

We were now approaching the area. I saw what he was talking about. I motioned to Steve. We developed hand signals in our military days. Sign language for when it was too dangerous to talk.

We were pulling into Flower Village. Off to my right, I could see a building protruding above the trees.

"Let me have Caden." I ordered.

The phone was passed back to Chad Caden. I could imagine him and the agent huddling under the President's desk in the Oval. Almost too funny. It could make a scene for a movie. Two brave men doing their best to secure peace.

"Yes."

"Sir, as the ranking officer for the FBI, do I have your authorization to assassinate the Four Star. The other officers? Save the President?"

"Joseph – my son – pull off a miracle. The plane cannot take off with the football. As to the Four Star and his accomplices, so ordered. Take the bastards out!" He ordered.

Chad Caden, still with the dry sense of humor. Caden never panicked. Never lost loyalty, love, duty or humor.

"Yes Sir."

The Four Star required a scapegoat. He absolutely needs to say the President gave the order. The general probably plans to execute the chief executive, afterward unleashing mayhem. He will say he did his best to prevent war – the President died in the resulting struggle.

I was out of the car running through the trees. One branch smacked me in the face knocking me to my knees. Momentarily, my cell phone rattled loose. I kept it in my hands by juggling it.

There was a fence to get over, which cut into my right knee.

"Come on Joseph," yelled Steve, who was pulling me over. In combat, he was always in front of me. Pulling and clawing.

Sister Claire was left behind. Steve kept leading the way – carrying two of the sniper rifles. One was my old reliable. I brought it across the country. Should I say – Steve was old reliable. He was the one who tugged the gun and me along.

As we broke into the clear, I saw the building in front of me. I didn't know if it was high enough. Or, too far.

"Steve, is my weapon hot with ammunition?"

"You bet. It has a long-range load, with your metered scope. No wind that I can feel," he said, speaking the sniper shorthand. Preparing for action. He was in his element.

"Too far for me. I could throw rocks at them with the same effectiveness."

"It has to be. In range."

"Are you going to try to take out the plane?"

We were now at the building, seeking a way onto the roof.

"If we cripple the aircraft, they'll still have the ability to authorize a full nuclear attack," I said, becoming somewhat winded. "They will say the IAM shot down the craft."

"Right."

"We have to take out the brass in uniform – the Four Star at a minimum."

I was still keeping the line open with the FBI's Caden and the sequestered secret service officers. I didn't know when, or if, I would need them.

Steve saw a ramp, with a ladder leading to the roof. He pointed.

"Over here."

A million things were running through my mind all at the same time. I knew the trip from the White House in the helicopter was only an instant of time. Were we too late?

"Everyone says the kill shot is impossible. However, I knew, 'all things are possible to those who believe'."

Steve and I climbed a ladder leading onto the roof. My buddy had fired a single shot at a lock which secured the route. Now, we scurried through the opening.

Steve and I emerged on top of a flat roof of the rusty metal building. We ran to the closest point to Air Force One.

"Oh my God," yelled Steve. "I can hardly see the plane from here. It's the size of a dime. Can't be done." He paused, out-of-breath. Then, he added, "Nonetheless, the plane is pulled forward a little – the protective barrier down. Expecting a quick get-away, I imagine."

My mind was still racing. Even faster. A billion thoughts trying to capture my attention. In my Green Beret days – and by training – I had been able to eradicate outside intrusion. But not today.

"I am trying to kill the leader for whom I had worked for three years. A man I respected. Not a man of God. However, still a son of God, nonetheless. The Four Star believed he could deal out 'fairdom' to the world by his brilliance."

What a dismal belief. How was he anointed as the one to vaporize a billion people?

I tried to still my mind, but the Holy Ghost was influencing me. Not allowing me to focus on killing.

I thought, "How had we become so tangled with brother fighting brother. The Muslims revere the Prophet Muhammad, born about 570 years after the birth of Christ. Muhammad prayed for revelation from God on his knees in a cave.

Not too dissimilar to our Mormon Prophet Joseph Smith, who received a visitation by God the Father and the Son, Jesus Christ in a grove of trees in the Spring of 1820."

God called Abraham as a Prophet, which is recorded in Genesis in the first book in the Bible. From Abraham flow the religion of the Jews, Christians, Muslims and Mormons. The same Heavenly Father.

God told Muhammad to lead his people to pray to him – God the Almighty — and to destroy the worshiping of idols. People in Arabia in the time of Muhammad were praying to a multitude of idols and Gods.

I knew, "Muhammad recognized Christ's virginal birth, and had faith that Jesus Christ was a Holy Man sent by God. He believed Christ was a Prophet. Believed that Jesus brought us truths sent directly from God.

The goodness of Christ was similar to what Prophet Muhammad told his followers that he had received. The message goes awry when men twist and alter the heavenly intent."

I looked out toward Air Force One. There still was not a chopper from the White House. No Four Star to take down.

"Why nearly 1,500 years after Muhammad's birth did Muslims believe the Quran told them to kill the Infidels?" I said out loud. "Kill Christians – and even Jews. God didn't tell that to

Muhammad any more than he instructed the Four Star to nuke the Muslims. Both notions are insane."

Steve looked at me very confused, as I had spoken out loud to myself.

I remember a special report to CNN by Jeffrey Weiss, who compares and contrasts the Jews, Muslims and Christian religions. Weiss says the most obvious difference is the Christian teachings about the Trinity – God, Jesus and the Holy Spirit as "one."

Weiss concludes that some Christians believe, "God is three separate beings who are also one." He says, "according to Christian tradition, God begets a son who is somehow also Him – but not Him – to atone for Original Sin."

I am not an expert on all Christian faiths. "However, I am a Christian with a fundamental belief that there is a Father in Heaven, and that Jesus – his son – prayed to Father as we read in the testimony of Christ's Apostles in the Bible.

To Mormons, God the Father sent his son Jesus Christ to earth to live a mortal life. Jesus atoned for our sins at Gethsemane, praying to the Father. He died on the cross and was resurrected three days later. Thereby erasing our sins by grace if we accept him as our Savior. Providing a universal resurrection.

So Jeff Weiss and I are not in accord. I thought that if we spent more time practicing Christian principles and less time fighting all inhabitants would benefit.

I know that Muslims believe that Muhammad was the last true Prophet of God. The End. They say, "Read Koran and you have all the answers."

"Why would God stop communicating with his children? We need him more now than ever. And yet many Christian religions – including Catholics – believe God said the Bible is the end. No more revelation. There would be no further word from God after Jesus Christ and the apostles."

The view comes from a mistaken understanding of Apostle John's words in Revelation – the last book printed in the New Testament. I know that Revelation is printed last – not because it is so great – but because it narrowly made it into the Bible. It had been rejected on prior occasions as "mistaken doctrine," and was included by only one vote, hundreds of years after Christ's death. Last not because it was more instructive, but because half the monks believed it to be folly. Last because they viewed it as less gospel and more dangerous. More prone to misunderstanding.

"Apostle John – who was beloved by Christ – said that any man who adds or subtracts from his writing in Revelation is damned," I said to myself. "John wrote while in prison on an island. Gave his instruction to keep the guards from destroying or changing 'his scrolls' when they were circulated to the faithful. Revelation was a singular document, certainly, not in the Bible at the time. Revelation was written to encourage believers in Christ not to bow down to the pagan Roman leaders, who self-declared themselves to be Gods."

I knew the Apostle's intent was not to say God "would never talk to his children again. That God would abandon us after he had sent his son to give us clear instruction on how to return to him."

I also believe John's writings to be the word of God, when translated properly. I have gained immeasurably from them; however, I know for certainty, John did not mean or believe that God would give up on us or fail to communicate with his children through Prophets as he had always done.

"Why?" I said to myself. "Why would God the father of all – who communicated with his children from the time of Adam – decide to cut his children adrift forever?"

I shook my head. Unconvinced at the absurdity. "The God of the Jew, or the Muslim, and all Christians is the same God. Sister Claire and I may belong to different churches, but pray to the same God."

The thoughts were infiltrating my soul with laser-like intensity, and as quick as rays from the Sun warm us daily. Thoughts from the Holly Ghost were uploaded to my brain in full chapters – rather than single sentences.

I have a strong testimony of the Bible. And of the Book of Mormon – another testament of Christ. Knowing that God is a loving God, master of consistency.

As a Mormon Bishop, I instruct the children of our faith to love all – without prejudice. A good friend of mine came from Africa, where he was born a Muslim. We share love – not hatred.

I have a severe headache – just above my eyes. So much information swirling in my consciousness.

How could I find myself on a rooftop? Ordered to kill a fellow American military officer? And how could he – the Four-Star General – have designs on erasing brothers with linage from the Prophet Abraham. Families who are Muslims?

How could a message of Muhammad be turned to hatred? God's words have always been the same.

"I am certain God's words to each of his Prophets were totally consistent when given to man. Despots like the Four Star prostituted God's kindness – destroying the way home to Heaven." I said again out loud.

"What brought me to this roof is the devilish creation of instruments of mass destruction. I want to be anywhere, but here."

The scourge of the modern age is the fastest growing religion, "A belief that some 'big bang' created everything."

They contend Darwin is all-knowing. They believe in the gene that came from nowhere. In nothing really – other than their own inventiveness. In fact, the Four Star's faith is measured by the advent of the drone and our nuclear superiority.

He says, "We have no relationship with the Muslim. God, Jesus and the Prophet Abraham are all myths. Borne by idiots."

Steve was shaking his head at me.

Just then I heard the whirling blades of a helicopter. At first, I thought back to my days as a sniper in the military. I was in a trance-like state from my ruminations. I started to duck believing we were under attack. That we were spotted.

Not so. It was the helicopter carrying our adversaries. Our President held captive. Presidents have been executed in office. Never before has one been taken by an adversarial group – until today.

I knelt on the roof which was burning to my skin. However, as I had always done prior to this mission, I put pain out of my vocabulary. I am finally able to concentrate of the single objective.

I sighted on the plane. There were some portable stairs – perhaps, 10 or 12 – leading to a ramp which gave way to the entry door.

That was not the normal loading procedure. The craft was pulled forwards from its traditional loading ramp – the protective barrier was pulled back, giving us sight of Air Force One. Perhaps, maintenance had been working or inspecting.

I saw the aircraft was pulled forward from the normal ramp area. I presumed the temporary stairs would be used by the men attempting to garner control of Air Force One.

"8,913 feet," I said out loud. That's what my scope interpreted the distance to the target.

"Jesus," Steve said automatically.

I said, "We certainly can use his help."

"Green Beret you have an unobstructed line of sight. No wind. Just too far," said Steve.

We were waiting for our target. I was afraid they would land the helicopter in front of me. Block my shot. However, they put the bird down slightly off to the left, which kept my view unobstructed. The copter was about 30 feet or so from the Presidential plane.

For some reason, they were taking time to maneuver between the helicopter and Air Force One. The copter's door opened. I was slowing my breathing, which had become erratic during our maneuvers. And even from my pondering.

Trying to alleviate pressure, I said, "Steve we're short of the world record for the longest kill."

"Would you like to move back some?" Steve said ironically. "Only you would recall something as minute as that at a time like this," Steve smiled, understanding my intentions.

"Incidentally, what is the longest sniper confirmed kill?" he asked.

I saw men starting to emerge from the chopper but still not at the right point to fire. I knew I needed to get them on the ramp, so that I could cut them off from the plane, and from retreating.

"A kill was confirmed kill in 2012 at 9,235 feet. We're a good hundred yards short of that record."

"You haven't hit anything yet. Maybe this one is more important, anyway."

"Certainly more targets." I said.

Just then, I saw the President of the United States, with his hands handcuffed behind him, being led to Air Force One. A gun in his back.

Two men were between the President and the Four Star. I could see the targets clearly through my scope. It was as if I was on a practice range. The men were moving as if clay pigeons at a carnival.

I already made a preparation for my kill by allocating the precise measurements. The distance between our location and the ramp to Air Force One was a clear shot. Maybe, too far.

"Don't let them reach the airplane," said Steve urgently.

I blanked out all outside noise and atmosphere. I aimed at the shoulder of the Four Star, realizing that my load might drop a tad – even with my precise calculations. He was walking left to right. I didn't have the chest at which to aim. His entire body that I could see was less than 12 inches.

"More difficult," I thought.

Then, blotting out the fact that I was going to assassinate an American general, I squeezed the trigger.

Instantaneously, I sent another bullet into the chamber.

Across the field from us, America's only Four-Star General plummeted off the ramp, dead before he hit the tarmac below. It was clear the bullet went through him.

There was bedlam. There were four other men heading to Air Force One. And one – the President.

When the Four Star fell like a rag doll, the other men became hapless, uncertain how to proceed. It had been his craziness that had propelled them. Without the fallen madman, they were petrified.

I fired again. This time my termination was the military officer pointing the pistol at the President. Although, he turned toward me when I hit the Four Star.

"A much easier shot."

"His head exploded like a melon," said Steve, as the dead officer was pushed backwards off of the ramp.

The President bolted forward into Air Force One. A lone secret service agent – stationed with the aircraft – jumped onto the ramp. His gun was drawn.

He fired at another officer on the ramp, who was hopelessly confused. The two still alive were trying to identify the sniper targeting them.

Their attention was not on the agent coming out of the door from Air Force One. They did not notice the President's astute move. The secret service agent killed one of the military adversaries while at the same time pulling the door to Air Force One closed.

"The last one is a sitting duck," I said to myself.

The remaining military terrorist appeared like a deer in the headlight of an oncoming car. He was frozen.

Steve said, "He can't believe it. He can't move."

It didn't seem sporting, but I had no alternative but to eliminate the threat. If he regained intellect, he still might attack Air Force One and the President.

"Where's the football?"

"Don't know," I said.

The final man threw down his weapon, raising his hands high above his head. He looked around unbelieving. I already sent a bullet his way.

"He's not going anywhere." Steve said.

Chapter 45

ଓଓଓଓଓ

SECURING THE FUMBLED FOOTBALL

All the while, I left the phone line open to Chad Caden.

"Sir, Air Force One secure."

"Where is the President?

"On Air Force One, without the generals. Secret service closed the doors. I've neutralized the threat here," I reported.

Air Force One was now taxing away from the ramp and onto the runway for takeoff.

"I have no way to communicate with the craft or the President," I said.

I reported the movement of the plane to Chad, who was still captive in the Oval Office.

"Now, how do we free you?" I asked. "Who's in command of the military? I've taken out a good deal of the leadership."

As the senior officer of the FBI's anti-terrorist task force, Chad Caden authorized the cold-blooded execution of the military officers.

He took his time answering.

"Are you certain, absolutely certain, that the threat has been neutralized?"

"Yes."

"The plane?"

"Sir, I can't see inside Air Force One. However, I can tell you, no military officer got onto the plane with the President."

Air Force One taxied to the far end of the runway. Someone on board maneuvered the giant craft away from the incident.

I asked, "How do we contact Air Force One?"

Chad Caden from memory gave me the on board, flight phone telephone number. Even in unbelievable circumstances the old man of the FBI could recall phone numbers.

He could hardly walk. Nonetheless, when the chips were down, you wanted Chad Caden on your team.

"You call the plane. Be certain the President is on board. Determine who has the football. I will call out a SWAT attack on the White House, once you confirm the President's safety."

With the instruction, the line went dead.

Then, behind us, I heard a loud noise. Both Steve and I whirled around in time to find Sister Claire emerging onto the roof. She looked like she was being chased by a swarm of bees.

Steve said, "You missed the action."

"We've got an angry mob below us. We need to secure the access to the roof, until we fight our way out of here."

"You have the roof access, Steve?" I directed.

"Yes sir."

I then dialed the number to Air Force One, which was roaring down the runway for takeoff from Andrews Air Force Base.

"You're not squawking a secure signal," said the person who answered on board Air Force One.

"I'm the sniper who took out the military combatants, who kidnapped the President. Please identify yourself," I asked. "And tell me if any adversary is on Air Force One?"

"No adversary is a board. The President is safe. One minute please. Stand by."

I didn't stand − I was still kneeling. However, I followed orders, waiting for the first leader of America ever kidnapped.

A beleaguered and tired voice, which I recognized as the President of the United States, came on the line.

"Who are you?"

"This is Joseph Smith, Mr. President."

"Are you the sniper?"

"I am, Sir."

"Who has the football?"

"I have no idea. I'm not on Andrews Air Force Base. Have no access. Presuming the Four Star had the ball, when I shot him, it fell to the ground. I can patrol the flight line with my rifle until help arrives."

"He had it."

"I can see something on the tarmac, feet from him." I said.

The President thought for a minute.

"Do you recognize the Vice President?" he asked.

"Of course."

"It may take a few minutes, because the Vice President is on the hill. Even so, I will have him with a security team retrieve the football. I will have him secure the area."

"Sir, who is flying the plane?" I asked. I was concerned. The craft looked like it was in for maintenance. Why was a pilot aboard?

"My chief pilot, of course. The general outsmarted himself. He ordered my crew chief here."

"Mr. President, are my orders to fire upon any person touching or coming near the football, other than the Vice President of the United States."

The President said, "So ordered."

"Mr. President, your secret service staff at the White House, and my commanding officer Chad Caden are prisoners of a military team. They're being held in the Oval Office."

"Hold the line."

We were not only holding the line, but keeping an irate group from below from attacking our position on the roof. The President was gone for a time which seemed an eternity.

Every couple of minutes a voice other than the President would affirm that we were still ordered to remain at our post and on the line.

Nearly a half an hour later a helicopter landed on the tarmac. I used my sniper rifle to sight the first man who left the airship. It was the Vice President.

He had no idea where we were. He, however, was aware of my orders to kill anyone other than him. Therefore, he turned around 360 degrees. Taking no chance.

"You see the Vice President?" The President asked, returning to the line.

"Yes, Sir. He's picked up the ball."

"That's right, son, football secured. You are free to stand down."

"What about the Oval Office?"

There was no answer. The phone was disconnected.

Chapter 46

ଔଔଔଔଔ

OVAL OFFICE - THE WHITE HOUSE

Now my mission was to reclaim my friend. The President had left the phone too quickly for me to get a clear picture of what was happening at 1600 Pennsylvania Ave. – the White House.

"Green Beret," said Chad Caden.

"Sir?"

"The White House is secure. I made calls; however, it was the President from Air Force One who made the orders extricating us. A group of 10 other treasonous officers are on the run. They won't get far."

"What are my orders?"

"Disappear."

"Disappear, Sir?"

"For now, the Bishop and the Nun are thought of as pariahs. I need the Sister and you to discreetly stand down. Until, or unless, there is another assignment."

"I don't understand?"

"The President cannot announce at a press conference that he was taken captive. Can't say the United States' top military officers activated a coup. He can't tell the world that our military was going to nuke all Muslim countries. Can't say America was going to take a pre-emptive strike," said Caden.

I had never heard his voice so serious – yet, apologetic.

"The two of you have targets on your back. Our government, and you're grateful President, must make this debacle go away. It never happened. Anyone connected to it will be hunted. There will be those in Congress and the military that will question my orders, assassinating militaries highest ranking officer, the Four Star."

"Why should you go through the trials and tribulations alone?"

"I was a captive. I was always seen as on the side of democracy and this President."

"I see."

I understood, but I didn't like it.

"What you don't see is that the Bishop and the Nun are identifiable with the national tragedy. You are both on everyone's most-wanted list. They believe the two of you were at the heart of the calamity," he said sorrowfully.

He continued, "Take this as a time to save your family. Your children, Joseph. They lost their mother. Gather your children – focus on them. Save yourself Joseph."

I said nothing.

"Sister, your brother in arms – my beloved Joseph – is going to need love. Support. A genuine friend. I knew his wife. When Joseph has time to rest – to think – he is going to hit bottom. Be there for him. Faith is one thing. The loss of family, and then shuttled into the wilderness by your country is another."

"I will, sir."

Chad said, "Someday we will meet. Happier times."

I asked, "What is the President going to do about the IAM? How is he going to avoid war?"

We were on the speaker. Claire and I could hear. Steve was keeping hostile neighbors off the roof.

"Now you see the problem, Joseph. The President needs to have this nightmare behind him, so he can deal effectively with the world."

Then, I did understand. The United States and the belligerent countries were still at an impasse. The President required solidarity at home.

"I didn't vote for him," said Chad Caden. "Nonetheless, he is a brilliant man. Now that I know him, I greatly admire his attributes. He stood up to the Four Star – the entire military establishment. The two of you just can't be in the way."

Be at Edwards Air Force Base in California, day-after tomorrow. I will see that the President as part of his cleanup of this aborted coup has new passports and transportation for the two of you to Rome, or wherever. Anywhere in the world. Plausible denial."

"Hard to swallow the order, but I've never disobeyed. I won't now," I thought.

There was a long silence. I could almost see my friend struggling with his decisive instructions.

"Joseph, you're a son to me. However, this order is paramount for our country. The Bishop and the Nun must disappear. Be off the radar, forever."

"I understand," I said, but not really wanting to disappear from my ward family in Camarillo, California. Not wanting to abandon my calling as Bishop. Walk away without a word. My friends would see the move as cowardice.

Let the world believe a Mormon Bishop and the Catholic Nun were traitors. We were trying to nuke Muslims. Or, however, they spun it.

"I'll see we don't go to war, or nuke our neighbors. Maintain your faith. Seek a new name and identity. Your country will call on you for additional service. I promise."

"Your promise is gold to me, sir."

Chad Caden was an avid reader. Although a devout Catholic, Chad read the Book of Mormon. He had respect for Joseph and wanted knowledge about his religion.

Chad said, "Perhaps, we should call you Nephi in remembrance of a Prophet of your faith."

I thought for only a second, saying, "Instead, let me honor all Christians. Call me 'James,' who was the brother of Jesus, and the writer of the Book of James in the Bible. Finding salvation includes both genuine faith in Christ – accompanied by works of a consistent lifestyle. Followers of Christ should not only 'talk the talk'; but must 'walk the walk'."

"You certainly have, my son," said Chad.

"This is Sister Claire Cogan, Mr. Caden. I am listening in, sir. See, Catholics have such a sweet spirit that I am already converting the Bishop."

"Sister Claire, don't believe that for one minute. Because, you will be vacationing in Salt Lake City.

To me, Chad said, "James, I love you."

Then, I heard the line disconnecting.

The End